I0825157

THE *WORDS* OF *DR. L*

ALSO BY KAREN E. BENDER

The New Order

Refund

A Town of Empty Rooms

Like Normal People

THE WORDS OF DR. L

AND OTHER STORIES

Karen E. Bender

COUNTERPOINT ✦ CALIFORNIA

First Counterpoint edition: 2025

Grateful acknowledgment for reprinting materials is made to the following: "The Shame Exchange" appeared in *The Yale Review* and *The Pushcart Prize XLV: Best of the Small Presses 2021 Edition*. "Helicopter" appeared in *Air/Light* magazine. "Messengers" appeared in *The Yale Review*. "The Extra Child" appeared in *Image*.

Library of Congress Cataloging-in-Publication Data
Names: Bender, Karen E., author.
Title: The words of Dr. L : and other stories / Karen E. Bender.
Other titles: Words of Dr. L (Compilation)
Description: First Counterpoint edition. | California : Counterpoint, 2025.
Identifiers: LCCN 2024057942 | ISBN 9781640095700 (hardcover) | ISBN 9781640095717 (ebook)
Subjects: LCGFT: Short stories.
Classification: LCC PS3552.E53849 W67 2025 | DDC 813/.54—dc23/eng/20241202
LC record available at https://lccn.loc.gov/2024057942

Jacket design by Jaya Miceli
Jacket image © iStock / hernan4429
Book design by Laura Berry

COUNTERPOINT
Los Angeles and San Francisco, CA
www.counterpointpress.com

Printed in the United States of America

1 3 5 7 9 10 8 6 4 2

This one is for:

my father, David Bender, and his memory

and

my mother, Mary Bender

The beginning, with love

Contents

THE WORDS OF DR. L

THE WORDS OF DR. L

The sky turned to night as I walked through the city, and the streets emptied in the blue dusk. I imagined the way the other women might walk as they headed toward this pharmacy, a casual, but brisk stride, and I tried to walk as they did, but with care; I did not want anyone to notice me. I was joining the great crowds of women in the country who needed the words. We were all, in our different cities, pressing forward, faces intent, as though on an errand. We were going to the supermarket. We were going to a meeting. Or that was what we said we were going to do. I watched the tall glass buildings fill with light as they did at dusk, many of the slim towers glowing, inside, a bright, identical pink.

I was at fifty-nine days, and I had until the sixty-fifth day, after which the words would not work. One friend advised me to go to Pelham's Pharmacy on Olive Street, a place that looked perfectly ordinary and was lit so harshly inside my eyelids hurt. The woman who staffed the counter at the pharmacy on Wednesdays, a woman with short red hair that ended right at her ears, could help direct me to Dr. L, who knew the words.

I had not been able to sleep the last couple of weeks, until I had learned how to find Dr. L. At that point my mind had reached a state of exhaustion so that it felt like a damp paper bag. The city echoed, a maelstrom of production, loud, steel girders always being slapped up, and the constant sound of ascension trembled in my throat. The air was gauzy with mist and as I walked, I could see the radiance of the letters PROTECTION atop several buildings, their pale brightness always visible in the dark air.

WHAT I KNEW was this: there was a series of words that, if recited in a particular order, would end a pregnancy. An hour or so after the words were spoken, the fetus would stop growing, be expelled, and that was it. There were a few doctors around the country who had been trained in the recitation of these words, and only they could tell you what they were.

The precise order of the words, and the fact that you could learn them and say them and stop the pregnancy in this way, was a new development over the last few years. A psychologist, Dr. L, had researched links between the mind and body, and discovered the exact phrasing, the thought that would stop the fetus from coming into the world. Why did it work? No one knew. Were the words—and the accompanying thoughts—so shocking to the growing cells that when they heard them, they wanted to stop? Were the words so persuasive in their honesty that the body had no choice but to follow along? How did the words make the fetus stop? There were rumors about Dr. L's research—for how had she known this?—there were murmurings that she was some sort of demon, there were rumblings that she had practiced on herself, that she had ended a few of her own pregnancies for the sake of science; there were other rumors that she had seven children and then, one night in which she was haggard and ruined from lack of sleep, had a thought so sharp and ferocious that it scared any forthcoming babies away. Some said the words worked due to science, some religion, some insanity. No one knew how she had devised this method, but that many women said it was effective.

The advantage of Dr. L's method was the lack of evidence. The words gathered in your mind, were whispered, and that was that. You could tell others about the loss and they would feel sad for you and you could weep, hands covering your face, receiving sympathy. You could feel sorrow too, but the inside of your heart was clear and pure as a lake.

The words left no visible mark. Your body was emptied. You were free.

No one knew the identity of Dr. L. She had never been photographed and no one knew where she lived. The rumor was that she moved from state to state, telling a few trusted aides the words and the precise way to say them. These aides then told others how to articulate the words, and then were transferred to a new location.

I did not want to become pregnant. I did not want to bear and raise a child. This thought sat in me with a polished certainty, like a gold coin. I was born right before the provisions enforcing motherhood were written into state constitutions, the laws that my friend Joanne and I knew but that we, at first, thought were irrelevant to us, a joke. In college, we were still encouraged to take classes in a variety of subjects. I had, one semester, taken a PE class, and I discovered that I loved how I felt when I ran, how I was fleeing the world for a short time, even if I wasn't, how I heard nothing then but the sound of my heart and my wavelets of breath. I loved feeling the expanse of nothingness, the sense that inside me was a wide, vast plain. I had been born, I thought, with a peculiar sensitivity to words; at first, those of my mother and the complicated advice she wanted to offer me. Then not just my mother—the school, the city, every institution telling me what to do. The words did not slide off me, as they did with most people; I tried to figure out why some conversations were ones I could just step into and inhabit and why others felt like they invaded me.

There was so much to be said for silence. I felt deeply myself when I listened to that silence, the feeling when no one was telling me what to do, when I didn't have to beat back the comments of others. The ability to not listen, to inhabit that nothingness, was to be free. Later, at dawn, coaching the girls on the track team, I liked the feeling of telling them how to run faster until that moment: "Until your mind is clear," I said. I didn't want to say too much lest I get in trouble. They looked at me with startled expressions, and I could tell which ones thought this was a sad state of affairs, and which ones, I think, understood me. I was glad to have been able to offer them that.

I did not want to have a child. It was as simple as that. Not at the moment we were captured, no. I wanted a moment to be a door, not a trap. And to answer another question that would be asked at a trial, if I were found out: Had I enjoyed the sex that led to this moment, this accident? I had. I did not want to get married. The man lay beside me, breathing hard, and my blood was made of warm, oozy caramel, and that was a moment in which the world was sparkling, languorous, bright. He kissed me deeply, with kindness, he was a nice man, and I had shivered at the way he gently kissed my shoulder, the way he tossed his dark hair. He was appreciative but eager to move onward to other activities. I too wanted the moments in my life to be a series of houses, doors opening and closing, one after another, to live in as many houses as I could design.

I WAS EIGHT weeks late. I had kept waiting, and hoping for the familiar ache, I kept imagining it was just about to happen, but it did not. There was a sourness in my stomach and I was tired; yes, it was hard to get out of bed, and I was well aware that each day passing was one day less to learn the words. But who could I ask? Not my mother. She didn't like the path I had taken. And certainly not my friend Joanne.

Joanne had joined the group Protection, which meant that I was now afraid of her. This organization drew women together to protect their fetuses from untoward thoughts. For when Dr. L located the series of words that would stop a child from forming, this sparked the fear in some people that they would say these words in spite of themselves. Immediately, organizations formed to help the terrified women who did not want to cause their fetuses harm. If there were rumors that Dr. L was visiting their part of their city, then pregnant women locked themselves in their homes, drawing their curtains shut. The mere sight of Dr. L could, they feared, spur one to terrible thoughts, could result in fetuses growing into babies with no arms or heads, with any variety of defects or malformations. Dr. L had discovered what they had all, in some way, feared.

Joanne and I had been friends for years, long before the takeover; we lived in the same neighborhood and often walked home together from school. I thought back to when I visited her house during middle school. She lived in a house that was clean in a way that felt like a rebuke of a former insult. The floors gleamed, hardwood, and her mother, who always wore long skirts that looked stiff even if they weren't, moved across it, oddly never quite making a sound. I listened to her closely, to see if I could detect anything, a rustle, a thud, but I didn't, to the point that I wasn't sure if her mother actually had feet. When she hugged Joanne, she placed her arms around her carefully, as though Joanne were wet.

WHAT I ADMIRED about Joanne, what I wanted to emulate, was that she complained, with a loose, airy ease, about her mother. Her mother glided around the house, tall and silent in an expansive way, except when she picked on Joanne, which happened briefly, and often, like an insect that swerved in to sting you and then disappeared. She could not bear the clunk of Joanne's feet as she walked across the house, she hated finding strands of Joanne's long dark hair in the tub. Worst, her mother laughed at Joanne when she showed her art projects from school. Her mother said they were embarrassing, but did not tell her why this was so. This hurt her the most.

For some time, Joanne became very quiet as we approached her house. Then, when she was fourteen or so, she began to make fun of her mother. One day, walking home, she turned to me, and said, "My mother wears the ugliest shoes in the world."

Her voice had the sharpness of a rock hitting glass. I wasn't even aware that her mother wore shoes. She looked at me, awaiting a response, and I laughed.

"She does," I said, carefully.

She brightened and added, "She also smells." It was a rank, undefinable odor, like old leaves, that could never quite be concealed with deodorant; her mother seemed to contain a rotting garden. She paused and continued. How bold we felt as she said this! We walked together and her complaints were, to her, a deep and buoying relief.

I wanted to join in, to talk about the failings of my own mother. But I could not complain the same way. My mother was voluminous in her proclamations, and all of them felt wrong. She had incessant ideas about when I should wear a jacket, or if I should have cereal or yogurt for breakfast, or the best exercise for losing weight or the jobs that would survive the current economy. She was terribly, powerfully convincing. But the worst thing was the story of her life, told often:

that others had told her she would be an excellent office manager, she had found a job, and then, a year later, was fired for an unspecified (and suspect) reason and had children and she wanted me to do the same thing. Or she did not say she wanted me to fail, as she had, but the way she described my future I always did. Her thoughts seemed weightier and more correct simply because she said them; I did not know how to stop from listening to them.

My mother was a woman with a delicate face, pink lips that, pursed, resembled a flower, and large, muscular hands that looked good for butchering something, though she generally did baking activities that involved fine motor skills, such as putting fondant on cakes. I always watched those hands with a kind of interest and wariness; I had dreams that they strangled me. She sat at the kitchen table, those enormous hands clasped, and regarded me with a love that was forceful but constraining; I wanted to absorb but didn't want to be what she thought. How guilty I felt about those feelings! Discussing recipes or current events, she looked at me with a combination of love and pity; I sat there, trying to balance the scale toward something more like love.

I STOOD IN front of the woman in the pharmacy, smiling as though I were a customer. I was advised to purchase something clichéd and feminine—a lipstick—paired, carefully, with a masculine item—a strong, musky deodorant. This was supposed to alert the worker to what I was really asking. An obvious, stupid binary; maybe it was supposed to be a joke.

Inside, the artificial light made everything pale blue. Outside, the world was remote and soundless, as though covered with snow.

She glanced at what I was purchasing, at me. I held still, not sure what expression to have. Her eyes moved briefly over the aisle of the store. She handed me my change and then leaned toward me, waited a long moment, and said, "Fifteen Logan Street. Twentieth floor. Wear a suit. A dark color. Hair parted on the left side." She added, "Monday between two and four."

"Thank you," I said. I sensed tenderness in her words, which I realized I craved, and I wanted her to continue. "A suit? Why a suit?" I asked.

Her face went carefully blank, her eyelid fluttering; deflated, I remembered I was not supposed to talk to her.

"Everyone should have a suit," she said, loudly. "They're having a great sale at Hansen's. Go right now."

JOANNE AND I went to school and wondered what our path would be through the world. We walked home and I remembered that route, the pure clarity of the air between us right before she went into her house, when our ideas and plans were arranged, neatly in our heads, before they were blown away like a pile of leaves, by our mothers' powerful thoughts. The moment when Joanne stood straighter, thinking, waiting for her mother's criticisms, bracing herself against them, and me carefully watching to see what she would do. I wanted to find a way to argue against the plans my mother had for me and I didn't know how. Joanne was my only guide through the muck, her criticisms the only strategy we had, and each mean comment she had seemed oddly hopeful; it made me think: maybe the world could be another way, too.

I felt shy and envious listening to her. We wanted wisdom so badly and did not know how to conjure it. Occasionally she would try to formulate motivation for her mother's behavior.

"She wishes I was not me," she once observed, crisply. It seemed terrible, but perhaps true. But who did her mother want her to be?

Joanne never, as far as I knew, shared any of these observations with her mother, only with me. I remember one time, when we were around twelve, at a school auditorium, to perform some song or another, and we saw our mothers talking together, and we watched them. Our mothers were standing in an aisle between the seats and chatting in an ordinary, amiable way. I remember thinking how beautiful they were, just standing there, how they were animatedly discussing something that perhaps had nothing to do with us. I remembered my mother making a chortling shriek of a laugh I'd never heard, as though she were young for a moment, and being aware of our two islands of time, the one they lived on and the one that held Joanne and me. I longed to be on that island with them, and I resented them for being on that island, which meant that I resented time, and that argument was pointless. Joanne watched our mothers, too, their brisk, sparkling gestures and shining hair, and she was silent and we could not hear what her mother was saying, but for a moment we imagined that she was bragging about her.

We did not say what, but I knew we were both imagining that.

But otherwise, mostly we walked home and she said everything she secretly wished she could say to her mother. And this. And this. I admired how she could just declare what she felt. Anything! What a skill! How could she do this? I listened, and I watched her walk taller, and above us the blue sky was like a bright piece of tin.

ONE DAY, Joanne's mother died. She had just finished cleaning, and the whole house gleamed. No one knew what happened; there was no sign. Her heart was working and then it was not.

We all attended the memorial, which seemed like a theater of a memorial, not an actual one, for what happened did not seem as though it could have happened; no one knew what to say. We all gathered at her family's home and stood in her shining green kitchen. I was aware that her mother had recently touched this room, had cleaned these counters and floors. The room stood, intact, but felt abruptly silent, as though we had all just missed a shocking and deafening sound. The light coming through the windows fell on our skin, warm. I remember watching my own mother with new, rapt interest. She was weeping but still ate a piece of chocolate cake, and I monitored her, acted like a servant, bringing her more items—grapes, cookies—to eat.

Joanne was dressed in a loose black dress; her face looked as though she had been emptied. I remembered the last thing she said about her mother; we were walking home from school and she resented, no, hated her mother for forcing her to wear a certain pair of dark-blue, practical shoes that had no visible heel.

That moment, the soft, cloudlike luxury of that resentment.

Now I noticed she was wearing those very shoes.

She stood, very straight, with the same posture of her mother; she resembled her mother, but she was not; she was trying to fit herself over something inarguable, innocuous. I stood by her, and tried to say anything, nothing: You were a good daughter. I'm sorry. I hugged her but she seemed light, terribly light, to not reside in her body; her abandonment of her self was sudden and complete. My hands held her shoulders, gripping her. She looked at me with blank gray eyes.

I felt more tender toward my mother after this, and sat in the kitchen with her, somehow more vulnerable to her proclamations. I listened to her to, perhaps, keep her from dying in this sudden way. But in my attempts to keep my mother alive by sitting beside her, my mother's thoughts crushed mine so that I could not think. I don't know how it happened. Sitting in the kitchen, she described her plan for me. I wasn't very good at many subjects, she said she could see that. (I didn't think this was true.) She had tried to join the workforce but felt her mind go sodden and dropped out. Perhaps I would be the same way. I could work for a year or two, but then stop to have two children, maybe three. I listened to her voice push through the dim kitchen, like a tractor pushing dirt. I was skeptical of my mother hawking her own life plan, for occasionally I heard her go into the bathroom, lock the door, and scream.

When she did this, I remained in the kitchen. I tried to come up for a plan for myself, but it was difficult. When I tried to think of my future, I envisioned a pale, hazy road twisting into the distance, but nothing surrounding it, no buildings, no houses, no trees.

Joanne and I moved through high school. I went to college, as that was where we were funneled next, that was everyone's obedience. But I did not tell my family about the classes I took. This was my first secret; it surprised me, and it led to a new, disquieting silence between us. I majored in physical education, I was a good, swift runner. For when I moved I was most awake. I ran, and my mind was free with blankness, and I told the team how to run, I found joy yelling orders at women kicking balls across a green field. In that way, I was perhaps like my mother. But not like her, too.

Joanne went another direction. She had trouble graduating from college; she never knew which courses to take. She kept changing majors and ideas, none of them cured her restlessness, none of them felt correct to her.

When she joined the group Protection, Joanne's demeanor was like a new coat, shiny as aluminum; she was more cheerful and alert. The group was formed shortly after there was news of the work of Dr. L; it was supposedly organized, spontaneously, by a group of women who wanted to support pregnancy, and encourage our minds toward it. The organizers were a slim, attractive group, with large white teeth and stubborn gazes, who appeared on billboards with arms around each other, laughing as though pregnancy were the most joyous event in the world. Their mission was to protect the fetus, and to coach us on the correct way to think.

Joanne loved Protection and loved it urgently, and without doubt. She joined at the beginner level, which meant that she sold merchandise. She quit her job and manned the flagship store in the Protection headquarters or went door-to-door selling tastefully designed mugs, caps, paperweights, jewelry, all emblazoned with the pink logo. The sale was easy to make, as everyone bought something; we all learned quickly that if you owned even one item from Protection, the busy officials from the government, who kept an eye on our behavior, would leave you alone.

Joanne and I did not see each other often now. She was quite involved in Protection and married another salesperson in it, a man named Greg. All I knew about him was that he moved with the slow floating elegance of her mother, and when they were together he always held her hand. Between her marriage and her job, it was difficult to get together. Sometimes we met for lunch. Each time we met she seemed taller. "I *love* it," she told me, a little breathless, as though she was constantly running up a hill. "I'm a top seller, did you know that? I had no idea I was good at this. It's what happens when you believe in the product, I guess. I feel very lucky."

She wore careful, glossy makeup now, her face always a little creamy. Her happiness had the stern, weighted quality of a vault; I was afraid of what lurked inside. It was not required, yet, that women join Protection, that they participate in the organization's mission, which involved both advantages—access to the nation's better hospitals and doctors, shining new schools, etc.—and threats, because Protection officers were always alert for women thinking bad thoughts.

But I was not a member and did not want to be. I had constructed a different life, for now, coaching the women's track team. I sometimes ran with them. I loved the sound of my breath in the silent fields, and I loved hearing theirs, and walking onto that field in the first light, ready to direct them, I felt content. My mother disapproved of this, which was why I did not talk to her much anymore.

"What about it do you like?" I asked Joanne, wondering.

She laughed, as though this were obvious. "The people," she said. "They are so nice. They think I'm a valuable addition to the organization."

I listened to her certainty and asked, "How do you know?"

"How do I know that they are nice?" she said, which was not answering the question I wanted. "They say I'm going to ascend in the organization. If I go to meetings, and all that." She folded her napkin and placed it by her plate.

Her enthusiasm had the shiny quality of a decoration; I did not quite believe it. "I'm glad," I said.

"How about you?" she asked.

I paused. "I'm good, too," I said.

I had mastered a certain glance when speaking to anyone who supported Protection, a kind of hard blink. Sadly, I employed it now when talking to Joanne; I was aware of myself blinking this way and was somehow ashamed of it; before, walking home from school, it had been easy to talk.

She paused.

"Good," she said.

A FEW YEARS AGO, I thought I noticed an officer from Protection wandering around the school where I worked—officers tried to emulate teachers, wearing beige blazers, sometimes (amusingly) carrying around textbooks, but I could always identify them by their slightly stiff, military manner of walking and by the expensive nature of their shoes. To appease them you were supposed to make eye contact with them, say (with enthusiasm) hello, not appear shy or irritable in any way, especially if you were a woman of childbearing age. It was also advisable to go to meetings and alert others that you were going. I made a point of leaving school one day to attend a Protection gathering with Joanne.

The meeting was in one of the central buildings downtown, which I never stepped inside; Joanne marched in with the confidence of one who belonged, heels ringing against the shining marble floor. We went to the tenth floor and entered a conference room, which was decorated with posters of smiling babies and mothers gazing at them as though they wanted to eat them, and enormous posters of children, faces frozen in laughter. I sat with ten other women on folding chairs. We wore name tags and everyone used their full name. The leader of this group, a Patty Sloan, stood in front of us. She spoke loudly, with a manner both upbeat and aggressive, as though the participants were objecting, even though everyone was somewhat timid and silent. At this meeting, she distributed baby clothes to everyone in the room.

The women in the room were in various lumpinesses of pregnancy; some, like Joanne, were not yet pregnant but intended to be. Patty passed around a box containing clothes sized for a six-month-old. The clothes included a picnic outfit, which involved crisp canvas overalls; a yellow party dress made of silk; a terry-cloth romper for the beach.

"Everyone hold each outfit for one minute," shouted Patty. A couple women lunged for the yellow dress. "One at a time!" she shouted. "No worries, everyone will get a turn with each outfit!"

Patty smiled as each person in the group passed around the tiny dress.

"We will do a series of exercises keeping your mind on your new baby!" she said. "Feel the clothes you are holding. Squeeze the little shoulders. Think about the joy you will know holding this being. Think, I will hug you, little baby! I will hug you so hard you will burst."

"I will hug you, little baby," everyone chimed.

"How will this baby fit into these clothes? Think. Bulky. You want a nice, bulky baby. Think that."

"I don't want a super-fat baby," said one woman, sounding sour.

"No criticism of the babies!" boomed Patty. "Turn the mind." Her voice was sharper, like a knife chopping a melon. She pressed a little outfit to her cheek. "If your thoughts start turning in any untoward direction, do this. Think, I love you little baby. You will be a big fat baby and laugh all the time. You will be happy and cute. Recite after me."

The women in the group all said this, together. "You will be a big fat baby and laugh all the time. You will be happy and cute."

"My baby will be beautiful," said Patty. "Say it!"

"My baby will be beautiful!"

"My baby will be a bundle of joy! Say it!"

"My baby will be a bundle of joy!"

"My baby is a precious diamond I will treasure! Say it!"

"My baby is a precious diamond I will treasure!"

The women's voices swelled. I mouthed the words but did not say them. When I glanced at Joanne's face, I noticed that it resembled the others so completely—the fierceness of the smile, the slant of her eyebrows—that I had to look away.

I WENT TO buy a suit, grateful for a clear, simple action. I walked by the building at Logan Street first to see what it looked like. It was a tall, glass office building, modern in that its street side tilted slightly like a pyramid. I told no one, of course, that I was going; I liked the idea that I was dressing for an official, even business-y, transaction. I was buying a suit.

"What is the event or occasion?" the salesgirl asked.

I considered. "A brunch," I said. "To celebrate an engagement," I said. This seemed like something all would agree on and celebrate; I picked out a suit that was a dark navy.

"Very sharp," the salesgirl said.

I turned around, examining myself in the mirror. I wondered what she saw in me, who she imagined I was. I wondered what anyone on the street would think if they saw me dressed like this. A successful person, they might think. Perhaps that was the purpose of this suit, to bolster the resolve of those who were wavering. It was a decent strategy. But I had no hesitation.

I regarded myself in the suit.

"I'll take it," I said. I asked her to cut off the tags; I wanted to wear it out.

I WALKED INTO the bright blue day as though it were silk. The others glanced at me, with a gaze of both admiration and suspicion—the admiration was new and the suspicion was something that was constant, like a low, burnt smell. I moved down the sidewalk in the suit, feeling the movement in my body, the shifting of my legs, cutting the world like scissors. I wanted to hurtle toward tomorrow, when I would see Dr. L.

I walked several blocks, slowly but not slowly.

Then, on the street I saw her. A gait that was familiar even from far away, that I knew even if a peculiar cheerfulness had infused it, a briskness that I did not want to see. The clapping of her sandals on the sidewalk. I saw this walk come toward me and then I saw her face and I knew it was Joanne. Of course. Then she saw me.

"Hey!" she said, stopping. She breathed a little hard, carrying some shopping bags. "Why all dressed up?"

Her eyes traveled up my outfit and down again.

"Just bought this. For a brunch," I said.

"I like it," she said. She set down one of her bags. She seemed to want to talk, and I wanted to just say good to see you and keep walking. But I saw her hands trembling as she looked for something in her purse, so I stayed.

"I need to decorate the baby's room," she said. She said it very softly, as though she were afraid of being harmed. "We are supposed to show photos of our room at the next meeting. Tomorrow." She paused. "I will be ranked," she said, "and it needs to be high."

"For what?" I asked.

"To get the best birth room. With the BestLove rating, I'll get it." If she received the highest ranking of love for her future child, she would receive the premier hospital suite when it was born, much coveted, which involved skilled medical personnel, a room with a soft bed and blankets, ample pain medicine during labor, a grand beginning to her baby's life. Not being a member of Protection meant that you waited in long lines to be admitted to the hospital, didn't always receive pain medicine or even a doctor, or were sent home to deliver on your own. In general, I made a point of avoiding hospitals, for there were always lines of women in labor, waiting, crumpled in pain, searching for a Protection officer and screeching about how much they loved their babies.

She took her phone out of her purse and showed me photos of the baby's room. The room looked familiar for a moment—then I realized, with a shock, that it was designed exactly like her childhood bedroom, the same orange curtains, the same lavender walls; the difference was that I saw a couple pictures of animals that she painted, a giraffe, a deer, set on the walls. I wondered if she understood this.

"Why did you choose that color?" I asked.

She looked more closely at it. "I liked it."

I could not tell her that it resembled the room where she

had grown up; this seemed too intimate. She was examining the photos with a grim expression.

"Will they rank me the highest?" she said. "Tell me."

I didn't know, but I quickly said, "Yes."

"I don't know what they'd like," she said. "I just guessed."

She was wearing her sales uniform, a crisp, pale-pink Protection blouse with the logo on the front, and she rubbed the scalloped collar as though trying to erase something from herself.

"Are you all right?" I asked.

"My mother would have liked this room," she said, firmly. "Don't you agree?"

I was surprised she mentioned her mother. I tried to remember her mother, and what I remembered instead was the way the bright sky seemed clangy and hollow, how it seemed to brush the tops of our heads as we approached her house. I remembered just one time Joanne's mother complimented her—she looked up one day when she was polishing a window, and said, "What a nice laugh you have." Neither of us knew what to say to that. How far away our mothers seemed, like remote, enormous planets, but also how close at moments, their immense heat on our faces. The singularity of the comment left Joanne confused and breathless. We kept wanting her mother to say something like that again. But, to my knowledge, she did not.

I wanted to comfort her, so I said, "I'm sure she would like it, yes."

It was clear that she was not just asking about her mother.

"I wish," she said, her voice soft and deadly hungry, "I wish you were pregnant." My body stilled. "Wouldn't that be perfect? Both of us. Sitting in the park. Knowing each other's children. Knowing them as they grew up together."

I smiled, a very careful smile, and stepped back, just slightly, from her. She was my friend but I was aware suddenly of the dangerous quality to her loneliness, its purpose, and I could see her wanting me to be like her. The prospect of loneliness, or forging ahead on one's own, was the true terror.

I had one thought. I had to get to my appointment tomorrow. So I said what I thought was my route to get there.

"You will be rated the highest of everyone. No one will come close."

I remembered suddenly what Joanne had been like when she was a child, before she lost her mother, when she whispered her critiques to me. I remember the clear sound of her truth, and how that precision was a thick rope, connecting us, how her words excavated the murkiness of the world. We walked beside each other, listening to each other, I could listen to her on and on. Now I had to get away from her so I could go see Dr. L; Joanne could not know what I was thinking at all.

"Do you think so," she said.

"Absolutely," I said. "You will be fine." How I hoped this was true. I stepped forward, put my hands on her shoulders so I was hugging her. The city, washed, a blur, around us.

THE NEXT DAY, I called in sick at work—a stomach bug. "I just need a day to rest up," I said, cheerfully; the administrator believed me. I might go see a doctor, which I said in case anyone saw me outside walking.

I walked through the city toward Dr. L. Since Dr. L's (illegal) success finding the words, others had seen an opportunity and wanted to benefit from this idea. There were giant billboards advertising Mr. Houseman, who said he knew the word that would make you thinner. He was a man in his seventies whose skin was burnished so he resembled an animated character. If you paid him a large sum of money, he would tell you the word that would make you decide not to eat. Slim women were featured on the billboards with him, looking pleased.

I walked past other signs: AVOID BLINDNESS! CALL 64521!

WE WILL TELL YOU THE WORD TO AVOID THE ONCOMING PLAGUE. This was to combat murmurings of mass waves of illness (rumored in other states) that would lead to one losing sight. There were flyers that cautioned one not to say a certain word, not mentioned, but implied, that might cause the person next to you to choke to death. I wandered through the icy shadows of the city, past what felt like a thick wilderness of leaflets, of warnings: MADAME JOAN HAS THE TWO EXACT WORDS THAT WILL MAKE YOUR CHILDREN STOP HITTING EACH OTHER AT SCHOOL or SECRET AND EFFECTIVE WORDS THAT WILL MAKE YOUR INTRUSIVE NEIGHBORS ANXIOUS AND JUST RETREAT INTO THEIR HOUSE or THESE SEVEN WORDS WILL STOP YOUR CANCER or DON'T EVER EVER SAY THIS WORD IF YOU WANT YOUR MOST HATED UNCLE TO STAY ALIVE.

The city lunged, grand and aloof, up around these flyers, the errant longings of the world.

Logan Street was not easy to find, and I set out to take a series of trains to get there. I wondered who else was looking for Dr. L, what other women needed the words. Were the women moving with confidence to see Dr. L, or with shoulders wilted, as though evaluating their own worth? Was that woman huddling by that building going to see Dr. L or was she just cold? Was everyone else asked to part their hair on the left side? Why was that? It didn't matter who was who, for even if my mouth was dry with the desire to tell someone, I couldn't. There was no one in the world I could tell.

I understood what Joanne had meant—she wanted someone to have the same thought as she did, she did not want to be alone in her pregnancy, her uncertainty about what would happen next. I had a different urgency inside me—to learn the words, end the pregnancy, and move on with my life. But as I walked through the streets, I realized that I also I wanted company, and wanted to know someone had the same thoughts as I did. My love for the world was coiled and intent as a vacuum. It was for the thump of my students' feet as they ran down the green track, the silvery joy in my throat when our girls won, the triumph in their faces, the way the world shimmered briefly in their hands. I loved the coolness in the air when we walked onto the field in the morning, the trembling silence of the new day, the sound of the buzzer when a race began. I loved their appreciation for me and for what they had accomplished. This was where I felt most myself, where I did not want to be anywhere else. How did anyone explain how they fit into the world, where you found your particular home?

I could not tell anyone I needed the words and began to feel sad for myself, for it seemed impossible that the words would work. I had but one life, and I was afraid I would lose control of it. It seemed that no one at all was on these streets, though it was crowded with people. The most dangerous thought I had just then, that dark trembling, that I was completely alone.

I KEPT WALKING. And I was aware of the women walking by, the ones who I imagined were going to Dr. L and the ones who were not.

I wanted terribly to find Dr. L. I wondered just then what Dr. L looked like. I had no picture of her in my mind. I suddenly imagined her entering a room and walking toward me; I could not see her face, but I imagined her placing her hands on my shoulders. I could, very clearly, with longing that made my skin feel thin, feel the warm solidness of her hands.

My phone rang. No. I let it ring a few times, but then answered.

"It's me," said Joanne.

Of course.

"Yes," I said, careful with my voice.

"They didn't like it," she said.

I could not remember what.

"The room, the crib, how I arranged it," she whispered. "They laughed at it. They laughed."

A plummeting inside me. "Oh no," I said, walking.

"I couldn't stand it. I wanted to run out," she whispered.

"Why didn't you?"

"I had to stay. Do you know what would happen to my ranking if I left? Do you know what would happen to me?"

I listened to her, my old friend, and I knew, and I didn't want to.

"They were wrong," I said.

There was quiet. "How do you know?"

I needed to convince her. "I saw it. It was a perfect room. Joanne. And the baby would love it."

She was quiet, I think absorbing. I wanted to tell her that her mother would have liked the room, but that wasn't true either. All I knew was what I thought, which was this:

"You will be a good mother to that baby. You will."

I had to say this quietly, for I was guessing. But I knew the sky-wide expansiveness of Joanne's hope. She would be kind to her child, she would be less critical than her own mother had been.

"I got a three. They knew what I was thinking. I was not properly focused. I don't know why I wasn't focused! My thoughts were straying, wrong."

I wanted to get off the phone and I wanted to stay on it. What could she do? Where was a door I could open so she could run out? I stood in the noisy center of the city, buildings soaring around me, everyone walking by me with their various locked doors.

"Come over," said Joanne. "Right now."

I wanted to plunge through the phone to her, to sit beside her, and I needed to keep walking.

"Please," she said.

"Joanne," I said. I could hear her tense waiting.

I took a deep breath.

"Later," I said, and hung up.

FINALLY, I REACHED the building where Dr. L was located. I went inside and took the elevator to the twentieth floor.

I walked down the worn, gray carpet that looked like it had not been washed in recent days, opened the door, and walked into the office. It both disappointed and comforted me in its utter and bland ordinariness. There was a conference room, with a large wooden table and seven black vinyl swivel chairs arranged around it, as though a group of businessmen were about to show up. A woman walked in, clutching a stapler for no apparent reason as there was nothing to staple. She glanced at me, as though from a great height, though we were eye to eye. I stiffened, and that seemed to answer what she wanted to know.

"She'll be with you soon," she said.

I sat in one of the swivel chairs. The gray blinds were drawn, and I could see the city light come through it, strips of dirty shine that stretched like ribbons on the floor. I had turned off my phone but I looked at it, wondering if Joanne was trying to call; the phone was warm, almost breathing in my hand.

After a few minutes, a person I imagined was Dr. L walked in. I stood up. She was a slight woman, and I was disappointed that her hands were regular size. She could have been a person in human resources, but she wore a white lab coat, perhaps to identify her medical status. She had a blank, regal expression. Everyone associated with her had mastered the art of the impassive face.

She regarded me with tired blue eyes, checking the part in my hair. Her work was so dangerous she had to see if anyone was going to arrest or kill her. I wanted her to love me, which meant that I wanted her to set me free. That was the love she distributed, to each woman who came to her.

"Do you want to know?" she asked.

"I do," I said.

Dr. L put her hands on my shoulders and whispered them to me. They were not unique words in any way. I can't say anything else about them.

"It won't take long," she said. "You can go into the bathroom," she said. "Say them quietly, but with conviction."

"Then what?" I asked.

"It will take about an hour," she said. "It will feel like a period. It may hurt, but there is aspirin in the cabinet and it won't take very long. Just wait and then it will be done. You can leave through that other door. Do not tell anyone. My partners and I have worked hard learning the exact words, said in the correct way, to create the result needed. If you need the words again, come back."

Then she lifted her hands off and I felt suddenly lighter and sorrowful; I was just here in this room, with myself.

I walked into the bathroom, and quietly said the words; soon I felt a pulling in my stomach. My body cramped, but it did what I wanted it to do, and soon it was finished.

When I was done, I went to the door and walked out.

It was the middle of the afternoon. The sunlight made the world resemble a cake that had just been iced. The brightness shone on windows, on mailboxes, on the tops of cars. I could still feel the grip of Dr. L, on my shoulders, and I wanted that feeling to remain. I walked quickly down the streets, and into the chattering noise of the day. I was walking home, I was just a person walking.

I went down one street, then another, feeling the roar of the city in my ears. The words had worked. No one asked me anything; no one noticed anything; I had the immense luxury of being nothing but a person coming home from work. I passed one Protection building after another, the secretaries sitting, staring, at the rest of us from the front desk, and when I walked by the offices, they knew nothing of me. I was the biggest secret, I was mine.

I was thinking of Joanne, and I realized I wanted different words now, too, ones that Dr. L had not offered. I wanted the words that would comfort Joanne, that would tell her that the love that was housed inside her was right, and I wanted the words to describe the particular shape of my own love and fear. The city rose, its cool shadows stretching around me; how I wanted to call Joanne. I tried to imagine us walking together, as we had in the past, our perceptions, our sentences, carving the air around us, as though we were cutting diamonds. But as I walked and walked through the roaring city, ready to call Joanne, a fact settled on me, with great clarity; I could not tell her any of this. My knowledge lived in silence, without words.

THE HYPNOTIST

He hypnotized me, and I loved him. This was a theory that came to me when I was eight, then was affirmed when I was a teen, and then simmered in my mind as an adult, but I remembered it clearly now, a few decades down the line, as I stood in the yard, waiting for news about my father. Years ago, we were sitting around the dinner table, harassing him for information about his patients, which he never revealed. My father, annoyed, sawing a piece of chicken, had mentioned this surprising skill.

"Do you know," he said, "a long time ago, during my training, I hypnotized someone."

My sister and I were meanly trying to guess his patients' various ills. We never could observe him at work, we didn't know what was happening when he closed the office door, so we threw out dumb guesses: your two o'clock might murder someone and flush them down the toilet, your three o'clock worries so hard her hair gets wild and birds land in it to make a nest. We wanted to feel superior because we were jealous, because the patients had a claim on our father that we did not; they were demanding ghosts who would be announced by the answering service. He would say, "Just one second," on the kitchen line and then went to his bedroom, slamming the door as though to emphasize the importance of his work. When he closed the door of his office, when he took calls in his bedroom, he turned his attention to his patients in a way that we could never be part of, could never see.

To end this unfortunate turn of conversation, our father said he had taken a class in hypnosis during his psychoanalytic training, that it was one of his favorite classes (though he had liked ones about catatonia and character too). When he was twenty-five years old, seeing patients at a hospital in Tarzana, he met a woman who kept chewing on red licorice. She ate so much she felt sick, she could not stop eating the licorice. It didn't seem that terrible, but she believed she could not stop herself and he wanted to help. So he hypnotized her (method classified) and told her to stop eating the licorice and she made a sour face and never ate it again. The hypnosis didn't involve a ticking clock or a ball swinging back and forth, I didn't learn the precise technique. I don't know why I believed my father at that moment—and now I wonder if it was a joke—but it felt like the most unsurprising answer to the machinations of the world. Everything seemed to perk up, brighter—the butter a gold bar on a china plate. He looked around the table, and said, "She didn't want licorice for a few hours. She just stopped. That was a great triumph for her."

My father gazed across the room, as though remembering

that moment fondly. I remember gripping my fork, watching him.

He tried to explain it to us. "Freud describes learning it from Breuer," he said. "He had a patient and hypnotized her and then told her to tell him what was bothering her."

He didn't tell us what you were like when hypnotized, though I wasn't sure I wanted to know. Did you just stare into space, or what? But when I learned he had done this, I thought that this skill actually explained everything.

Would that explain (I thought, as a child) the fact that I wanted to believe what he believed? I wanted a theory to explain the helpless force of love I had for my father. I had my own thoughts, which curled in my head like fragile green shoots, thoughts that no one had ever thought before in the history of the world. What, for example, was this thought, that I wanted to kill my friend down the street when she laughed at my sneakers with the gold fabric stars on them? What was this thought, that I wanted to press my lips to that boy's soft ear to see if it tasted like a marshmallow? What was this thought, to wrap myself in a dress made of the fire in the fireplace, because I imagined it a brilliant, glowing skirt? My mind was breaking open each morning as I looked out at the dusky gold sunlight in Los Angeles and wondering how to describe the general explosive sweetness of the new day.

There was a feeling, with my father, of the sun cast out more brightly onto the world. The sun was different around him, illuminating each blade of grass, each camellia, each car windshield. Everything felt part of a grand plan, meaning life seemed to have an actual direction. The way he nodded at my various little perceptions, as though they were important, the way we walked together, the way he called me "the president," with affection, because I apparently did not sleep at all as a toddler and directed my parents to sleep beside my bed. The way he described how stunned he was by love when he saw me as a baby; he couldn't believe it! It was just there. His laugh, when I did various funny things, like rub spaghetti in my hair. How could I exist! I was accustomed to this thing, existing, but he couldn't believe it. That laugh rushed through me like a froth of silver. My small stride rushing to keep up with his.

It felt easier, as a child, to sometimes borrow his thoughts. When I was eight, we went to watch a UCLA basketball game, and I did not know what to look for and he said, "Number seventy-five. Watch. He has the best dunk. It looks like he's climbing up a staircase in the air"—and I watched seventy-five and I thought he was right, it did look like a staircase, and here was a thought I could think over and over, he looks like he's climbing up a staircase, and it was his thought, but I borrowed it, and told someone at school about it. "Then he twirled like a tornado," I said, adding my own flair to it, which was a little thrill. But to cleave my thoughts to his felt like a gift; it felt like love.

Why did I think he had hypnotized me? I was embarrassed by the force of my feeling, wanted to find a reason for it. I missed him when he was not around—when he went away for a conference, for two nights, with my mother, when we were six, seven, eight, the nights felt long, like enormous dark lakes I had to swim through, a deep sluggish mud that made it impossible to move. Not missing, that was not the word. How was I to be in the world without them? What magic had they, or he, conjured so that when they drove away I felt the burden of each moment, the light tarnished, everything harder to perceive? My sister and I watched TV and needled each other and watched the babysitters, a series of lanky, distracted girls who viewed us through bored eyes; we felt that boredom in the way they crunched potato chips, savagely, with their teeth. Over the course of the night, we sometimes forgot about our parents; we stood on chairs and grabbed cookies out of cabinets, our minds went to other topics, an untethering that seemed disloyal but a relief.

But when we heard the door open, and they were back, a radiance seemed to suffuse the hallway. There were the sounds of them entering the house, the key in the lock, the shuffle of their shoes on the wood floor. The sounds I had memorized. I understood that a part of me was dedicated to supporting myself while they were gone, and now I did not have to support myself this extra way. The world felt uncertain sometimes, and my parents weren't perfect, they got mad, like sudden bad weather, about random dumb things, but their presence made the floor feel impenetrable.

Then I was older, eleven, twelve, and I boarded the bus, the RTD groaning up to the stop, picking me up and depositing me to the places I wanted to go around Los Angeles. I never could quite believe the bus would go where it said it would, the banners across the front saying: SANTA MONICA, MARINA DEL REY, but when I leaped onto the bus it seemed like the rest of the world crumpled, dragged along like a sash.

It was like it vanished until I returned. I could not believe this other world, my world belonged to me, it was mine. The bus moved past the stores and trees and parking lots I knew and I looked out the smeared window, wondering if the bus would in fact get me to where I was going—a dance class, a McDonald's, the beach—the world felt like it was glistening beyond the window, made of cotton or paper, but the bus just moved, with the same one determined thought, to its destination. And I remembered when the bus passed the building where my father's office was, and I didn't know what he was doing but knew he was there. He was invisible, but he was not. I fell into a sort of calm, I was tethered to something, even as I lumbered out into the day.

I had my own thoughts. I was noticing things. The goal was to keep these things a secret. How thrilling a secret felt, cupped in my hands like a fragile, translucent balloon. Crouching with my friend Gloria behind a hedge at recess, so we could avoid dodgeball and getting slammed by the hard rubber balls, listening to the teacher call our names until she was hoarse, as though she thought we had been kidnapped. There was the great triumph of that misunderstanding, our hands knotted together, knowing the truth: we were here. The teacher yelling at us when we emerged. Walking through the door of our house, this secret zipped silently in my throat. Could my father know that the teacher thought I had vanished? I eyed him when I walked through the house, watched him sort through the mail or sit on the couch and watch the news. How could he not know? I watched him as he pretended not to know. It was a brilliant act.

"How was school?" he asked, offhandedly.

I tried to harden my skin against his knowledge, to trick him, but he stood there, pretending to wonder. He did not know. Or did not admit that he did.

When I was older, he snapped at me to remember not to go to the party in the canyon where two cars ran into a ravine, killing all four teen passengers, I said of course—but then I did ride there. On the ride, my thoughts were suddenly thick and violent as branches, thrusting into the air; I was determined to be myself, I would not think what he thought. But there I was, with my friends, frozen in the back seat, that warning like a glowing neon sign as the car crawled up the soft black magnolia-fragrant hills. What was wrong with me? Why couldn't I shut it off? I knew what it was: I had been hypnotized, while the other kids seemed to forget their parents and what they said, with glorious ease, leaned out of the rushing car and screaming into the warm night. This was, I deduced, a problem with hypnosis—his thought was there, lodged in my head.

LOVE IS A feeling but it's also a thought, one that emanates from the center of your body. It's a form of knowledge, a feeling that tries to answer everything you crave about the world. So when I fell in love, I tried most to form my own thoughts. This was when I'd claim my own mind, I would let these branches reach toward whomever they wanted. My mind would be an open sky.

My father sensed some disruption in the hypnotic field.

When, in college, I dropped by the house, we sat at the kitchen table, and talked first about what he thought I should study (he thought history or political science, maybe literature, not business), what part-time job would work best with my class schedule. Then—the prospects.

"May I suggest," he said, "Hal Silver's son. Just graduated Stanford, three years ago, has a growing PR business, and a yacht. Wouldn't that be fun, going to Catalina on a yacht?"

Then he sent me possibilities in the *Jewish Journal*. "This guy, studying to be an anesthesiologist, looking for someone who likes to laugh, that's you! Someone who likes to put people to sleep wants to be woken up. Let's see, you just write to this box number—"

"No!" I said.

"Why not?" He looked bewildered.

It seemed obvious.

I couldn't decide if these ideas were serious or not, but they were numerous, and each one felt somehow abhorrent. My mind shut firmly against them. My shutting down felt like a great and lame triumph. My attempts at love would be a rebuttal.

Yet I let myself be hypnotized by a range of fools. I loved one guy because he enjoyed ridiculing the world, which was funny until the ridicule was turned toward me. Another: a man who ate only frozen hors d'oeuvres and said so little he created an aura of great depth and intelligence, until I realized he actually had little to say. The gymnast who moved in an unearthly way, who I imagined would clutch me the same way he held the bar, but who slept curled up, away from me, hunched in a cocoon.

I felt like I was in a tunnel, grabbing who I could, looking in their eyes for something that I knew, and did not, kissing mouths that tasted like coffee, breath mints, candy, darkness. The beauty of secrets, the silky triumph of sleeping naked beside another person; I could do that, too. I threw myself forward, looking. I told them nothing.

My father was full of questions! He was like a shark, moving through the water, smelling the faults seeping from these men like blood.

"This guy you talked about, Carl? He did what, studied anthropology and he is evaluating people's behavior in pubs? Does that mean he works in a bar?"

"The other day I was just thinking of the one you mentioned, Jeff? He didn't mention his parents? Is he estranged from them?"

I reported on my life as though I were a spy. ("We went to dinner." "What kind of dinner? Where?" "A good one." "We saw this new movie, a thriller, really good." "What movie?" "I'm not remembering, but it was set in Paris.") Sometimes I did not remember, honestly, the information flew out of my head.

My father felt left out. This state filled him with a lot of energy, like a carbonated drink. I sat at the kitchen table and he made tea. The blue flame fluttered under the kettle. I was in my twenties, hurtling toward something, afraid some goldenness about life would slip through my arms. I could not bear his bewilderment, but also required it. The suggestions about the men with glamorous lifestyles were then accompanied by a series of carefully researched warnings, offered with great politeness. "You do know that a large percent of skiers break their legs each year." Or, "The fact that he does not give you information about his relatives is, well, not a good sign." These thoughts were scattered among otherwise reasonable conversations; they exploded in my head, weaving a lattice around me, as we sat in the kitchen, the kettle boiling. I was just with my father, the hypnotist, but I did not know how to protect my thoughts, and how to structure them, peering through the lattice so I could still see him, sitting at the table, smiling at me.

I FOUND MYSELF hypnotized by a man who had my father's laugh, which felt buoyant and right, but wearing a costume of a someone else, with vigorous hand gestures and dark hair and large white teeth. His name was Armand. I was hypnotized with my whole body, a hypnosis of electricity, of waiting for him to walk through the door, my mind full of him. Thank god no one knew this, that no one had access to my mind. The glorious hypnosis of being held while approaching orgasm, the safety of showing him when I was ridiculous, trembling. What is better than that gift?

My father shaking hands with him. Their palms touching, that weird feeling. Armand's hand had been inside me! What would happen? I waited for the sky to crumble to earth, but my father sensed nothing. Shaking hands as though closing a deal. There was an embarrassing, ancient quality to the shaking hands. They were polite, too polite, my father bringing Armand a cup of tea with honey, asking him about his job as a publicist for a type of fancy car no one bought. They faced each other across a table, talking about the world like regular people, and I wondered if he was hypnotizing Armand, I had that thought, and with a slight panic, wanted to warn my lover. Stop! You don't have to think his thoughts! I wanted to tell him. What shape would my father's hypnosis take toward Armand. Would Armand suddenly feel deeper feelings toward me? Or would he want to flee? What would be my father's desired outcome here? Armand didn't have a yacht but was a good dancer and enjoyed his job trying to create interest in unwanted cars. Would it be: Get away from my daughter? Or: Welcome, don't stray or I'll come find you and beat you up? What did my father want for me as an adult? But more, more, more—why the hell did it matter? I wanted to flee them both. My father, wearing a blue sweatshirt, sitting in what I thought was his professional listening position, one leg crossed over another, hands clasped across his chest. I saw Armand nod, his foot jiggling, wanting, sweetly, to be liked.

I could not guess what my father thought of Armand. He kept everything sealed in, craftily. It was annoying. He did not appear to be the powerful person that I knew as a child; he was just sitting and talking to this man beside me.

When we left, I held Armand's hand and asked, "What did you think?"

I looked into his eyes carefully, trying to see if he, like me, was hypnotized. But Armand saw my father simply as a regular person, who talked about things like who was the best player this year on the UCLA Bruins or the best air conditioner to get for the size of the room. He knew a lot about all electronic devices, and which delis in West LA had the best matzo ball soup; Junior's better than Zucky's, no contest. He didn't even eat matzo ball soup that often but liked being an expert on it.

"He told me don't even go near any sort of chicken soup at Izzy's, my god. A bland nothing. A travesty of soup," he said.

Later I asked my father what he thought of Armand.

He became suddenly busy with the refrigerator, bringing out half-opened yogurt containers, smelling them, throwing them out. He and my mother loved to throw out food if they thought it was spoiled. They did it with a kind of exuberance, as though hunting down a monster on the cold shelves. It was a horrible waste.

"He seems nice," he said. I heard the word seems, though I don't think he was deliberately leaning into it.

He found a yogurt that had, shockingly, not been opened, flipped off the plastic top, took an emphatic and somehow ominous bite. I thought that being hypnotized by my father meant that I sometimes believed I knew his thoughts—his sour chuckle when he overheard a political lunatic on the TV, his sharp, furious sigh when he heard me complain about a boss who had demeaned me. The hypnosis of a daughter meant perhaps that I understood him, too. But at that moment I had no idea what my father was thinking, what he thought of Armand, and that was both a relief and made me feel as though I were alone on an island—a place of adulthood, whatever that was.

A few months later, Armand decided that our run was over and that was that. "You are not it," he said, and left. It was shocking, waking up without him, as though he could make this decision, after we had writhed around in the buoyant velcroed state that was love. It seemed as though this world was not the world, that the real world was existing behind a secret glass door. This was not the world, yet it was, the tattered story about grief, yet deeply new.

I had entered the dark of the world fumbling, trying to locate its seam, finding none. There was the feeling of shame, that this form of hypnosis had not worked, that I had failed in my own attempts to conjure the attention of someone, that my father had somehow won in some race I did not know had been established. I felt competitive because I had lost.

My father slumped before his tea, sad in a way that felt like a terrible offering. I did not want him to look that sad, and I did not want to be the object of pity.

"How could he do that to you?" he said. "A scum. If I run into him I will beat him up."

This was an absurd statement, as my father was a gentle person, though he liked the concept of himself as someone who would pummel Armand. What irked me, perhaps unfairly, was the idea that he wondered how Armand could vanish, how this could happen to me, in that I had stupidly thrown myself at this person who decided, well, not me.

I had never missed anyone bodily, and somehow I missed Armand, his bony feet, his red lips, his shining brown hair. I missed the warm weight of his arm on me in bed and how we did not want to depart from each other into sleep, I clung to my longing as evidence of my separation; it was mine, even if there was no one to hold with it. My thoughts wound around his invisible body, and I almost liked him more as an absence, for then he was pure, unknowable.

My father, of course, wanted to talk about it, and I did not.

Armand was a stupid dream and my father was here, on the patio, describing all the ways he wanted to harm him, with a sort of fierceness and delight, as though he wanted to shoulder the anger for me. It was somehow self-congratulatory, as he and my mother had lived, mostly successfully, on the boat of marriage for thirty or so years. It seemed a gift and also ridiculous. I looked down and hoped my father would not see my shame.

MY OWN LIFE continued, that peculiar conveyor, I was twenty-five, boarded a plane and floated across the country, and I met a man, Ben, who I wanted to wrap around me like a coat. The strange thing was that he wanted to wrap me around him, too; somehow we both understood the other as essential shelter. At night, when he held me, it was as though I were a baby. I felt that comfort, that desire to be nowhere else. We lived on the other side of the nation, and he did not meet my father until we were engaged; then there was no room for debate. When Ben met my father, they did not shake hands but hugged, as though trying to feel some similarity in each other. My father sensed that he was not to be kept out but invited in.

Ben was not hypnotized by my father; he was a little shy around him, wanting to make a good impression. My father wanted to do something to make a connection, and knowing that Ben was a fan of walnuts, he gave him a walnut cracker that had belonged to a great-aunt.

DURING THE WALK down the aisle at our wedding, my hypnosis was useless. I had no idea what my father thought at that moment, or he had no idea what I felt, either. We had no words for each other; my arms linked as I moved to my beloved, carrying a love created from my mother and father, to present to someone else. The swish of white silk, the sweetness of roses, my father lifting a glass of pink champagne and declaring a toast, suddenly stammering, tearful, unable to speak.

THE NEXT THIRTY years: the slow and long span of adulthood, the arc of one's family, its mirror and departure from your own. The way my father held our children, looking at them with a kind of bewildered love, that again he was clutching a baby, but that it had entered the world through his daughter, an impossible fact. He looked at them as though at comets, dazed, blinking.

The children outgrew clothes, they sang in recitals, they graduated from school, they wore onesies and then T-shirts and then jackets and high heels. Their procession through the years was an echo to him, he was attuned to that, opened his mind to every memory he had about me when I was their age. It was as though he wanted to fall back into that time, that those years were when he felt most himself, most powerful. But I was tired of being a child, I had done that and now I was looking down the telescope the other way, astonished: it seemed a great and puzzling triumph.

But my own children did not listen to me the way I listened to my father. They doubted me early on. "Clean that up!" I'd say and they'd laugh me out of the room. My own skills at hypnosis were clearly faulty. It was embarrassing, really, and I wondered if their ease of inattention was a failure of my parenting or a success. They floated away, bright balloons, buffeted by the wild air.

I watched our children watch my father. They rushed toward him when we visited, a moon pulling a tide. They did activities perplexing to him—shouted at Nintendos, scrolled through photos of friends on their phones.

When we left my parents' home, the children sometimes had precise observations that made me think they were seeing him from afar, from an island across a sea.

"Why does he not understand a phone?"

"Why did he get mad when you moved that chair?"

The children entered the house as though it were merely a house. They ran through it, looking for hard candies, random toys, old photos they could laugh at. They went to my father like a magnet, but their eyes were sharp. They wanted to know reasons.

MY ADULTHOOD HAD first been a large, oversize outfit, and now was adjusted to fit more firmly on my waist and shoulders. I looked in the mirror and was surprised. My father and I talked every week. He wanted to know was happening with my life, with the children. I told him what I thought was everything, covering the children and my work and what I was cooking and he laughed and listened and sometimes asked, "What else?"

I didn't know what else. He seemed to believe I was hiding something from him. I wanted to offer him something else, the what else.

My father gripping the phone at fifty, sixty, seventy. What else. He flung open the door and we examined each other. "Hello! You look great!" The hypnosis of love is that, even as we all hurtle southward, we see the version of the person that we want to see. I saw him open the door at seventy, eighty, his shoulders thinner, his beard fading white, and I noticed the father, sharp elbowed, black haired, walking quickly beside me, shutting the door to talk to his patients. I could see him as though through a telescope, perfectly. He looked at me, in the slump of middle age, and he saw a tiny sparkling girl. What a trick that hypnosis was, what a joyous shared deceit! He loved that deceit. As I trudged in, he saw that girl and sensed his power over her, and his laugh bellowed, delighted.

IN THE BLUE dusk of night, in my fifties, I sat on the patio. My parents wouldn't let me in the house. They were afraid of the virus. They were afraid of me, and they were right; I had been on a plane, god knew what I brought with me. My visits now meant that I came to see them and sat on a plastic chair on the stubby green lawn. They peered out and waved and I yelled so they could hear me through the screen door. Sometimes they came outside and sat on the patio and we called to each other.

For a few months, I visited this way. It was still Los Angeles, so it was warm, and at dusk, I pulled on a sweater. Sometimes I sat in the yard, on my plastic chair for a few hours and after a while my parents remembered tasks they had to do and disappeared into the house. I was reluctant to leave. I stood by the glass windows and watched them, my father and mother moving through their living room, through the piles of things they had accumulated. The couches and chairs were the same as they had been fifty years ago, the couches covered in beige tweed, the chairs in gold velour, with stuffing coming out of their arms; my parents had not repaired them. The injured furniture sat with an indifference born of a sort of joy. It was as though my parents were still waiting for us to run through the house again as children, in those small, sweet bodies, that by maintaining the furniture as it had been they would conjure the past. If they left everything in a form and shape we would recognize, their children would return.

There was mail, an ungodly amount of mail, there was a pile of expired 20 percent off coupons from Bed Bath & Beyond, there was a package of seven unopened Brooks Brothers shirts, there was a box containing a sweater I had sent them six months ago, there were catalogs and magazines on the fireplace.

I was sad and mesmerized as I watched them. I had the uncharitable thought that they didn't mind me out there, in some way, that they liked being watched behind the glass. Or they liked the idea that they could disappear into the house.

"Let me come in and clean up," I asked.

My father, low lit by a brass lamp, stopped, sorting through some envelopes. He said, "No. It's not safe. There's no need to clean up."

"With a mask. Fifteen minutes?"

No.

"But how can you find anything? What if someone trips?"

He looked at me with a rare stern expression.

No. They were fine. Stop telling them what to do.

When they were out of the room, I pressed close to the screen and imagined darting in and grabbing some junk mail and dumping it. Would another person have just barged in and done it? They were old, but their brains were still sharp, or sharpish. They would know. Any piece of six-month-old mail that I tossed they would ask for, and they would feel cruelly betrayed. Or maybe the hypnosis was still active, keeping me on the patio, waiting for them.

My father came to the door and sat on a folding chair. He wore a sweater, even indoors, and he always offered me a jacket. We stared, him behind the glass, me sitting on the patio, in a sort of détente. He always offered thoughts on improvement of some sort, some way to protect oneself: a vitamin I should be taking, a safety recall he had seen on the news.

My father settled in his chair with a proclamation set in his mind, something he had been thinking about, strategies so I would be safe in the increasingly bewildering LA traffic. He told me which streets to take from 4:00 p.m. until 7:00, and the streets and intersections to avoid, in low, hushed tones, as though it were a military maneuver. "Never Wilshire and Westwood at five p.m.," he said.

I sat on the darkening patio, in a posture of listening, though I knew all of this. The hypnotist straight in his chair, pressing his spine against it in a position of vigilance. He was glad to see me but wary, as though I was about to ask him a difficult question.

I SHOUTED, TENDERLY, at my father and mother through the glass for a couple visits and peered through to the growing clutter in the living room that they would not let me fix. Then one day in spring, my father was tired but wanted to go on a walk. He did not go on walks every day but wanted to show me that he could still do it. "Let me get a sweater," he said. He pushed down on the arms of his chair and slowly raised himself, holding his arms out for balance. Then he left the room. I talked to my mother, who was chatting brightly about her friends, through the glass for a while. The yard sparkled in the sun.

My mother stood up. "Let's get some lunch," she said. "I'll make some sandwiches."

"I'll bring one out to you," she said. They fed me outside, as though I were a dog.

"Hello," she called. She went deeper into the house. She said my father's name.

There was a silence, and for a few moments it was a regular silence. I don't know when it became another sort of silence. One moment, then, two, then the current of unease. I stood up and moved close to the window and tried to hear. I heard them talking. Then I heard my mother say, sharply, "Oh no."

I looped my mask on my ears, pushed open the door, and went inside. It was strangely easy. The dust sparkling in the light. I felt myself move like a person through the house.

Then I saw my father in his room, lying, still on his bed.

"What happened?" I asked.

"Don't come in!" he said, with surprising force.

"Are you sick?"

"Go!" he said. "You're not supposed to be in here."

"Um, you have a black eye."

"It's just a little fall. It's nothing! I must have hit something."

"Are you okay?"

"Get out!" he yelled.

"Back on the patio!" my mother said.

"I'll call the—"

"For god's sake, don't call anyone! Just get out!"

I didn't know what to do. Did I stay, as I thought I should, or go out, which he was clearly screaming at me to do? Other smarter, unhypnotized offspring would ignore what he asked, would rush in and bring him water, or check him over, or do whatever hapless children do when their parents fall. But he did not want me to. He was very direct. He lay on his bed with a black eye and he wanted me out. So I went to the patio. I stood there, staring at the glass.

"Hello," I said, stupidly.

In a few minutes, my mother came out. She had a frozen stare, as though she had been hypnotized in a different way.

"Would you like some strawberries? I just got some from the market. They're good," my mother said.

"No, I don't want any strawberries! Is he okay?"

"They're good with yogurt," she said.

"No! Can we just go to urgent care," I said.

"He says he's fine. He says don't call the doctor now. He said he is fine. And he knows just what happened."

"How does he know?"

My mother rolled her eyes and vanished back into the house. I followed her, the trespasser. He was still on the bed, now with his eyes closed and an ice pack on his forehead. He was, however, alert enough to hear me tiptoe in, and raised his head slightly.

"Out!" he said. "You can't be in the house."

There was a terrible, real fear in his eyes, something more frightening than what had just happened to him.

I stepped toward him, wanting to get a better look, but he half sat up.

"Out!" he yelled, his voice hearty in its outrage at my presence.

I stopped feeling weepy and was now mad.

"I'm going to the yard," I said, "Talk to me through the window." He glared at me but didn't object.

I headed out to this new discussion spot, outside of their bedroom window, stepped around a cloudy tangle of camellia bushes and, standing in the dirt, tapped on the glass. The yard smelled like honey with its camellias and gardenias. Inside, my father slowly sat up. I gripped my cell phone, ready to call every ambulance in the world. He turned toward the window, squinted, trying to see me through the smeared glass.

"I know what happened," he said.

I stood amid the camellias, trying to hear him.

"I stood up too fast," he said. "So what. It's not anything. It happens. You don't have to think it's anything else."

He slowly turned so he was facing me, looking directly at me. His eyes were startlingly bright. And I understood, then, that he was trying to convince me of something. I felt a tremble in the hypnosis, for I did not believe what he said. He presented his opinion with such confidence I almost admired it, his belief, his perception that all was okay, that what he thought was true. But I did not. I did not think that was what happened to my father. And at that moment I knew that something had severed, that the hypnosis depended on a sort of innocence, a bargain between parent and child. I stood in the dirt; my father was upright and tense with his own theory of what had happened. I understood, fully, the theater of parents and children, the way we acted to maintain our roles, a thought I was not supposed to have—that we were together just temporarily, that we would separate from one another, that my father did not want me to infect him, yes, but that he also did not want me to know what was happening inside the house.

I touched the glass. It was dusty but hard, and my father continued talking, but I understood that I was not listening as I had before. There was the peculiar sensation of some elemental part of the hypnosis vanishing. He was not always right. How had it taken me so long to understand this, or understand it in this particular way? How a part of me had always wanted in some way to believe this, that he was a lighthouse, casting brightness into the dark endless sea of the world. I was hypnotized, perhaps, by the desire for him to know everything. I knew that of course he was not always right, that my thoughts were separate from his, that I floated along in my own way, a happy scrap of a person. But just then I understood that he did not quite know what was happening, and it was the clearest and most terrible thought that I ever had.

I did not believe him.

But I pretended that I did.

"Okay," I said, leaning close to the glass.

He rubbed his forehead. Did he know I was lying? I couldn't tell.

The bruise on his face darkening, he was trying to figure out what to do. I knew that I could not be part of that figuring.

What was wrong with my brain? I asked myself. What had been wrong with it all these years? It turned to love, it did that eagerly, happily, that was the rich and living part of my brain. But my brain was too small, too meager to comprehend the other thing. No human brain, truly, could. There was no medication, no pill, that would unlock the understanding of his decline, of his future passing; we stood, dumb, hapless, in the face of it. We stared at each other through the smeared glass and neither of us would mention, not now, and not months later, when we sat, waiting at the hospital, by his bed. I could not tell him that my brain was a spectacular failure because it could not hold this, the brute fact of our separation. This was a thought I could not have.

Now I stood in the dirt, the yard's rank, honeyed smell, watching him.

"It happens," he said, looking at me. Sitting up now. A curious look, eyebrow lifted.

"Okay," I said. The room was dim. It was hard to see anything. I pressed my forehead softly against the cool glass.

SEPARATION

The ships would rise all at once; the day would be celebratory and historic, silver flags fluttering on the dry field. The takeoffs would be coordinated, one after another, a series of shuddering rockets heading up into the air. The dust from the ground, a yellow shimmer. There would be a brass band, maybe several, on a vast field, playing anthems of bravery, and television crews would run across the field filming the rockets as they separated from earth. A major holiday across all nations. There would be T-shirts and posters and other merchandise, and there would be, for the first time in years, an unnatural, exuberant feeling of hope. Everyone, Dawn said, would be grateful, for doing something this brave, this dangerous, for strapping ourselves into these silver ships. Those left on earth would lift hands in salute as the ships cleaved into the air, gigantic and shining, and everyone would watch, the rockets growing smaller and smaller, as they faded into the sky.

I had only learned about the ships through information we received in school. Each year, on the educational day devoted to preparation for the Separation, the teachers marched into the classroom wearing long coats that resembled aluminum tents; the government manufactured them to show us what we would wear in our lives on Mars. Each year, we received a newer and improved version of the outfit and we left school, a flock of silver shining gowns, shards of light hurtling through the yard. On the icy landscape of Mars, the coats would, supposedly, protect us; we pulled them tight around our bodies even though they made us sweat. We would receive pamphlets describing that year's progress, the latest developments with magnets and on and on. The main point was that the explorers would be sent to Mars first, ahead of the general population, to do necessary investigation, and then return for us. Then the rest of us who had waited on earth, watching their ascent on giant screens, would be retrieved. The rockets would again lift off the earth, carrying all of us through the dark to our glorious new futures.

Everyone she knew, Dawn said, had a list. There were thirty-seven people on her family's list. She was not supposed to tell anyone, she said, but she knew I could be trusted, so she was going to tell me who was on it.

Dawn told me about the list the day her mother drove us to see the ships. It was a great privilege seeing the ships, greater because my parents hadn't seen them. I was going to see something they never had, and as we moved through the gates, I felt a cool, unexpected joy on my arms. The ships were set in a field outside the city: eighty, a hundred, arranged as in a parking lot. They were supposed to haul the first brave explorers into the sky. I was surprised how easy it was to drive into the lot, if you had permission and knew where they were. They towered, great and silver, spread across the huge pale field; we ran past dozens of them, like giant lipsticks, columns of silver light. "Let's go," Dawn said, with a shocking casualness. They were, to Dawn and her mother, ordinary. She had been here many times.

It surprised me that we could just run between them, that the rockets, which we had heard about for years now, were just sitting here, that we could even walk up to them and put our hands on the hot steel; the reason we could do this was Dawn's father. He was famous, an investor in the rockets, in the future. We did not know much about him, but in photos he was recognizable because of his smile; he was a businessman always photographed in a crisp blue suit and who had a smile that looked as though it had been installed in his face, in its startling, fraudulent brightness.

I was an intruder in that lot, but also invited, and my heart was divided, like a cafeteria tray, into equal parts pride and unease. We stood in the blue shadow of the tallest one.

"So, you know," she said. "I can bring someone."

Her voice was cool, matter-of-fact. We both knew the difference between us; her family would lift off as part of the Separation, while mine would wait for them to return, but I sensed her hesitating. I stood, leaning forward, a posture of listening.

"One person," she said.

WE LIVED IN the last American city. It was located in the upper Midwest and had grown in size over the last ten years. The nation's population had recently surged toward this city, toward the enormous, precious lakes, which held everything necessary to live. No one I knew had seen the lakes, or swam in them, though photos of them were everywhere. The lakes were projected, blue, trembling, all over the city—on the sides of buildings, on billboards, on the sidewalk, in images so clear, and realistic, it seemed we could walk up to them and step into the clear water. The photos were supposed to, I think, cheer us up. Some of us thought the lakes only existed in photos, as access to them was so restricted as to make them seem unreal.

Dawn and I became friends because we both said we could smell the ash from the fires, that we could smell the world burning, even though the fires rimmed the continent hundreds of miles away. There were nightly trackings of the fires on the news, there were experts discussing whether they could stop the fires or how the smoke would smother the world, and sometimes they went out but they always erupted again, somewhere.

The three precincts, which radiated out from the lakes, were this: the investors lived in a circle around the lakes, the workers lived in the circle outside that, and those who grew food in the remaining farms lived beyond this. We were in the city—my mother was an engineer and my father was a reporter for the newspaper. We did not live by the lake, but we appreciated those who did, as they were the ones developing the rockets and our future on Mars. We were expected to appreciate them because we were told to often, and with great enthusiasm. And we felt assured they would return for us. We wore shirts and hats that celebrated the coming Separation in glittering letters; we awaited the day of the launch, we awaited the day of their return; we awaited our own launch into the new future; across the world, the fires burned.

MY MOTHER HAD, my whole life, had a watchful demeanor, as though always expecting some foolish person to walk up to her and present a theory or solution on the world's bruised state; she would always correct them. She was full of information and had her own plans. She told me that if things reached an emergency state, meaning if the fires spread north and approached us, if the Separation had not yet happened, or if they had not yet returned for the rest of us, she had a secret route to get to the lakes: "I know this city," she said, "I know the lakes. I have, let's say, expertise." Her comments carried the tenor of bragging, which I was noticing more at my age, and made my arms feel that something sticky had been thrown on me. She seemed to take up all the room of knowing, and I wanted to know things, too. But she kept murmuring about this, as though wanting to reassure me of something I had not asked. She had detected some hidden sewer tunnels under the current ones, and she had measured and tracked them to the rim of the lake; one day, we walked by a manhole and she shuddered just slightly and whispered, sharply, "Keep walking," as though we had done something criminal. I didn't know what she was doing. I didn't want to tell my mother I doubted her but doubt was flourishing inside me, like a new, dangerous light seeking answers about the world.

My mother was a solid, tanklike woman, who wore the same sad, scuffed navy blazer every day to work, and who had spent many arduous years trying to set up the water distribution in the city in a way that seemed efficient and fair. She talked about fairness a lot, as though trying to reassure herself of something. This was not a kind thought, but it's one I sometimes had. Those who lived on the edge of the circle received less water, only enough to bathe once a week. My mother tried to figure out ways to reroute and direct it, even when her supervisors told her enough, stop, but I recently noticed that we always had enough water; her definition of fairness meant that she always found enough for us.

My father was practical in another way. He focused on how we would breathe. The fact was that we would begin to choke as the smoke unfurled over the country. We were told about buildings that acted like trees, buildings equipped with filters that would breathe for us; the teachers showed us photos of these buildings, which expanded and contracted like huge lungs, and which honestly looked sort of fragile and ineffectual. They would stretch out, miles long, and would shelter us until the ships returned for us.

My father was claustrophobic and did not want to be stuck inside these buildings with masses of people waiting to be saved; plus, he was suspicious of them, so he set himself the task of finding the best protective suits to move through the city during times of heat or smoke. He was strategic; he was a writer and for a magazine he wrote an article about the most advanced suit, a hilarious golden cube that was highly protective and looked ridiculous, and he wrote a glowing article about the suits, after he deemed them effective, and then got three for free. He stored those suits, gaudy gold blocks, in the downstairs closet, locked with a key only he held. We would wear our suits as we scrambled through tunnels and somehow we would reach water.

My parents were extremely prepared for a single and precise moment of danger. However, they did not tell me the rest of the plan, I thought, because they had none.

Dawn and I met at a Peak Performance athletic training class, a combination of gymnastics and dance and running that was designed to get us into top athletic shape. The idea of peak shape in response to the fires was, perhaps, pointless, but there was the hope that if we were in this shape we would do better on Mars. In any case, it felt good to practice something.

We were eager for the Separation, but we were also, somewhat inconveniently, afraid. We were not supposed to feel this, for when the first explorers returned, we would all be lifted to our future, but I was starting to notice the fear in my classmates. There were those who believed the transfer was imminent, and listened to anything that confirmed this hope; there were those who constantly purchased things—custom apparel to prepare for the launch, clothes, masks, ventilation equipment—some questionably low-budget. There were those who were paralyzed with worry, prone to silence and weeping, and so as not to distract the others, they were allowed to stay home from school.

Dawn and I became friends because we shared the shape of our fear. We all despised each other's fear, as to see it in others was like seeing the raw tender inside of your skin. But I wanted terribly to find someone who held it the same way I did.

I noticed Dawn's fear, and how it resembled mine, when I saw her watching the fires on the screens. Others tried not to look at it, or made fun of it, but she was motionless in a way that was comprehensible to me. She was trying to control the fire with her hope. I recognized that expression, that deep focus. I did it, too. When I saw her counting, I knew that she too was so afraid she felt invisible. When she saw me looking at her, her face reddened, and I knew I was right.

"Stop watching," she said to me.

"Ten," I said, a little viciously. I too had counted to ten, hoping miraculously they would stop.

She looked away, ashamed. I wanted to stand with her. I said, "I agree," and stared at the screen. Nothing stopped, but she saw me watching with the same ridiculous intensity. We were not the same, but I wanted to be, wanted to be lurched out of myself, and I saw that she wanted something like that, too.

DAWN'S HOUSE WAS located in the part of the city that was by the lake, or what we were told was the lake, and of course it was guarded. Guarding was not exactly the word—for there were three layers of security to get to it.

So I was lucky now, in a new way; I was leaving the city for the first time. I gazed at the buildings as we waited for the car that would carry us to her home. I mostly just walked by: the buildings were concrete, hulking slabs, riddled with cracks from the heat. We ignored them because now no one would repair them, because what was the point. The government buildings were scrubbed a little cleaner and were encased in thick clear sheets of material that would withstand fire. (Why wasn't everything encased in it?) Thin, tall plastic trees were arranged around the city to give it a natural feel and set up sections of shade; there were squares of fake grass, in many colors, around the city that were rolled up and frequently changed.

The route to the lakes was long and circuitous, and the car looped back to drive through all the precincts. It drove us through the first precinct, which was an expanse of dry, brown, hairless land, what most of the nation now looked like, and to see it, undecorated by the fake foliage that the government had arranged at picturesque points around it, was startling. Then the second precinct, which was not visible to the passengers, the highway encased in a tunnel to create a darkness so crushing and profound nothing was visible, which made me feel like I was dissolving, and I cried out. I heard Dawn laugh in the darkness and she said, "Wait," then when we drove into the section where she lived, she slowly rolled open a window, and stretched out her arm.

The air felt different; it was cool, there was an undertone of dampness to it, as though under the air there was something sweet, something clear and glorious murmuring; almost living, a dragon, an invisible tongue. I had never felt air like this, ever, and I wondered what it was to live in it every day.

The families who lived beside it did not know what to do with the lake, it was so precious, and no one was allowed near it, to swim or use boats on it, no one could do anything to disturb it. It felt not as much a lake as a museum of water.

But Dawn, who lived on the edge of it, told me to follow her the night I was staying at her house. We rushed through the darkness to the lake, ducked into a place near her family's pier, where we, because of her father, were allowed to dip our feet in the water, nothing else. My mother had taught me to swim in case we ever made it here; she pressed a hand against my back in the bathtub and taught me to float. I remembered her palm on my back, flat, perfectly steady; then she withdrew it and I was floating, I was suspended on the clear skin of the water. I never thought I would have the chance to use this skill.

Dawn was wearing shorts and a T-shirt and waded out into the water, to her waist, and lay down on her back. I did, too. We were floating in the cool water, in water, so much of it, the buoyant blue coolness surrounding us, this pleasure, I had never felt quite this cool, the feeling of the world around me, not a threat but generous, giving, liquid, wet, suspension, air. I felt an enormous longing for my life, wherever it was, for the possibility of life itself. I envied her then because she believed she had the right to run to the water, to float in it when forbidden, which was something I had never quite felt, and my whole body stretched out on the water with the unusual feeling that it was filled with air; I was lifted, briefly, by the world.

SHE SAID THERE was a list.

I didn't know what this meant at first. The day after we ran among the ships, she showed me the sketch. "This will be my room," she said. There would be thirty-foot ceilings so it felt like they were outside, in the sky, there would be trees brought up from earth, real trees, with dirt from earth, and the trees would spread out their branches to fill the room. The room would not have to be built but would be shaken out and inflate upon contact with the Mars atmosphere; it would then harden to seal out the cold. That was how the settlement would be built. The houses, folded in their compartments, would be brought to Mars inside the rockets. The families did not want to bring up construction workers, they did not want more bodies than the ship could hold. A couple of workers would whip out each house like a giant plastic bag.

I was silent, listening.

The sound the city would make, on Mars, when the workers stood in the door of the rocket, that lit square in the endless darkness and began to shake out the city onto the silent landscape. Quieter than any quiet we had ever known. The buildings would shudder onto the landscape like great silver sheets of water that would, when they touched the land, form into homes, and a central dome for everyone to meet for parties. The sound, the rumble, the city would make. She said she often thought about it. Like the sky was coming unzipped.

"Can you imagine it," she said, in a wistful tone that I could clearly identify as a boast.

I never knew how to respond to her descriptions of her ascent to this other place; I wanted to hear more and I was left out. "When will you come back?" I asked.

She made a very slow gesture, smoothing her long, straight dark hair, and she didn't look at me.

Her mother said there would be parties. The scientists and maintenance workers and pilots would still be working, those who monitored the floating magnets to maintain the atmosphere and grow the food; everyone else could just relax. There would be parties envied by anyone left on Earth. Everyone would gather each weekend in a dome, and they would float down a long tunnel to a building that would glow with the setting sun, with pale red light. They had not figured out yet how to adjust the gravity of the planet, so everyone would maneuver, with grace and difficulty, through the air, some swimming through it horizontally, some stepping forward, trying to hold themselves vertical, as though on a tightrope, pushing through it, trembling, suspended in air. Everyone moved very slowly. There would be dresses especially made to accommodate this new way of moving, dresses made with lots of fabric so they would trail behind to resemble comets or birds. The women and men would wear clothes that, she said, took full advantage of the fashion possibilities of floating. I thought of the lights of the dome, a bright-yellow lozenge in the immense dark.

This was too much, all of it.

"When are they coming back to get everyone else?" I asked again.

Her eyes turned vague, cloudy.

"You can't tell anyone," she said.

I leaned closer.

"What do you mean?" I asked.

Her large eyes blinked, slowly.

"Never," she said.

WHAT DID SHE mean?

She meant never.

The explorers would go up in the rockets, start settling Mars, and then?

Then nothing.

What was this nothing?

There wasn't room for everyone, she said.

They would leave us here on this burning planet.

They would not return.

I WAS TRYING to absorb this terrible fact when Dawn told me there was a list and that she could bring one person. One. That admission seemed to unlock some gate within her, and she began to talk. It seemed that her admission made her feel closer to me, that she was happy about the fact that I listened and accepted it, that she had been harboring this fact, like a decaying nut inside her, for some time. She was unburdened and we were bonded now, in some deep way; I had been chosen. I had been extracted, really, from the sad plight of everyone else. She was a good friend, maybe now very good. She seemed glad at my acceptance of this fact. I did not want to think too hard about any of this. I did not want to think at all.

Now she was sparkling with generosity; she wanted to give me things.

"Do you want this shirt? I grew out of it," she said. She tossed it to me.

"These shoes. Boring color. Take them."

I slipped on the shoes; they were sneakers, a blue I didn't like. I didn't want them, really. I looked at them and tried to want them. But I was afraid of the shoes.

"I don't need them," I said.

"Oh," she said, taking them back.

The rest of the day was ordinary considering this development, to the point that I wondered if I had imagined it. She wanted to go about our day as we always had. I watched her show me how she had mastered a difficult flip we were learning, sit in her family's new car, discuss the merits and flaws of our classmates, which made me very alert, stand at the edge of the lake and feel the water and its miraculous coolness at our feet. I heard my laughs swerving into a pathetic, high-pitched sound like a seal; someone was laughing, but that someone was not me.

My mind crumpled. I was ashamed of my want and wondered if Dawn could sense it. And there was something I wanted to ask. What did it mean to be invited and aloft on Mars, striding in our gowns through the darkness, would I feel as light as I did here in the lake? And, more to the point, what did she mean by one person? Was she inviting one person, me, or would the invitation include my family? Or anyone we knew. I wanted to ask this all day. I wanted to ask it when we stood by the lake, I wanted to ask it when we ate lunch, I wanted to ask it when I followed her through her house. The question was like a car, wheels spinning, stuck in my throat. I wanted to ask but believed that when I asked and when she answered, the world would cleave into two parts, and I did not want to know what I would say or be when I heard her answer.

EVERYTHING I HAD been taught about the Separation was a lie. My mind felt sharper, now awake. Our teachers had been fed the wrong information, but worse, they had accepted it. We had been fooled, each year we had put on those aluminum coats, running out of the classroom with them, a glitter of students rushing into the sun. Each year, we had dutifully put them on and examined the latest improvements. Each year, we saw the photos of the breathing houses being built, great rows of houses. I thought of all of us in those flimsy silver coats and I thought of all of us now standing on a barren earth, scanning the sky, waiting.

How could this be?

Each step brought me closer to my parents and me knowing something they did not. The entire world seemed transformed by this secret, as though a bomb had silently gone off. The car that drove me from Dawn's house to our neighborhood took me past everything I had known—the school I attended, a worn concrete building, the offices where my parents worked, the park gray with the shadows of the plastic trees. For a long time, I had wanted somehow to unroll my parents like scrolls and compare what was like me and what was not. How unfair it seemed, that they, my parents, held all the secrets and pretended to know the mechanics of the world. Now I knew something that they didn't. It was a small, potent triumph. I sat very still in the car, through the darkness, through the dry land, my small heart blooming larger and stronger: Now, finally, I knew everything. Now, finally, I knew how I would be able to live.

OUR BUILDING WAS a bland cement block like the others, several lines of them in a row, and we were in Row B. Some of the buildings were starting to flake, like old skin. There were a few versions of manufactured trees—palm trees, pine trees, sycamores, and some tree designers had gone a little wild and created trees that did not exist anyplace but their whims. We lived by a slim, lush tree with lavender branches and blue leaves, and its shade made our apartment cooler. I stood outside our building for a few minutes, my knowledge about the list, my future escape, about what the Separation really meant, like a hand around my throat.

When I walked inside, my mother was hustling around the kitchen, making dinner. It was never very good, but she threw herself into it, as though engaged in a dream of cooking rather than the act itself. We did not have that many foods to choose from, but she did her best. She was clicking her tongue against her mouth, which she did when she was concentrating. She must have felt the weight of my gaze on her and she looked up.

There were so many things I wanted to ask but was afraid to; first I wanted to tell her this.

"I saw the lake," I said.

She paused, remembering where I had gone.

"You did," she said in a measured way. Her face was damp from the heat of the stove. "What was it like?"

"Oh, I went into it," I said, casually. "I floated."

It was better to admit this lesser crime than to reveal the other potential one.

"You went in?" she said, leaning forward. "No one's supposed to go in—"

"Just for a second."

"You'll get in trouble."

"Dawn does it all the time."

"You're not her."

We stood in silence for a moment.

"What did it look like?" my mother asked.

"It was huge. I stepped in, I couldn't believe how cool it was."

She sat forward, her face burning in the yellow light. She wanted to know more.

"Amazing," she said, and I felt a thrill of pride that I could tell her something she did not know. "You were a good floater," she said. "I taught you to swim."

"Yes," I said.

NOW I LOOKED at everyone I passed on the street, wondering who would be left behind, who wasn't on the list. The knowledge divided me into two people, the one who people saw and the one who knew everything; the two mes made me dazed, as though I were looking at a place where the sky had, imperceptibly, been lowered, just enough to feel it slowly squeezing the light from the day. The air held that watery shade of grayness. I walked and I practiced not breathing, as though that would be helpful, walked and breathed and then just stopped and continued and felt that pressure rising in my lungs to take a breath, that longing that could not be stopped. I walked and I noticed the slight rise of everyone's breath in their chest, their shoulders, I noticed how people sighed. I did not want to notice it. I walked, holding my breath until the last possible moment, and then, when I felt dizzy, exhaling and breathing, in a sudden, cold gasp.

NOW, WHEN I went to Dawn's house, she wanted to talk about the parties. She brought out outfits we would wear on Mars and we tried them on. We had similar bodies, so I fit into her clothes. Our faces were bright and astonishing with makeup. She liked outlining her eyes in a smoky gray and gold. The clothes were a relief, as they gave us something else to think about. We did not look like ourselves. I in a red chiffon dress with my shoulders gleaming, in a black gown that showed the shadows between my new breasts, in a pale-orange miniskirt that hit the midpart of my thigh. I was utterly new in these outfits. I was in love with the vision of us, in the future, the potent sweet blankness of that future, the hard fact of it, each of us dressed for it, ready. I was in love with the feeling of the dresses on my body, of how I would move through the red dark air of Mars to the person I would love. I did not know how I would get there but these dresses seemed a route from my own smallness. I wanted the chance to love, to blur into the skin of another, to be kissed and pressed against a wall, to be opened slowly, like a box revealing a pale, rose-colored light. To feel that light shining on everything in the world. To see everything made gilded, clear.

I felt I understood everything when I wore those dresses.

One afternoon I put on a particularly beautiful dress, a silver sequined strapless item with a slight train in the back. I was twinkly, like I wanted to be touched. I looked at myself in the mirror and I maybe liked the person looking back, maybe didn't, but what I understood, fully, was that Dawn had a future, she would grow up and become old. Then I felt a tremendous sorrow that heated me like a furnace and I could not keep it back, I could not.

"I want to go," I said.

The moment felt long and hellish. Then her face broke into a smile and she said, "Good!"

That was it, oddly simple, almost as though I were just visiting her house, but on another planet. Could it be? Did she have the power to just say I could get on the ship? I craved that power, I envied it, I wanted to don her like a coat, to possess it. What kind of thought was this? Did it mean I just wanted to escape? The silkiness of the dress on my body made me feel wild, reckless. I could just go. I could get on that ship with everyone and feel it tremble and soar from this burning earth.

I imagined leaving my parents, oh, everyone I knew, and shutting them out of my mind. Yet my mind was like a steel door that would not shut; I hated her for making me try to shut it. I thought of them standing on earth, watching me rise, and I closed my eyes and then I opened them and looked at Dawn and I said, in a rush, "I want to bring someone."

She was like concrete, as though she had been waiting for this question.

"Who?"

I didn't want to say it or even admit it. I felt she should not make me ask. Then I said, "Two people."

She didn't get it, so I said,

"My parents."

As soon as I said it, I wished I hadn't. How embarrassing to admit that I wanted to bring them. I wished I was the sort of person who wanted to leave them behind. There were parts of them that I loved so much, my skin hurt: my mother's hurtling around the kitchen in the morning, as though every day was the day of the launch, but setting a bowl of oatmeal tenderly in front of me; the soft way she put a hand on my forehead when I felt sad; my father's cry of joy when I came home from school, as though I were a celebrity. I wanted to stuff these elements inside myself, hold them there.

There were aspects of them that knocked within me the wrong way—the way my mother's hearing seemed to shut off when I disagreed with her, the way she furiously brushed my thick hair so it always stuck up, like a hedge, in back, the way my father laughed, a sound that made me think he was choking, the way he hugged me, in a clenching way, as though he sensed I wanted to go somewhere far. Ha. They had no idea how far. They were a catalog of things I wanted to avoid. And a secret part of me thought perhaps I could not tell them. I would wake up the morning of the launch, make my bed, and just go.

"Your mother eats too much."

I jumped a tiny bit, as though slapped on the feet. My mother did like to eat, especially desserts, and she liked making them for me. Sometimes I brought items she made to Dawn, whose mother did not cook, and Dawn ate them, with gusto.

I answered, carefully, "Not all the time."

"Well," she said.

She glanced at me and must have seen something troubling.

"I don't know," she said.

I tried to make a regular sound of communication, like, "Oh." But I couldn't.

Then she said, "I'll consult my mother."

I EXISTED IN two realms, awaiting Dawn's answer. I walked through the realm of lies, where we lived, in which we gazed at the enormous screens showing the bustling, productive cities on Mars, the communities set up in the hazy Mars darkness, houses that resembled our own, the neighbors waving to each other, all of them smiling, fools, smiling! The screens were on office buildings, highways, in waiting rooms, everywhere, selling us this. I used to search the screens with interest, for details of our new future; now I rushed past them, arms tensing against the idiocy. I also existed in the realm of truth, the rockets plunging into the dark, leaving us. Did no one really know what was going to happen?

Now, when I sat with my parents in our apartment, I watched them to see if they would show any signs of their own ability to save me. I observed them coolly; I was both traitorous and also perhaps resourceful. They did not know that they were lucky and that soon would, in fact, owe me a great deal. Did the way my mother walked me to school indicate a swiftness that would help us in a moment of danger? What about those suits in the closet, what would the golden cubes actually do? How long would they protect us from the fires if we were abandoned here on Earth?

I wanted to test them. I wanted to be precious and the next moment I wanted to be ignored so I could just go. I woke up one night with a scream and waited for them to run in to comfort me; to my aggravation, they slept through it. There, I thought, there's my answer, and fell asleep, discomfited. But when I woke up, I found a shirt I had been desperately looking for folded neatly on my bed and somehow, ridiculously, I wanted to weep.

My mother and father went to work, they came home, cooked dinner; we sat outside. I always thought the sky held a slightly burnt smell that existed somewhere beyond the flattening heat, or maybe I imagined it, but it still had a color that could be identified as blue. I felt myself try to take in each moment with them like a pancake absorbing syrup, was aware suddenly, terribly, of their sweetness, even if I wanted to escape it. I wanted to stop each moment as it happened. I felt their bodies breathing beside me, and I felt my love for them thick and despairing, a rope.

DAWN'S MOTHER HAD said hello to me on occasion, but briefly, and (I thought) with a slight suspicion, but maybe it was indifference. I was spending more time at the house and the air was a little troubled, as though someone had been ripping it, and then I identified the disturbance: someone was arguing here.

I did not trust completely that Dawn said she would ask her mother, so when she went one day to do this, I followed her. I walked slowly so she would not see me, but I heard her footsteps and her mother's. I could not tell one from the other.

"Stop," her mother said. "I can't ask him again—"

I heard the soft sounds of Dawn following her mother, and I did not know the rules here, and then there was shouting and then she was walking alone, through the hallway and she headed toward me with the regal, shabby gait that meant that she was embarrassed.

We were friends, we did not know how to look at one another.

"Wait," she said.

THE PRESIDENT BEGAN appearing on the TV more than usual. He sat at his large desk, the flag of our country behind him, and led cheers. The cheers were to prepare us for the launch of the rockets, so we would all have something to say as they lifted, roaring, into the sky. In the past I cheered, but this time I didn't. I wanted to admire him, like the others, but now I did not know what to think. I wondered which ship he would ride, where he would live. The thought unfurled in my mind—if I were to take a seat on the ship, if I too joined the explorers, I might run into the president, or others selected for their desirable qualities. I pushed this idea away when I had it, for it seemed almost too fun to imagine, and sometimes I saw myself walking through the glowing, inflated buildings and running into the president or famous figures from the world down some hallways and it was true that I felt this: I wanted to be important, I wanted someone to say my name in the golden corridors of the new world.

THE NEXT TIME I visited Dawn she went to the kitchen to get some snack, and was there for a long time, and I was hungry and went down the hallway to find her. I heard the tear in the air again, I felt that disturbance, and this time I heard voices. One was Dawn's mother and the other was a voice I had not heard. "Two is enough on our ship," he said.

"We need four," she said. "At least."

"I told you. They will self-repair. They are made for this. The engineers are unnecessary."

"Let's just have extra—"

"No need."

"Please," she said.

"No need," he said.

"I trust you."

"Then stop asking. Stop asking."

There was a clatter of shoes and I stiffened, in the pantry where I had stopped to listen, and I saw a man in a suit whisk by, his face gray and intent. Dawn's father—I had never met him. I had only seen him in pictures. He looked like himself, but lesser, as though he had been through some sort of machine and was bleached. I was perfectly still. He had a demeanor about him, as though he were about to vanish into a cloud, and a slightly disheveled look, his beard unshaven, his hair a whoosh of gray, uncombed. I held still, not reassured. He looked unhappy with everyone in the world; I had never seen such direct and simple unhappiness, complete in itself, as though it were a sword. He darted into a bathroom directly across from me. The door was open and he picked up a toothbrush and started to violently brush his teeth. Somehow this unnerved me. He brushed his teeth for what seemed like forever, but it was perhaps just ten minutes. He spit into the sink, once then two more times, and the sound of spitting was harsh and guttural and then he smiled at himself in the mirror. His teeth were not white, nothing like they appeared in the pictures, but gray like the rest of him and he frowned. I barely breathed. He dropped his toothbrush into the sink and dashed out.

MY MOTHER WOKE me up at some hour deep in the night. She and my father were dressed in dark clothes and had backpacks that rose on their backs like tiny clouds.

"Let's go," she said.

She handed me some clothes the same color as theirs, as though we were all bank robbers. They were cold and masterful. They wore small rubber caps.

"Where are we going?" I asked.

"Hop to it!" she said, sharply. "Let's go."

I did not know what was happening, so I did what she said. I put on the black clothes and followed them swiftly, silently, out of the house. Finally, I thought, as we passed the other houses shuttered against the darkness, finally, I thought, as I heard our footsteps crackle against the gravelly street. I didn't even know what I meant by this finally, as though I were trying to hold myself above this with my weariness, for I did not want to go anywhere I would miss the launch, or maybe I did, maybe I did not want to make the decision. It was just a word I liked and clung to: Finally, I thought. I followed my mother and father, the three of us moving together through the empty city at night. The city flashed, windows on in some buildings, like jagged teeth. We moved with a kind of understanding that none of us mentioned, as though toward something important and good.

And then my mother stopped, glanced around, and slipped down a side street. There was no light, the dark was full and weighted like a terrible thought. I could barely see her figure moving through the dimness, and I rushed forward, afraid I would lose her, and she stood before a manhole barely visible, by a tree. She lifted it and slipped down.

"Let's go," she said.

It was hard to say no to my mother, who seemed simultaneously both grim and cheerful. I was just following her.

How monumental this seemed, and also, strangely, like nothing; we were just lowering ourselves into a manhole in the street. I was going to my future or I was not. I went in just because I did. Each moment I wondered if I would break away. The concept of my life was like a bird swooping around the sky, wild and directionless. She lowered herself down a ladder and then I went down, too, my father behind me.

I was suddenly thirsty.

"I need something to drink," I said.

"Not now," she said, a little out of breath.

"I need water," I murmured.

I needed to get out; my throat was suddenly dry, and I made a weird sound that scared even me; she stopped.

"Let's go," she said.

My father, who was above me on the ladder, climbed up onto the street, and reached down to grab my hand. Lifting myself out of the tunnel, I took large gulps of the air. They handed me some water, and I drank it. We rushed through the night; we were heading home, and I wondered if we had forgotten some essential object, but we had not, and it became clear that it was not time, we were not rushing to the lake. When we were home, my mother took off her cap and sat down and said, grandly,

"That was practice."

Now I felt ridiculous. The night slid forward unperturbed, like a cat.

"Through that tunnel," my father said, "we can get all the way to the lake." They were inordinately proud.

"Then what?" I asked.

I watched them the way I watched everyone—as though they were wearing a costume, and I needed to rip it off, to locate what was true under what they said.

My mother's hands sliced the air: "I spent twelve years thinking about this. We have to get to the water. I know all the swerves of the tunnels. I know this: how to get to it and how to wait. If we are by the water, we can find a place to wait. I know tunnels, you know I know tunnels, I have been thinking about this for years. We have plans—" she said, firmly.

I did not feel reassured, no I did not.

"What about the fires?" I said. "What are you doing about that?"

"We would try to put them out," she said. "We'd extend the border of the water through irrigation, flooding techniques. Finally, we will take over the lake. You know, Dr. Payson? He thinks we can live in tunnels by the lake until the fires go out. And you know, Professor Marton has learned how to freeze-dry foods for extensive periods of hiding—"

My mother was full of details, different details than Dawn's, but energetic in the same way. They both wanted to live. But they were propelled by different things. Dawn spoke with a calm, knowing she would be saved, that others would arrange this for her, that she just had to pick out what to wear. My mother spoke with a low, spiky anger. She was making her own plans.

I suddenly wanted to know something.

"Can Dawn come with us?" I asked.

What was this? This just came out. I wanted to shut it

back into my mouth. But I wanted my mother, abruptly, to say yes. It felt right to ask; Dawn had asked for me. She had found my life worthy; now I wanted to test the expanse of my parents' generosity, or my own.

"Your friend?" my mother asked.

"Yes," I said.

There was a long moment. Then she said, "No."

"No," my father said. She nodded at him; in the low yellow glow of the kitchen she looked exhausted. I could see the vague outline of her bones in the light, and it startled me, like an affront. There was me and there was not me and I felt the not me of them was something filthy in the room. I stared at them, and they probably thought I was just looking at them but I wondered if I picked her up if I could break her, and then my father, how strong I could be. They could not see any of these thoughts and that seemed both sad and a good thing. Then I remembered that I could just walk onto that ship.

DAWN SAID THAT she had something to tell me. When I arrived at her house, there was the buzz of preparation. There was a date, she said, for the launch. She had her clothes out on her bed and was going through them, deciding what to take. She could not stop touching the dresses, her hands trembling, as though trying to locate a flaw in them. She held up one, a green sequined dress with a skirt that poufed out.

"Tell me," she said, her voice serious. "This one? Or that. What is the best?"

The window let in a square of golden light. The sky was

a hard, glossy blue, like a plate. Outside, some of the staff who worked at the house stood on the green lawn for a photo. There were about twenty of them and they were dressed in work outfits. A photographer stood beside Dawn's mother; she held up her hands and yelled, "Smile!"

"What are they doing?" I asked.

"They are taking photos," she said.

"Everyone turn to the side!" Dawn's mother said.

I watched. The photographer snapped photos of the staff from all angles. Facing front, side, from the back. He leaned toward them and took close-ups. The workers seemed flattered by the attention and turned around, posing. Dawn's mother watched.

"What is going on?"

Her eyes flickered, annoyed; more dresses tumbled out of her closet. "What do I do with ones that don't fit?"

"Give them away. Throw them out."

Her shoulders stiffened. "I can't," she said.

I noticed Dawn's mother walking very slowly around the various staff members; she was taking notes.

"She's choosing," Dawn whispered.

I looked at the staff, standing very straight for their photos, and smiling. I didn't ask how many, but she added, with strange smile that went with holding special knowledge,

"Two."

Two.

I saw one woman in the group, who I had seen washing a window in the house, lift a hand and smooth her hair.

Her hand trembled. Something unnamed gashed me like a knife.

Two.

"Two," I said.

I stood up.

She blinked. "Oh," she said, leaning forward, "I need to say—"

"Wait," I said.

I went out the door of her room, down the hallway, walking as though I knew where I was going, I was walking at a regular pace and then a faster one, each foot settling on the floor, watching the members of the staff flow back into the house after their photo session. None of them knew what was going to happen. Each staff member looked entirely distinct from the other, one walked by with red hair, one with a pouf of brown, another with high arching eyebrows, another who was bald, each face unique, themselves but suddenly each looked like my parents. I stared. How could this be. They were not my parents, and they were, my parents located in each of them, in an eyelid, in a smile, in the swiftness of their walk, and I saw them perfectly—they were my parents and they were me. My whole mind wrapped around this thought. And I felt my heart crumbling and expanding with this, and I wanted to grab them, but I didn't, and they didn't recognize me either, and we were just walking by each other, we were walking by.

I was frozen, a piece of snow. The earth spun through the endless darkness and I could feel it, thin, under my feet. And there was my friend, rushing toward me. She ran past them, not looking at any of them, and stopped, breathless, in front of me.

"I had to tell you," she said. "Your family can come."

THAT NIGHT, I was sitting with my parents watching the news, which had information about the launch. The ships would lift off in two weeks. We saw a few silver ships being carted to the launch site, the long vessels floating by cheering crowds.

I was going to tell them that we all had seats on the rocket, we would be able to go with the first explorers of the Separation. I kept waiting for myself to say it. I waited; it was taking me longer than I expected; the words were sodden in my throat. I did not want to hear myself admit this, that I wanted, so terribly, to live. But, finally, I did.

I moved close to my mother. I listened to the sweet sound of our breath, together.

"Listen," I said. "I know something."

She turned to me.

"I'm going there," I said. Her eyes narrowed, wondering. "I'm going to be on a rocket," I said. "I'm going to be on the launch."

Her face fluttered, maybe winced, and she turned to me. "What?"

"Dawn told me to come with them. And—they're leaving forever. The rockets are never coming back."

I let this hang in the low dark air for a moment. I added, quickly, "Don't worry. You can both come, too."

On the screen, the rockets gleamed. I did not know what I wanted from her, but I waited for a response: for gratitude from her, to be noticed.

My mother laughed. A short, hard sound. This surprised me.

"What's funny?" I asked.

She shook her head.

"Nothing. You can't go."

I immediately sat up, affronted. "Why?"

"They're never coming back," she said. "But for another reason."

"What?"

"It can't work," she said.

She put her hands on my shoulders, but I stepped away.

"What do you mean?"

"Everyone knows but the investors," she said. "They can get to Mars, but they're not going to be able to live there. They've paid some scientists very well to advise them, but are the scientists getting on that rocket? No, they are not."

I thought of Dawn in her dress, floating in the darkness, a yellow silk dress aloft around her, like a parachute, glorious, silent.

"They'll live there a week or so, then their bones will break from the lack of gravity. Their bodies will not sustain it. They are not thinking." She was speaking faster now, as though she had been waiting to let this out. "They thought they had the answer."

"The houses," I said, slowly. "They had houses they could shake out—"

"They won't work. And they were paying scientists a lot to help them figure it out. But anyone can see it's fantasy. It won't work."

My mother stood up.

"They think they had a great plan." She paused. "They think they found a way out. They thought they had a way to keep everyone calm, waiting for them to return. But they didn't."

I stood up, sharply, as though I would go out and warn Dawn, anyone going up, anyone. But I did not. She touched my hair and went into another room, rummaging for something. I glanced out the window. The night was dark, in a way that was utter and complete. What was out there, what was the future? Was my mother correct? How did she know this? What would we be, left here, how did we maneuver around this burning earth? I wanted to run to Dawn, to grab her, to tell her, to bring her down the dark tunnels under the city, as we ran toward the cool of the lakes. I began to walk to my mother, but I did not want to see her face, and I said, quickly,

"Can I bring—"

But it didn't matter what my mother would say. I knew that Dawn would walk onto the launchpad with her parents, and she would step into that rocket with them. I ran out of the room and looked up at the sky, at the darkness, at the faint froth of stars, and I felt the cool distance between me, on the trembling earth, and the rest of the universe, the weight of the air. I looked at the distance, so huge it was beyond comprehension, and I wanted to reach through the vastness, reach through the sky to her hand and grab it.

THE SHAME EXCHANGE

No one knew who originally proposed it; the government would mandate an exchange of shame. Citizens who held too much shame, which interfered with their productivity, would come to an official site where their shame would be handed to a government official who had none. Many people, in both the government and technology sectors, were involved in organizing this exchange, and it had not been easy to agree on the terms. The government was, for years, not sufficiently responsive to the needs of its citizens, and this was what a panel finally decided to do.

The citizens would be selected by lottery, interviewed, and examined with an ultrasound machine, and those who were unduly burdened by their shame would be told to participate. Being quite shameful, they had trouble saying no, and could always be convinced. Psychologists had created a technique in which they could detect a person's shame through the ultrasound, and transform it into physical, hulking thing. It was, on average, the size of a large pillow and resembled a raw steak. Their shame would be removed, using noninvasive laser technology, carefully packaged by professionals, and stored in large refrigerators. The shame still belonged to the participants, but during the exchange would be presented, in a controlled environment, to those who had none.

The event would take place in a large warehouse somewhere in the middle of the nation. Though there was much interest in the details of the exchange—who gave what to whom, etc.—no one outside of the participants would be allowed to watch. The proceedings would be heavily guarded. No one was allowed to meet or speak to one another. Everyone was instructed to wear a mask—a simple plastic one, constructed in the shape of a lion, dog, rabbit, or other animal—to conceal their identity. They would all be told to dress professionally, in clothing suitable for an office.

Elected officials would be required to undergo a test. Those officials whose shame did not reach a certain appropriate and decent level were ordered to the warehouse at the appointed time. Every member of the legislative, judicial, and executive branches would be required to take this test, and some would try, cleverly, to impersonate shame when they had none. But the test had questions that revealed these attempts. Psychologists had worked very hard on these tests, and all attempts at false shame would be detected.

As word spread, more and more citizens signed up to hand over their shame. They could drive themselves or were provided a pleasant, air-conditioned bus from their home to the warehouse. More buses were quickly added, as citizens, in buzzing, excited numbers, signed up.

As soon as certain elected officials were informed of their low scores of shame, they were escorted to locked vehicles that would transport them to the warehouse. No one quite knew what happened in the locked vehicles, though rumors spread that the politicians were, during that final ride, given anything they wanted. This had been negotiated, with much back and forth, in backroom deals. The vehicles sped across the country, not stopping until they reached the warehouse.

The ones with no shame entered a large, empty, light-filled building and stood across from the ones who were handing over their shame. The two rows of individuals stood across from each other, wearing masks, which made it appear that everyone was about to engage in a dance. Armed guards, screened for their capacity to resist bribery or threats, stood around them all, watching. The ones with no shame moved slowly, coolly—but under their masks, they appeared to be scanning the room, trying to determine who was here.

Those in Row One clutched their shame, the bags heavy as though they contained broken, dripping melons. Some people had double-bagged their shame, as shame had a tendency to leak. There was a sharp and bitter odor of rot. They looked embarrassed, shoulders hunched, even if they were handing over this burden. They understood, all too clearly, what this entailed. They could not meet the eyes of the ones in Row Two. Some even seemed reluctant to hand over their shame at all, to burden another with it. But that was what they were here to do.

"Row Two, hold out your hands," announced a voice.

The ones with no shame refused to follow instructions;

they did not hold out their hands. The guards had to grab their hands and forcibly lift them up. The guards pried open their curled fingers. No one said the recipients had to accept the shame willingly. A few of them screamed, and a couple of large security guards stepped in to stop some from running away. A couple individuals in Row Two chuckled, as though not believing this would actually happen.

"Row One, place your bag into the hands of Row Two."

Those in Row One, some weeping or trembling, lifted their own bulky packages of shame, and placed each one in the hands of the person standing opposite them in Row Two.

There was a deadly quiet in the warehouse. The guards pressed the heavy packages of shame into the palms of those who had none. The ones in Row One stepped back. They looked at each other and laughed. They were advised to keep just a handful of shame for themselves, not giving all of it up to the ones in Row Two. A handful of shame would help them get along with family, friends, work. A handful, that was all.

The warehouse was silent for a few moments, and then echoed with the sound of one person laughing, then another, then everyone in Row One. The pure sound of being unburdened, relief. An ice cream truck, offering vanilla, chocolate, and pistachio, was set up outside the warehouse, so that they could celebrate. Some of those in Row One literally skipped out the door.

The ones in Row Two clutched the packages of shame, or more accurately, the guards fit their hands around the packages. There was a deep silence, though some officials began to cry, in a choking, confusing way; it was the first time some of them had cried. Everyone in the warehouse watched them with interest, wondering what they would now be.

Everyone in Row One left the warehouse, zipped out to the rest of their lives.

The ones in Row Two had their hands full, forever. Shame plinked onto the concrete floor.

The warehouse was almost empty now. Outside, drivers stood by the vehicles that brought them here, waiting for the officials to come out. The drivers of the cars had been gathered in small groups, chattering with each other, but they quickly went to their respective cars and stood very still. In a few minutes, they would drive the officials back to the capital, where they would return to their work governing the nation.

Now what? Unfortunately, those who had organized this exchange had no further plan. All the research, planning, had brought us to this day, to this trembling hope: that the ones in Row Two, now chock-full of shame, would govern with sensitivity and in a kindly way. Would this happen? They checked that the locked vehicles held food that the officials had requested, though some might be so distraught they would not eat. Had the locked vehicles been cleaned? Were skilled therapists on board each vehicle? Were people knowledgeable about a variety of policies ready to ride back with them? Now that they were burdened with a great deal of shame, the officials needed to be treated with a bit of tenderness.

"This way," said one organizer. The ones in Row Two filed out, slowly. The shame was now part of them and the packages could be taken to a sterilized and locked facility.

Organizers in hazmat suits took the shame from their hands and set the packages into a special truck. The politicians moved slowly and with deliberation. They would not remove their masks until they were safely inside the cars; many people here were afraid to see their faces. So much work had gone into this exchange, so much planning. Was this, finally, the strategy that would help the nation? The organizers watched the officials get into their cars. The cars started, turned, and drove onto the highway. Those at the warehouse stood, watching the cars vanish into the distance, and then everyone—carefully—cheered.

THE EXTRA CHILD

We dropped our last child off at school and drove a thousand miles home. The school was a university. The buildings were massive, concealing the children's futures within thick, enduring walls of brick and concrete. The parents filled the student dorms with objects: blankets, shoe racks, handheld vacuums, tiny refrigerators, coffee makers, as though propelled by memories of their own sorrowful need. They wanted to prepare their children; they did not want the children to want anything. Then the parents left.

She was the second of two. We stood with her outside the dorm and inside it sounded like a war was going on, but she laughed and identified it only as joy. Lights spangled on and off in the old buildings, their red brick dull in the evening light. She wanted to vanish inside them; that wanting was a gift. She stepped toward the dorm, said goodbye, and that was that.

We drove home, a thousand miles, our hearts tender as glass.

We opened the door to silence, and we went to the second one's room. It looked like someone had ransacked it, taking her posters, her jewelry boxes. It looked like violence had been done. I made the bed, tucking in the edges carefully, because I did not know what else to do.

Twenty years ago, we had brought the first child home. We held him, and the silence before us then was the deep vast thrum of all we didn't know. We were suddenly parents. The silence weighed down the air like boulders on silk. And then, of course, he cried.

Soon the children bounded up and ate food and broke things and cried out in the middle of the night. There were toys they wanted and discarded; they ate candy that made their teeth blue. There were screams and slammed doors and arguments and many sentences that froze in the air, glittering meanly, and that I wished I could grab and smoosh under the bed, embarrassed. The times I had not been able to help, when they asked, or didn't, the times I had been on a call, the times I was too tired.

I stood, listening to the wild, quiet drone of their childhoods, finished.

I WALKED INTO the living room and there was a third child sitting on a chair. I screamed. He startled and looked at me with brown eyes that seemed like a baby's, new. He had dark hair, like me, he was curled in the chair, clutching his body as though cold. His legs were thin as a deer's.

Who are you, I asked.

He shivered.

You know.

Who, I said, chilled. How did you get in here? I'm calling the police.

Stop joking. Stop. You know.

Where are your parents?

I live here, he said. There was softness around his eyes. Then he said, terrifyingly, *Mom*.

I did a quick look around the room but obviously he was talking to me. Me. I was his mother. Suddenly, I knew it. I had given birth to him, clearly in some sort of haze, and then I had forgotten him. The others had taken everything. They stumbled into the world, glossy and beautiful and greedy, distracting us for years. I did not realize the house was this large or, for god's sake, had this many unswept corners.

He scratched his knee. His shoulders wilted a bit, unburdened. He was wearing an old T-shirt I recognized from our son's closet. He smelled a little rancid, of sour, damp cotton.

I wanted to say, I never had you, but it seemed a terrible thing to say, and there was the nagging feeling I always had as a mother, that I had forgotten something, and here it was. I had forgotten this child. There was the low, rumbling fear of forgetting: forgetting to pick someone up at an activity, forgetting to buy the gold stickers for the art project, forgetting to pay the registration fee, forgetting to give someone their lunch, forgetting the dentist appointment. I was a supreme artist of forgetting. Not just the children, but my husband, the person I wanted to be with during this life. I had forgotten to pick up his toothpaste, his favorite ice cream, I had forgotten to ask him about his concerns; to be fair, he had not remembered mine either. The house was a vault of stale air and missed opportunities.

I looked at the child. He did seem familiar. I could see his eyes, his mouth resembled my mother's, that precise red blossom. His long dark eyelashes were like my father's. I trembled, bracing myself for years of hidden love, or something, to tumble down upon him. I sensed it, gathering deep inside me, a giant, sodden, fluttering chaos-haul of trash. The immensity of it would bury us—or so, perhaps, I hoped.

He walked with me to a corner of the garage and showed me a pile of rags and a baby blanket. It was neatly arranged. He said he had slept here for ten years. I shivered. This child, my child, had been sleeping on rags while we raised the others. I had not taken care of him. And now here he was.

I want my own room, he said.

I wanted to hug him. Arms emerged from my sides. I held out my hand, and he grabbed it. His hand in mine lit up my arm. On the drive home from the college, I had felt my body dim, even though I knew better, even though god knows I had numerous other activities to pursue, even if I had made eager, sputtering lists of all my plans when they had left.

I felt his back moving up and down, breathing. In other bad news, I had forgotten his name. I wanted him to tell me without me asking. I looked for a hint, initials: saw them scrawled on the edge of his shirt: CB.

Are you hungry? I asked C.

No, he said. C.

Your nickname, I said, watching him.

I guess so, he said.

C, I said.

He lunged forward and wrapped his arms around me, ferocious, fingers lurching into my shoulders, like he was slipping off a cliff. I held him, tight. I craved that desperation like an evil drink. My children had not held me like that for some time. This was now how they held their friends, boyfriends, that same clutching. I knew it was right and just and I did not want them to clutch my hand forever, I did not. But what was it like now to live in that forever?

I thought it was over, that brief, elastic falling in love, shaped one way around an infant, another as the child began to walk, stretching to contain the children as they run and leave. The endless, tender flexibility of that parachute. That parachute now taut, I was not sure how to stretch it, form it. I listened to his heart beating, slowly, a dark sound of thunking, beside mine.

I want food, he said.

I didn't know what he liked so I gave him everything. A peanut butter sandwich, apples, tuna, cookies. He grabbed a handful of tuna, and I had to show him how to use a fork.

He piled food on my plate. Here.

I'm not hungry, I said.

Yes you are, he said.

OUR DAUGHTER CALLED.

I am fine, she said.

We stood, awkwardly, holding the phone.

Do you need socks. Do you need a coat. Do you need Kleenex.

I hate the meat loaf, she said. My roommate tripped on her shoelaces and fell out a window. She's alive, but barely.

Well, I started, the first thing—

She hung up.

THE EXTRA CHILD was used to slinking around in the darkness. He had done it so skillfully for so many years. It was strange for him to be out in the light, to be seen. I took him shopping for clothes. He looked to be about ten but he clung to my hand like a toddler.

How about this.

I held up a gray sweatshirt.

Yes.

This.

A pair of sneakers that were a strange orange color but sturdy and a good price.

Yes.

The mall was neon, electric, roaring. He put his hands over his ears. He looked around, blinking, at all the items in the store. He was, oddly, not a demanding child. Anything would do, any piece of clothing was an improvement. The chipper salesmen were like new seedlings. They did not realize what they were really selling. They glided through the store with their bright smiles, so helpful, but as they knelt before us urging feet into shoes, we knew what they were really hawking here. Time. The briefness of our time together.

Everything we could gather to avoid it. The mall a giant box of distraction. The roaring in the mall and inside of me.

I bought him the most expensive pair of shoes.

HE SAID YES. He agreed with the clothes I showed him, he agreed with the hamburger we bought at the food court, he bit into everything with a tiny, terrible sigh of relief. His agreeableness scared me. The others had been appreciative in short flashes, those moments when the entire house lit up like a bomb with their joy, but what I remembered, what resided in me, were the moments when the house dimmed with their sorrow, when friends were mean or when they didn't understand algebra, the times when the world slapped them around and we couldn't help, the times when everyone stumbled around and no one could see anyone else. He took everything, and I offered him what he asked for. Thank you, he said, thank you, thank you and I was suspicious.

MY HUSBAND DIDN'T seem surprised at the arrival of the third child. He had always thought the house was a mess, and now here was the rationale. Now that the third child had revealed himself, there were no more suspicious crumbs in corners. He was glad to be proved right.

He's asleep, my husband said. Come over here.

We grabbed the darkness and cocooned it around us. We crawled through it with that wet hunger and hardness and stealth. Those waves we grappled onto, the foaminess. Our hands grasping our bodies; we loved that shared reaching, the long soaring; we felt young even if we were not; we gave each other that gift of blindness. Of forgiveness.

Still, we waited for a knock. Still, we had to be quiet. We listened for him. But there was nothing. He went right to sleep.

At the day's first light, he was at the kitchen table, waiting for breakfast. Now that he was a citizen of the house, he was up at dawn, ready for anything. He wanted to be served. I poured some cereal in a bowl for him. How grateful he was for that gesture! He smiled at me, a smile that no one had seen for years. His teeth were strangely white and perfect, those of a presidential candidate. His gratitude was a magnet; every morning I awoke it drew me to sit with him.

I ENROLLED HIM in school, which meant I lied. I leaned across the desk to the vice principal and tried to explain his arrival. We lied to the pediatrician, telling her he had just been sent to us, which was not terribly untrue. The pediatrician, sodden from overwork, was surprisingly gullible. C was in good health amid a flood of cases of strep throat and whiny parents; the pediatrician signed forms; he slipped through.

C was eager for the lunch box, the backpack, wanted to select the right one. He held each one, tenderly, in his hands as though each would inform him about his future and then chose one with a photo of a family of giraffes. I packed three peanut butter sandwiches and five cookies for his lunch, for he was concerned about becoming hungry during the day, as though the school was a much longer journey than it was.

Walking through the school doors, he slipped into this new world as though he had been buttered and slid down a chute. I was here, my children grown, away, and it was as though I had been laboring for years in a rusty factory of parenting. Now, the world of parenting involved standing on a deserted landing strip, scanning the empty sky. I had stories and advice and I felt like a pro, I was oddly calm. The newer parents rushed in, worried, worried about everything. Their hearts beat so furiously with worry I could almost see them through their coats.

We did not know the other parents, as he was much younger than our other children. Hello, they said, eyeing me. Are you new to the neighborhood, they asked.

Yes.

THE DAUGHTER CALLED, crying, the roommate who fell out the window was back and had become extremely controlling about any socks dropped on the floor. Plus, the daughter hated philosophy, the professor was a terrible explainer. Plus he was mean to her.

The first thing to do is, I said.

She hung up.

The son called. He and his lab partner in chemistry had dated for three weeks now and she was his ideal woman. He got the top score on his anthropology exam. If his girlfriend got pregnant (though she wasn't), they thought they would keep the baby in the top drawer of her dresser in her room. All would be fine.

The first thing to do is, I said.

He hung up.

C WOKE UP early, was dressed and ready to go, walked briskly to school, came home and did his homework. We received notes from teachers. *He makes me glad to be a teacher. What a student! Such a great learner! Like a sponge.*

How easy he is, we marveled, strutting. Maybe we are pretty good at this.

The three of us, at the dinner table, sawed away at our food. My husband and I, oddly quiet. We were glad that C had something to say. C talked about what he had learned that day. He had consumed his giant lunch, every crumb of it, and each day he was slightly taller. He did not look ten anymore. He was eleven. Twelve. Each day he seemed older, each time he returned home he was bigger, it seemed he was, there was a swell of muscle on his arm, his pants were shorter, his new shoes stretched and split.

Each night, we sat around the dinner table, and he told us what he had learned in a crisp, oddly articulate voice. He sounded not like a boy but like a television commentator. He read and read. He was done with the fifth-grade curriculum within a couple weeks. He was speeding through *War and Peace*, telling us the plot in specific and somewhat arduous detail. We listened to him and were awed by his focus and energy, which surrounded us like an unseen light we could feel, glaring, physically, on our arms.

How was your day? he asked.

What? my husband asked. It was a shocking question. We just shoved through our days like quarterbacks, with as little bruising as possible, to the other side.

How was your day. Good, bad, middling.

My husband cleared his throat. I hate everyone, he said. Now I'm here.

C's eyebrows lifted. He seemed disappointed by this answer.

Oh, he said. Well, tomorrow make it better.

He turned to me.

How was your day? he asked.

My coworker refused to work. I had to do everything she didn't, I said.

He looked baffled.

Why do you let that happen? he asked, coolly.

What was he talking about, let? This was life. It was a dreary, opportunistic slither. We did our best.

Well stop it, he said. Just stop.

He spoke so that it seemed he did know everything in the world. We regarded him, moved and afraid. That certainty of the young, residing within him like a brightly wrapped gift.

I'm your mother, I said. Don't speak to me like that.

THERE WAS, OF course, a shift. The moment he saw us and did not want to be us. The moment he saw us and we switched from beautiful giants to tiny, unfortunate rocks to be kicked. We were trying so hard! But we were, of course, found wanting. He was watching our movements like a director evaluating a play with terrible actors. He wanted us to have different lines.

I wanted to tell him I understood the watching, I did, and I ruffled his hair in a kindly way. But no. His gaze was like a mouth trying to eat the world, to nourish himself with what he needed. He was trying to be different. He was trying to be himself.

EACH NIGHT, HE sat at the dinner table, a little larger, more muscular, and yes, sweatier, the beastly sweat of an ox. We opened windows as we felt too shy to say anything, so as not to insult him, even if he was our child. He consumed his meal in a few gulps. He ate everything. He wanted more.

My various failings, big and small, seemed to personally injure him. He sat forward and his eyes glowed with the serene, immense hunger of an alligator.

Come on, he said. Just stop. Walk faster. Don't eat that bread. Tell the person who won't work to work. Stop being depressed. Just tell her.

We had been through this with the others, but each time, it was surprising.

Don't talk to me that way or go to your room, I said.

Now, a few weeks in, we swerved from tenderness to fear. We got through dinner quickly and warily bused our dishes. We kept an eye on him as he soaped his dish. We were watchful, light on our feet in case of sudden movement. I thought of, in an emergency, hitting the smoke alarm for a fire we could not see. C oddly wanted to help clean up. He moved around the kitchen briskly, wiping down counters, sweeping the floor, but his grip on his sponge was fierce and he was scrubbing the stove a little too hard, and we watched him, wondering what he wanted to erase.

Good night, we called as he went to his room. You okay? Do you want anything?

He slammed the door of his room, and the house shook.

MY HUSBAND LOCKED the door to our bedroom. We couldn't call the police, for what would we tell them? His mere presence in our household appeared to be a crime. Maybe he would calm down and read something. We locked the door while we tried to figure things out. A locked bedroom door was an invitation to each other. We were stiff, afraid at first to move.

Now we were not protecting him; we were hiding from him.

I thought I heard knocking. I jumped.

He was not knocking on the door. He was shattering something. There was shattering; we jumped up and opened the door a tiny bit and peeked out. It sounded like a dish and then there was another dish and he was yelling at all of it, but what? What was he saying? Were we supposed to punish him?

Was this the punishment for all we had not done?

Now we pushed a dresser against the door. We waited.

His anger was one-note, directed, enormous. His anger pulsed through the house, a bomb. He hit walls, there was that pounding, we could not call the police, we held each other and locked the door, and I felt his rage invade me, lighting me up, a hunger coiled deep. I understood it. C was a person in the world, with all those all those awful realizations: that he was sealed within himself, that he would age, that we were parents, solid, muscular, but also worn like cardboard, paper-thin. What was he knowing? What could we offer him, with our chewed-up, hopeful hearts? What could we all do in this brief island of time?

We waited. We love you, I said to the door, hoping he would hear it. The darkness surrounded us, and we felt the sun rise.

SOMEHOW, I SLEPT, and when I woke, I did not know what we would see. When we stepped out of the bedroom, the dishes were cleaned up, swept; he was out of the house before we got up. He had poured his own cereal for the first time. The kitchen stank of his sweat, an entire locker room of bitterness, so strong we could taste it. The kitchen sparkled. We wandered through the gleaming, pristine landscape of the kitchen, fearful, searching for his anger. Open, shutting cabinets. Nothing.

Clutching our coffee, we waited for him to return.

THAT NIGHT, I worked late, the frenetic, meticulous way one does when reluctant to go home. There are times when no parent wants to face their child, when their demands feel like a cloud made of lead. I was nervous about what I would find. I stopped at the supermarket and filled my cart with peanut butter and jelly and milk, as we were low. In front of our house I paused and gazed at the lights glowing within, not knowing what resided there, if these lights denoted happiness or someone who wanted to explode the world.

I opened the door, very slowly, ready for mayhem. But C appeared to be the only one home, sitting at the table, which was clean and perfectly set.

What is happening? I asked.

Hello, he said. I thought I'd set things up.

I walked in and lowered myself into a chair. C folded a napkin with great care.

I defrosted some chicken, he said.

He did not seem to be apologizing, just growing. This too was unnerving. The chicken sat on the counter turning wet. I said, Let me show you how to cook it, and he stood beside me, watching. I handed him a fork and he moved the chicken around in the pan a bit.

The other children floated somewhere; he and I stood together here.

I waited for his anger to crawl out from under a rock. I was oddly eager for it, its buoyant life and clarity; you could not mistake the anger for anything else. He sauteed the chicken with unusual tenderness. We put it on a plate and sat at the table, and I unfolded a napkin. He regarded me, with a slow, careful glance—almost clinical.

I picked up the salt and shook it onto the chicken. I noticed his eyes; they were watching my hand. They detected something. I set down the salt and glanced at my hand, which seemed like a normal hand to me.

He swallowed.

What's wrong? I asked.

You're older, he said.

His directness unnerved me.

Well, yes I am, I said.

I covered one hand with another, suddenly self-conscious.

I need more clothes, he said.

We can get some this week, I said.

THAT NIGHT, I was about to go to sleep when I went to check on C in his room. I opened the door and peeked in. How small he seemed, quiet. His thin arms clutched his pillow, and he shivered.

THAT NIGHT, MY husband kept our door locked. We trembled at any sound, we waited for the shouting, we waited for something to shatter.

But there was nothing.

OUR DAUGHTER CALLED to say she was fine. She was fine. She was crying so hard we could not understand what she was saying, but it was nothing. We didn't need to know.

What. Tell me.

Nothing.

Honey. Slow down.

The long useless stretch of arms, of branches, how they stretch toward air.

The air troubled by the sound of your child weeping.

What can we do?

Nothing.

But she did need some new sneakers, could we put money in her account for that.

BACK AT THE mall. I was slightly stung by the hand comment, accurate as it was, and to throw around my clout, I wanted to buy him whatever he wanted. He was anxious for new clothes, and he could not fit into the ones he had found, so here we were, walking through that dull flat light, that roaring. He had enough with the kids' clothes, the T-shirts with trains or animals on them. He walked through the aisles swiftly, focused, and he passed the junior-size outfits to pause at a rack of button-down shirts. He picked out a light-blue shirt, removed his T-shirt, and slipped the shirt over his shoulders. Then he stepped back and looked in the mirror. He could not take his eyes off himself. He was in love with this, a semblance of authority, this crisp, new stranger. He was growing up. I felt pride rush through me, that warm light.

This, he said.

HE SEEMED NERVOUS and excited as he dressed the next day, turned around and examined himself as though about to meet a beloved. What was the event? Who was he meeting? He had a new, quiet dignity about him. He asked me if his tie looked correct, and I was glad that he wanted my opinion. I said yes. He headed off to school in his blue button-down shirt, his face sharp with expectation, lunch in hand, walking.

THAT DAY, HE came home late. We kept looking out the window, nervous, waiting, he had never been late before. Setting his backpack on the table, he sat down, he had trouble meeting our eyes. He did not want to look at us.

What now? What had he done? Where had he been? There was another feeling I noticed in him, he was not angry—it took me a moment to identify his expression and then I recognized it as guilt. He went to bed early. I heard sounds in his room—not breaking, but something different—organizing. Packing.

THE NEXT MORNING, he was up early. We heard him bustling around, preparing an egg, the smell of hot butter and yolk. When we joined in at the table, he had set it again, was shaking salt onto a fried egg.

I need to tell you all something, he said.

We waited.

There's been a mistake, he said.

Alarms went off, familiar and not familiar.

I am in the wrong family, he said.

What!

I thought I lived here, but I did not. I'm sorry for the inconvenience, he added.

The word *inconvenience,* of all words.

But. Wait. Weren't you here? All these years? You said you were here. Somewhere.

I thought this was the right address, but, he said. Apparently not. Houses look alike.

We sat, frozen, trying to figure this out.

He paused and said, I made some calls.

So wait. You weren't here?

I wandered here. But this is actually not where I am supposed to be.

I stared at him.

Now that he was not who he said he was, I gripped the table, eyeing him, and wondering what he wanted. Or what to feed him, and so much else.

But we are your family. You lived with us.

I felt again an enormous rising inside me, a dismantling, and the peculiar vanishing of my arms.

I did, he said, and thank you for all your service. He said this with irritating primness, as though he'd gotten this phrase out of a book. Service. What was this? This was not a word we had taught him. He glanced at us and I could see the love in his eyes, I could. But now he wanted to go.

Is this—I wanted to ask, is this.

Thank you for all your service. I have to go.

HE WAS JUST a child. But he was a determined one, and he was one who had shown up in ways I could not explain. He now said we had no claim to him. The other family was waiting for him. They were great! He had an address. They were now eagerly setting up his room.

Can't we call them? Can we check? You are a minor!

He shook his head. He had grown quite a bit overnight, he was taller than we were. Maybe he wasn't even a minor! Who was he and what were we?

Now I wanted to call the police but for different reasons—I could not keep track of all the possible crimes going on here now.

You hate us, we said. Is that it.

No, he said, firmly. Stop that. I just need to go.

He didn't want to look at us. Something about us filled him with shame. Or did he want something more? We had raised him, in this brief period, to want to get out there. He wanted to see the world. Snowcapped mountains. Blue water rising on a beach. A dim bar. A pair of red lips.

Life. Anything.

HE PICKED UP his backpack and a tote bag filled with his clothes.

Thank you all, he said, as though addressing a convention. But it was just the two of us, standing in the living room. He had an almost gentle, tolerant look about him, us melting before him. He had liked us, in his way.

By the way, you bought me too many shirts, he said. He left a couple of shirts on a chair. He folded them, as evenly as he folded the napkins, a surprising new skill. When he hugged us, I thought I felt that clutching, that grip he had held us with just a couple of months before. Or perhaps I just imagined it. How could a child blow through your house, conjuring all these feelings, and then just go?

We hugged him back, a quiet, fierce knot.

Call when you can, we said. We want to hear from you.

Then he was off.

I SAW THE shirts he had left. I took off my shirt and slid the new shirt on. My husband watched me. I buttoned it, slowly. He had left us this, a gift.

We were aware of each other, we were aware of the sun rising, and the shifting quality of the light. I heard my husband breathing. There were our children floating in their lives, they were away and in their orbits, and I understood that while yes, in some way they had left us, they were moving on to what they needed to do, C had understood that someday, we would leave them as well.

I clasped my hands together. My vanishing arms. Each day took us farther away. Each day, we were closer to leaving them.

The children, I think, knew this.

I walked to the window and looked out at the sunlight, the way it lit up everything, the way we were all held in its blossoming and waning light. There was the sidewalk, a shining ribbon, there was the brightness glinting across the green leaves, there were the tops of cars, glimmering, and there was all the beauty he was going to, all the light he wanted to gather, there was the light we walked through too.

The sun stretched out across the day. All of us, located somewhere, in its bright gaze. My husband touched my shoulder very gently, and we stood together at the window and watched him walk and walk and walk.

HELICOPTER

The helicopter was large, thick and brutal in a slightly military way, with a curved brown window so dark the pilot could not be seen. It was veering, with its deep guttural sound, toward our apartment building. I thought the helicopter would fly over the building, it would move on to its duties, but it was coming closer to the building, yes, closer—and then the helicopter was hovering beside my window, here.

There was nothing between me and the helicopter but a pane of glass, which seemed now very thin, so thin it concerned me. I waited for the helicopter to crash through the window, that would be a natural course of events; the helicopter had that hulking potential.

My bedroom was not very clean. I was alone and I did not know where my wallet was. Where was my ID? It seemed important to have it. How could I board a helicopter without it? I was naked and unknown. The cats were on the bed; one licked the other on the head. How happy they were over nothing, their happiness innocent and extravagant. The body of the helicopter was very still, as though parked on an invisible lot, but its blades whirred until they blurred; the vibrations they made, on the other side of the thin window, trembled within my body, through my neck.

Why did the helicopter pick this moment to pause by my window? I didn't know; in any case, I was naked, I did not want whoever was there to see that. Or perhaps I would give them a surprise. The previous night, I had had an orgasm so strong, I felt now the stirrings of my period, or what was left of it these days. It was as though my uterus was yelling, a final yell. I could not hear it, but the sound it would make would be glorious. I pulled the sheets around me as though to show I was modest, but this was a lie. I did not want to be modest; it was only what I was told I should feel.

Every day, I watched helicopters sear across the pale sky. They seemed to be on a definite mission, but I didn't know where they were going. Perhaps this helicopter had made a mistake and was visiting the wrong floor. Perhaps someone on another floor had summoned it, perhaps there was an emergency within the building that I had not heard about. But the helicopter merely floated here, suspended, like a hummingbird, in the air.

That day, the supermarket was low on food. The trucks with supplies had not arrived and some of the shelves were bare. Everyone was throwing the cheaper foods into their carts, particularly the perishables. "Everyone, don't push," said the clerks, speaking with confidence; they were waiting for the trucks to rumble in. "There will be more peaches.

There will be more carrots. It's all on its way." There was plenty of canned soup, surprisingly, but no one took notice of it. Everyone wanted the peaches, the blueberries, the sweet fruits that were edible for a short time. There was no visible emergency, or none that we had been informed of, there was food, they said, coming in from somewhere else, there were trucks rolling down the highway. We had to be patient, the manager said. We had to trust the trucks were coming. Of course, no one trusted this; nothing was coming from anywhere. We trusted only our ability to hoard.

I heard a woman, older and sturdy looking, tossing bell peppers into her cart, chatting with another. "We're moving to Idaho," she said. Another woman asked why there. "It's the people," she said. "Their friendliness. We went and visited. I just felt so comfortable there. The beauty of the mountains. But really, we were there just for a week, and I loved the people." She spoke with a belief in the goodness of others that was surprising to me. I envied her certainty, her love toward those who were really still strangers.

I listened for the sound of sirens, but I heard none. The traffic flowed on the highways, in a sweet and naive way. People were driving to their work, to appointments, and no one knew the food was about to end. I knew this. Longing hung in the air. I could not identify if it was theirs or mine, but I could feel its presence, soaking everything up. I felt an anticipatory hunger, before I was hungry, and wanted to quell it before it subsumed me. Yesterday, it was my birthday, and I went early to make sure I could get ingredients to make a cake with strawberries in the frosting. The sweetness of birthday cake had been created for a reason. You wanted that taste in your mouth as you looked toward what would come next. I found that cake and then, full of a brassy confidence, I had approached the last box of strawberries in the store. An older man, his hair a translucent white flame, his hands gripping his supermarket cart, had been shuffling toward the box and I swooped in and grabbed it. I wanted the strawberries more. That was what I told myself. First was first. I had stolen a pack of berries from the too-slow grasp of the old man. I saw him turn away sadly, and I tried to feel unaffected by that sadness. I imagined offering him some strawberries but was afraid things would get out of hand. I wanted them. There was nothing complicated about this; I just did. My aging year was different from his aging year, not as dire, or perhaps more. Aging was about proof of some illusion of certainty, and I wanted to prove that I could grab first. How did the shape of our wanting reveal who we were now, at these various stages? Now the box was hidden in the refrigerator behind some less appealing items—a bowl of old spaghetti, some celery sticks. I had grabbed those strawberries, and I was savoring their red sweetness, one by one.

I stared at the helicopter. I did not know its intent. Was it there to save or kill me? How sad that these were the only two choices I could imagine. Why couldn't I believe it could just take me on a nice trip? Was that the problem with everything, the inability to figure out intent? The way the frail old man had glanced at the strawberries, the sound of shoes clattering across the produce section as people pushed forward and grabbed. I had not thought I would be one of the grabby ones, perhaps I had not been. Perhaps the man had stepped away, interested in other food options, allowing me to lunge. Perhaps I had handed him some strawberries too, we had shared them, in a tender moment of communion. But that was wrong, and I knew it. It was what I had done. It was only a matter of time before the army filled the streets. There were a couple soldiers by the supermarket, for an unknown reason—they looked like they had recently been brought in. They had thick beige bulletproof vests, and they held in their arms long rifles. They were young enough to be my sons. I was far away from my own children. We all stood and pretended to ignore each other, but I knew we were aware of each move. Our attempts to ignore one another were pretentious and ridiculous. They stared at nothing, feet planted, cradling their guns. Their faces were young and dreamy as though inhabited by clouds.

NOW I INCHED forward, sheets clutched to my chest, eyeing the helicopter. The cats stirred, their mouths opening like tiny caves. They began meowing, sensing something.

When would the war start? I wanted to ask the person in the helicopter, the one I could not see. Would someone tell me? I squinted, but the black dome was impenetrable. We all agreed on the fact that there would be a war, we all knew it was going to happen, it was just a matter of when.

The helicopter trembled by the window. Was the helicopter, besides the pilot, empty, or was it carrying another person? Or more? And how was I supposed to get into it?

It seemed a mean sort of dare. The pilot had to know that I couldn't step through the glass. The helicopter would have to crash through, the window shattering, glass everywhere, the cats probably leaping through the broken window, hurtling to their deaths. I loved the cats and did not want anything bad to happen to them. We gazed at each other and when one climbed on my chest, our small hearts beating against one another, we were both happy; it was the most unifying feeling in the world. I loved the clichéd aspects of it. I wanted to protect his furry, thrumming self. Be careful, I wanted to tell the pilot, sternly. Do not hurt us. We will not tolerate harm. I had practiced all my life to say this. Perhaps the helicopter would carry us to safety, to land on the top of a cloud, to the mirrored surface of a lake, its ramp unfolding into air. A location I did not know. I wanted to believe in the buoyant surface of clouds, in safety. The room suddenly felt claustrophobic and terribly hot; my cheeks were burning. I had to get out.

The helicopter hovered, silent.

The helicopter was not being helpful. No one was telling me how to get to it. Panic flared in my chest. What was the helicopter going to do? There were already dozens dead somewhere in the city, all people who had done nothing wrong; I did not know where they were, but I knew. There would be more, and I wanted to help them, but I did not know how to start. The old man was perhaps wandering by the strawberries and I wanted just then to know his name. Where was he, was he as hungry as I was, did he feel the same trembling inside? Who else had found the strawberries, and what were people storing in their vegetable bins? What could we offer to anyone else? If I flew inside the helicopter, perhaps I could find him. The helicopter was turning, the air stirring in great clear sashes around it. "Stop," I shouted. "Wait." I wanted to fly it. Which was ridiculous because I had never flown a helicopter in my life. I believed I would be a good pilot. My hope was a great shroud of deceit, but necessary. The pilot could not hear me shouting through the glass window. Perhaps the pilot could see my mouth shouting, but that was easy to ignore. "Wait," I shouted again. "Let me try." I put my hands on the glass. "Stop. Don't leave yet. Let me try."

The helicopter turned on a pale sheave of light to leave, the propeller beating the air, and I imagined myself inside it, gripping the controls of the machine, guiding it with my hands, the helicopter rising and falling as I surveyed the glowing, broken city, and wondered, among the wreckage, what it was to be victorious.

MESSENGERS

Our community was encircled by walls that were eighty feet tall. We had been sealed here, in this compound, for over a hundred years. Our district was spread out on land that stretched for miles; there were farms and stubby gray fields and a large clear blue lake. The community was built in concentric circles, so our homes all faced the center square, a flat concrete yard with long, blue shadows cast by the founder's statues, where we gathered most nights in the cool dusk.

We were a successful community because we had claimed this wild land many years ago and, with some strange luck, started growing a plant. It resembled a walnut but tasted like raspberries, and its fruit produced a very healthy jam, and its leaves could be ground into a substance that was valuable in war. The land was vast, and the soil was gray and dry and sometimes difficult, and our community was surprised and grateful when this plant blossomed under our care. We heard about the first years the plants flourished, when trucks rumbled out the gates, carrying loads of jam to the outside world, bringing back food and supplies that helped build our community. Those years, everyone was busy and productive, and our leaders said we had a responsibility to those who lived outside our walls, those who eagerly awaited our items; we could not let them down.

For several years, we had bountiful seasons. The plants broke out of the earth and opened, twisting, green and glorious, into the sun. We woke up, we brushed our hair, we went to the farm or to work or to school; the roofs glinted as each day slid into darkness. When our parents and neighbors sat in the center of the town, they told us that the seasons were not always this generous. They told us about the years when the soil was stubborn, when plants pushed out of the earth but did not flower, when the trucks idled, empty, and when nothing came in. Sometimes when we were assembled on the concrete square, waiting for the day to end, waiting for the sky to flush a deep blue, someone might softly mention the Confusion. We noticed a stillness in the air after this—then someone wept or coughed or walked away.

"What happened?" we asked.

The Confusion—which apparently happened more than once—was an event that made everyone wilt with embarrassment. No one wanted to discuss it.

But they did want to talk about another topic, which generated a kind of low, dark excitement, made people brighten and lean forward: the appearance of the messengers.

The community was surrounded by a vast number of districts. For a hundred years, messengers had come to our community and gathered outside of it. They arrived annually, during the deep cold of winter, and stood on the other side of the huge wall, their voices echoing through the silent, chill air as they called for us to accept an envelope and read their message.

The point that everyone agreed on was this: the community had never accepted any of the messages, ever. We had a great deal of pride about that.

IN SCHOOL, WE learned that our community was created after a war, after activities that were unspeakable, and the story we were told was this: Mr. Van Worth had discovered the uses of the plant. He had been running along a river, under the cold, steel sky, exhausted, starving, and as he tumbled to the ground, he picked up the scaly green pod. It looked inedible, but Van Worth, that genius, decided to crack it open with his teeth. There were casts of Van's mouth in classrooms, so we could see close up the teeth that somehow understood the task of survival. We were proud to have brilliant white teeth that could crack anything apart and sometimes cracked fruits at our desks in class, applauded by our teachers. They were most appreciative of those who, through evolution or masterful dentistry, had developed teeth that resembled fangs. We sang songs in honor of Mr. Van Worth, whom we were all named after—Van1 or Vanda1 through thousands. We remembered the bravery of those who joined Mr. Van Worth on this unpredictable land, who set up the community and constructed the walls protecting us.

Our teachers marched us down the streets of our district, singing songs praising Van Worth. They pushed us to sing louder, especially as we walked past the main buildings of our district, the slumped old buildings, the dark, crumbling sides. They had been constructed, squat concrete structures, decades ago, and there was a sort of suspicion built into them, the blocklike structures with few windows. After the plants first blossomed, there was a time of flourishing, and the walls were first erected to protect us from anyone who wanted anything we could not provide. We had survived, they told us, because we had worked together so effectively, because our community had used our land and bounty; the teachers told us this as we stepped carefully through the cracked streets.

When the messengers arrived, they held an envelope with something urgent to tell our leaders, and they said that the community needed to listen. The decision to turn them away was made immediately and was resolute. The community spent all its extra money, that some said could be used to develop our old buildings, our rutted roads, to build our walls higher, bolstering them. The walls thickened and grew, their solidity a point of pride for the community. Certainly, we thought, those in the less successful districts around us, those who had not coaxed their land with our ability and skill, viewed us with envy; we believed their messages were full of malice and threats. So we refused them and waited, with great anticipation, for the people of these districts to try to destroy us.

Every month, a siren pierced the air, and we ran down stairs located beneath closets in our homes. The stairs led to corridors under the city, clean, solid concrete tubes with dim lighting that made our faces look blue. These were, besides the walls, the best-maintained structures in the city, the corridors that would keep us safe. They wound down under the streets, and when the sirens blew, everyone in the community clattered down into the halls with a low roaring sound like thunder. We were supposed to be perfectly silent as we huddled in the concrete corridors, which stank of everyone's breath. Some of us were good at crying, muttering with anxiety; one of our history teachers had a splendid, terrified moan. The imagined intrusion was so vivid it seemed as though it had actually happened. We climbed out of the tunnels and resumed our daily activities, but we remembered (even treasured) these moments, the gauzy dark light in the tunnels, the brimming silence, the mesmerizing, living quality of our fear.

WE COUNTED THE months, marked by the drills, and in the dull cold of winter, when we went outside and our lungs stung in the chill air, we waited with fear and hope for the arrival of the messengers. It was a fear that made the lights brighten inside our homes. Who would approach the wall? How would they try to present their message? In what manner would they be turned, again, away? There was the simple method, in which we ignored them and went about our lives efficiently, responsibly, knowing the messengers were outside the walls of the compound, desperately wanting to say something, waiting, unheard. There was the more active strategy in which members gathered on the wide flat surface of the wall, glared at the messengers, and screamed, "Go!" We would sometimes pause in class to listen to their screams pierce the air.

The knowledge that the messenger was out there, waiting, while we were inside the compound made us all feel a prickly clamminess, a combination of fear and pride. The messengers wanted to tell us something—maybe something we did not know. But it was absurd to think the messengers could tell us anything new. Our teachers, our parents' supervisors all emphasized this—if we needed to know something, we would have learned it here. Yet we all waited, with a kind of eager trepidation, for the messengers and their thwarted visits. The messengers' relentless determination over the years, our ability to turn them away, made us feel, it seemed, that we were worthy.

First, there was a messenger who came once a year and was turned away immediately. There was the messenger who walked barefoot to the wall and surprised everyone in the community by singing. No one was fooled by that, though the few people who remembered his voice did say that they admired the way he held the final note of his song. They remarked on his talent, but, they added, there had been no need to let him in. We heard about the messenger who was extremely thin, almost skeletal. Some kind members tossed her a few biscuits; she stood outside the walls of the community for two days, waiting, and they described how they watched with interest to see whether she ate the biscuits, but they did not let her in. There was the messenger who was beautiful in a way that people still talked about. She had blue eyes that were luminous and pale as though she were staring through a darkness we could not see, and some people gathered just to witness that stare; they talked about how her stare made one of the Vans nervous, and the story was that he actually took the envelope, just to look at her eyes one more moment, but then, of course, crumpled it up and tossed it to the ground.

When we became used to the frequent incursions, they began to arrive in groups. There were two messengers waiting in the shadow of the massive wall encircling our community, then three or four. Was their message longer, requiring more than one person to deliver it? Or was it more pointed, more urgent? What could they possibly want to tell us? And now that they were standing out there, how long were they going to wait? Were they going to rush the walls, grab us, force us to hear their message, whatever it was?

IT WASN'T SAFE for children to go near the messengers; when we approached the walls, we generally were told to stay away. But that day, we hadn't *decided* to go see the messengers. It was simply something that happened. We sat at our desks in school, and we knew they were out there, clutching their envelopes and waiting. We did not want to go, of course we didn't, we had exams to study for, there were all the tasks ahead of us, but it was distracting, thinking of them out there, knowing they wanted to speak to us. We were going to check on the situation—perhaps that was what we planned to answer if any teacher asked us why we were going, but it was not an answer because we had no need to answer, because there had been no decision.

Van657877, tall, with a long, emphatic stride and glorious, fang-like teeth, walked first, for he knew how to get to the top of the wall; his father had a job repairing it. His tongue moved lightly across his sharp teeth, the way it did when he was nervous before an exam. We ran up the stairway that would take us to the top, and we were in a rush, which felt strange because there was, of course, no need to rush.

It was not the first time I had seen a messenger—I had caught glimpses of one or another a few years before. But this was the first time I examined them at length. They were young, in their late teens, and they looked vaguely similar to us, as though we were seeing our own faces distorted, far away, through a telescope. They were two girls and a boy. One girl had a face that held a similar determined expression as my father's, as though they had been born in the same dream. The messengers all had limp bronze hair that stretched down their backs, and they were thicker than us and shorter than I had imagined. They saw us, and one blinked in surprise, a fluttery blink, as if to reconcile the real and imagined versions of us that lived in a blurred overlay in his mind. Another held up an envelope.

"Here! Read this!" they shouted.

They stood in the patches of dirty snow, shoulders touching, as though trying to warm each other, and that intimacy was somehow startling, not what I expected to notice. They all clasped hands.

Their hands disturbed me. The clasping, the huddling

together—it felt like a reproach, an answer back to some statement we had made. We stood on top of the wall, casting our thin shadows onto them. Next to me, Van657877 inhaled slightly. I turned to look at him. With his height and his teeth, I'd always assumed he was fearless, but now I sensed a fragile aura about him, as though he were a stack of twigs that had just been assembled.

"Go!" Van657877 shouted down to the messengers, and there was his voice. So loud. How peculiar it sounded, soaring over them, but they did not seem threatened. They rushed forward and tried to thrust the envelope in his hands. "Here!"

Their voices rumbled over our ears, and their faces were convinced of the importance of their message; the conviction seemed a peculiar, awful costume thrown on them, and I wanted to tear it off. I looked to Van657877 to see what he would do. His tongue flicked over his teeth.

"Stop holding hands! Just go."

They looked up at us, and we looked down at them from the top of this hulking wall.

Then they laughed.

Their laughter. We had never heard it before; it was a bright sound, like aluminum cubes clattering. A circus-like sound, a sound I had never imagined them making, never imagined would be turned in our direction. The messengers were not supposed to mock us; they were supposed to be sent away. Van657877 stepped to the edge of the wall, paused. We weren't sure what he was going to do—jump down, which would have broken his legs; dive down, crushing his skull; or weep. For that moment, any option seemed possible.

And then, quickly, he turned and ran away from the laughter, ran through the sparkling, clean streets of our community to our homes, ran toward the dusk stretching dark over the silver roofs. The rest of us tumbled after him. We sat up straighter in our seats and were grateful the next day when our teachers reminded us that our job was not to listen to the messengers. And we were grateful when the three messengers were gone the next day, their envelope left in the dirt and swept up, disposed of as always.

THEN IT WAS spring, and the plants stretched out their leaves—the green stalks unfurled their long arms, studded with the tiny gleaming flowers that would become their fruit. We gathered at dawn to watch the plants grow—they grew so fast you could almost see it—and we shivered as we watched them bloom. The vast dark-green fields glittered like an eternal lake in the sunlight.

We watched the leaves grow, and we went home, and we returned the next day to see their progress. But as we walked toward the vast fields, we saw people running. They ran alongside the rows and bent down and shouted and then ran a few feet and stopped and bent down again. A peculiar green dust hung over the field. Dust, we thought at first, blown in from elsewhere, carried in on the air. Then people started pointing at the plants, and it slowly became clear that the green in the air was the plants, that some of them had become dust, and that they were dissolving.

No one predicted that the leaves would start crumbling

off the stalks of the plants. Just a few plants dissolved at first. It was a mutation, they said, or the sun hit them a certain weird way, or there were murmurings that the visit from the messengers interfered with the fragile growth of the plants. No one could describe the biology of this last interaction, but everyone spoke of it with conviction, so it appeared to be true. The plants had flourished in this community for so many years. Still, the next week it happened again, more leaves crumbled at dawn, the bright-green dust rising softly from the fields under a hard, glittering blue sky.

We began to receive daily reports on the plants: how many were growing and the proportion of leaves that crumbled. We still went to work and school, everything continued, but after school, we went to watch the plants. The dissolving of the leaves was mesmerizing, a glossy leaf present and then suddenly not. After a lifetime of drills, disaster had finally arrived, but not as we predicted, not from outside our walls. The sirens sounded, we gathered, silently, in the cold corridors below the city, and we went through our familiar gestures of dread, the ones we had rehearsed for all our lives. But we did not look too closely at each other's faces.

AND OF COURSE, the messengers kept coming. Van657877 and I were in the fields together one day, checking on the plants, and heard the usual commotion. Van657877 was agitated, covered in green dust.

"Why are they here?" he asked.

"They are always here," I said.

"Why are they here? Now?"

They were here because they were always here, but this answer was not enough.

"Come with me," Van657877 said. "I want to show you something."

There was a small door that led to the area beyond the wall. No one was supposed to pass through it—only select members of the community, to evaluate the climate outside the walls, to sometimes gather supplies. Van657877's father, a high-ranking member of the district council, went through it at times, and Van657877 once saw him, and now he found it, in a section of the wall surrounded by thick gray bushes, and we pushed through it, through a damp concrete tunnel, and then we were outside, and we were looking at the messengers, right in front of us. There were four of them. Their breath was like meat and musty, as though they ate different foods from ours. Their nearness, the heat of their breath, was shocking, and I did not know where to look. One held an envelope out.

"Hello! Van? You can read this! Here!"

He had said our name. One of them pushed close to me, and I could feel his breath, and then he put a hand on my arm, gently, as they pushed toward us. I jumped a little. I had never been so close to a messenger, never felt a messenger's hand on me, and I thought, Who are you, and I thought, Who am I, and then, What do you want to tell me, then a little flare of interest, and then I thought, You cannot tell me this, whatever it is. I was so close to the messenger, I could bite him, though I did not. I noticed his eyelashes, long and dark. His eyelashes startled me; I don't know why they reminded me of my eyes when I saw them, but they did. The same eyelash curl, the same color. I was dizzy, I was not the messenger, and he was not me, but this little bit of us was the same, and somehow terrible. I blinked, hoping the eyelashes would look different, that the me-ness would vanish, but then I heard the messenger click his tongue, which was not a sound I had heard before, and fear flared in my throat, and I trembled.

We were all blurred together, the messengers shouting, and then Van657877 shoved one of them, shoved him so he fell to the ground. The air seemed to riffle and bend; the other messengers knelt by the one whom Van657877 had pushed, and then a fist hit Van657877 in the face, and then there was blood coming out of Van's mouth—he was missing one of his fang-like teeth.

The other messengers yanked the one who had punched Van657877 back, and one started to speak sternly to him, while another still held the envelope out, in a ludicrous and stubborn gesture of hope. But Van657877 was focused now on one thing—he lurched over to the one who had punched him and hit him so hard that the messenger collapsed. I had never seen Van657877 so mad—his fist came down on the messenger again and again, like a hammer, and the others tried to pull him off, but they could not. My heart was bouncing around in a confused way; there was a great jostling, and I did not know how to stop him; I did not think I was supposed to stop him. I heard someone shrieking, and I believed it was me. My shame was both a knife thrust in me, an assault on me, and fluttering somewhere in the air, away. I was not me and Van657877 was not Van657877 and also he was, he was who he was, and the world weighed a thousand pounds and also nothing. Van657877 was strangely silent and focused in his battering, as though he had been practicing for this all along. I saw something sharp on the ground, and I lunged for it. It was Van657877's bloody fang-like tooth. I put it in my pocket.

The messengers finally slipped in and pulled away the one getting battered. The messenger's face was broken, the ground was dark with his blood, and he was completely still. When I looked at him, there was a knife in my throat. My hands twitched, holding nothing. The messengers murmured to him. Their whispers were urgent, limned with fear, but they were quick, efficient as they lifted him in their arms and walked away.

Van657877 ran back through the door into the community. I followed him. He had his finger in his mouth and was rubbing the empty space where his tooth had been.

"Look!" he said and opened his mouth. I peered in and saw the gap, and his mouth was full of blood.

"Where's my tooth!" he said. His finger was bloody, too; he was breathing hard. He looked at the wall, and I thought he would go back out there, searching for his prize tooth. This idea made my heart beat faster.

I found myself standing in front of him; he stopped.

"Van. You're bleeding. Let's get back."

My fingers touched it in my pocket, that curved knifelike point. It was mine.

VAN657877 HAD BEEN, out of nowhere, attacked by a messenger; that was the story he told, and everyone believed it, especially after they saw his missing tooth. He had been attacked, so unfairly, and they would all return. Of course, the message was this! That they would knock our teeth out, and worse; this was what we had predicted, and this was what happened when we stood too close to them—imagine what would happen if we took their envelopes, if we let them in. For a few days we did not discuss the plants and how they were dissolving; we did not discuss how people were going into the fields and grabbing the fruits that were blossoming and storing them away. Instead, we prepared for the return of the messengers, after they had attacked Van657877, one of the most popular young men in our community, whom the best dentist outfitted for free with a gleaming new tooth.

TWO HUNDRED AND seventy-eight members of the community climbed to the top of the wall, and they sat in chairs in the hot sun, waiting for the messengers to return. The top of the wall was thick, about eight feet wide, and they set up umbrellas and rolled out blankets to rest on, and they looked out. They were allowed to leave their homes, their jobs, to camp out on the wall and scan the land day and night for the surge of messengers. Guns and other weaponry lay across their laps. There was a great relief in the community that they were sitting on the wall, that they were looking.

A few days, we thought, and the messengers would arrive.

One week went by. Two weeks. A month.

The fields twinkled with plants growing and vanishing.

People ascended the wall with great excitement but tired after a couple weeks, dazed by the glaring sun, and were replaced by others.

The officials organized parades for those sitting bravely on top of the walls, on lookout for the messengers. We marched by the walls, blowing horns, shouting our appreciation for them, waving colorful flags.

Two months. Three. Four.

We felt a subdued but clear craving to hear the messengers, to be able tell them to go. It was the structure, the shape we were accustomed to, and now its absence gave me a shivery feeling, as though I were not quite whole. We were all possessed by a great restlessness. "Can't you feel it?" a neighbor said with conviction, rubbing her bare arms. "They poisoned the air."

In the fields, green dust lifted into the blue sky.

THE FIRST ATTACKS happened in the fields. It was, they said, a misunderstanding. It was Van657877's father who tackled Van998126, who was, opportunistically, scooping extra berries into a bag. Then it was a group of adolescents who got in the way of a few others entering a market, who claimed they did not have a clear path inside. Then it was a scuffle between two women at a clothing store, who knocked over a shoe display in their determination to grab the same shirt. There was the moment the sirens sounded, and we all rushed into the corridors beneath the city; all the lights went out, causing a brief panic, and in the darkness there was a shriek. When the lights sparked on, several minutes later, Van109876 was on the ground, his jacket torn and his face bruised.

There were misunderstandings, the newscasters said. My parents listened to the broadcasts, to the community leaders who commended our bravery in this difficult time. If we behaved appropriately, there would be special jam distributions and other rewards. Here was bounty, beyond the walls was threat. But people had started locking their doors, and my parents brought boards from a closet and hammered them on the windows, expertly, as though they had done this before. Sometimes, when the sirens went off, the members of the community did not rush through their escape doors but remained in their homes, pretending not to hear their loud drone.

We began to eye one another. Mostly we eyed each other through our windows, for we were becoming afraid of going out into the street. We did not venture out to the fields, where most of the fights went on, for we didn't know who would rush up and pat us down for something; we didn't know who might come up behind us and begin to hit us, looking for some sign of our diminishment.

THE SAFEST PLACE to sit was, oddly, the wall, for no one harmed any of the brave people who sat there. They had to switch out every few weeks, for the sun and the boredom depleted them. The leaders called for more people to sit on the wall, to look for the messengers. Soon it was my turn to scan the landscape with the others.

I sat under a frail umbrella, holding a gun. I was, it turned out, an excellent watcher. The others who sat on the wall beside me were an excitable, impatient group, believing they saw the messengers coming, believing they saw danger when they only saw the slow rippling leaves of a tree, the glimmering shadow of a bird. They were glad to have a purpose. They wanted a purpose as much as they wanted to live. They told me to tighten my grip on the gun if they saw a particular shift in a certain tree's shadow, that a certain circular flight of the birds meant that they had spotted a person in the brush. I was, they said, a diligent watcher. They complimented me on my hard gaze, the way I stared, at my clearly intent absorption.

I didn't tell them what I was really looking at—the sky, the glossy and wide blankness in it. I noticed the variance of the colors, the pale rose of the start of the day, the fading light blue, the midday aqua, the way it slid to darkness at night. It told me nothing, but I could not stop looking at it. They did not know that I was pretending to press myself into the sky, not in the community or outside of it—I was a great student of the sky, of nothingness; perched on this wall, not looking for the messengers, not looking at the community, the dusty, dissolving fields, behind me. I imagined the sky and clouds gathering into new forms, forms that defied physics and the laws of weather, that rose into columns and swirls and fountains and towers, into new cities that I had never seen before.

I told no one of this. I did not quite know what it meant, myself, but I imagined taking myself apart and becoming absorbed into the clouds and sky and these cities, becoming not me, not here.

I felt the concrete roughness of the wall under my feet. Sometimes I put my hand in my pocket and felt Van657877's tooth, which I had kept for a reason I could not explain. Carefully, I ran my fingers along it and felt it, knifelike against my palm. Sometimes I wondered what I would do with it.

ARLENE IS DEAD

Sylvia had, perhaps forever, told us about the problems with Arlene. The two friends had both lived in this building for almost half a century. They were the first residents, moving into the brick tower on the East Side of Manhattan during the 1970s, the building slapped up to inhale the middle class back into the city. They were mothers together, they loved and hated the building together—the browning red brick, the corruption of the maintenance crew, the fact that they asked for help with the dishwashers and were ignored, or at least ignored longer than the couple in 3B, who got the attention of maintenance, and how? Why did 3B get assistance with the dishwasher and not them? This they agreed on. Over the years they had, at various times, gotten along, sworn they would never see each other again, sometimes within the same hour, tenderly knocked at each other's doors, presented offerings of cookies or bottles of wine, owed each other money, accused the other of owing money, disagreed on the amount of money owed. Sylvia Goldstein was eighty-six, Arlene Moscowitz was eighty-seven.

We had heard about the dinners together during which, Sylvia said, problems occurred because Arlene made too many demands of the waiter, because she had been an actress and also at times, shockingly, a therapist (shocking because, as Sylvia said, Arlene never shut up), but had been a bad saver and now, on her small budget, never got to eat out, while Sylvia had a generous pension from her university teaching job that allowed her to eat out often—more than, she said, she should. But Arlene, because she ate out so rarely, yearned for her meal to be perfect. She had many substitutions and preferences. The tomato and lettuce on a hamburger needed to be on the plate, not on the burger. Mayonnaise never spread within the sandwich, was always in a small dish beside the plate. Cheese was never, ever, found in the designated location. She gave the waiter these instructions as though giving strict details for a medical procedure, though she proudly declared she had no allergies she was aware of. If they added ketchup when she said not to, if the cheese was not offered in a cup by the side, that was just it. She sent it back, with a torrent of accusation and a deep, sorrowful disappointment. One time, after a particularly arduous lunch at a popular French restaurant, Sylvia had later looked over her receipt and found an extra charge for a "challenging guest." She had never seen this charge on a bill before.

"THEY CHARGED ME for Arlene," Sylvia said. "Can you believe it?" This incident had happened in the vague recesses of past decades, but it was one of the memories that pierced the surface of her mind now, recounted with vividness and the same residual anger. There were a few stories we heard over and over, because now we were living with her. It was December 2020, and there were four of us, her son, daughter-in-law, two grandchildren, packed up from a state where people ran through supermarkets barefaced, breathing. We argued about who should sleep on the foldout couch in the living room, we set up Zooms in a room that doubled as a storage closet, delicately positioning work meetings so that others would not see the archeological morass of dresses, pajamas, and underwear from the 1970s onward piled against one wall.

"Why are you living here again?" she asked us.

"We moved here three months ago to take care of you," we said. "The rates are high, and we can work here. Your aide, Bianca, went to a party! Sylvia, it's too risky. She can't come in."

"Risky why? Is she going to steal something?"

"No. Worse."

"I want to go out to the coffee shop. Let's go."

"No, can't. Too dangerous."

"It's just a coffee shop! What are you afraid of?"

We spoke passionately into screens, we hunched over in the thin gray light, we tried to be useful to our places of employment and prayed they would not call us back. We were living here to do everything: to cook, to soap her back, to grab her hand as she stepped out of the shower, to dole out the pills stored in little compartments, to talk to her.

SHE SAT AT the kitchen table and there were certain things she remembered, or remained consistent. The handsomeness of her husband, his shoulders, and his ambition, but also the fact that he left her—through death, a few years ago. But when she examined her collection of rings, stored in a shoebox, she was suddenly certain that he had given a couple (The turquoise one! Where was it?) to some other woman, one she had never properly identified but somehow took his attention away from her. When she remembered this, she was less sad about his death, though temporarily. There was the loss of her youngest sister when she was six, the sister she shared a bed with during her childhood. Her sister, Opal, who loved eating babka, who left crumbs all over the kitchen. Opal, whose head was shaved because of a skin disease, she couldn't remember what, just that sometimes she stared at Opal's head beside her, like a small moon, put her hand on her head at night, feeling the soft velvet curve of her skull. Opal had been sleeping beside her one night, perfectly fine, snoring a bit too loudly maybe, and then the next running into the street, the shouts, the tires, the way she had lain so still. How did I know, she told us, that she was not pretending, making a joke? For months she woke up, arm reaching toward Opal's side of the bed, shocked each time by the empty space, by the nothing there.

What had been wrong with the love she had given? She could not quite identify what was wrong with the love returned to her, for she had loved her husband, her sister, her children, gloriously, all of them. She could name many of the presents given to them each birthday over the years. Now she awoke at night sweating, certain that her husband had snuck into her shoebox one night and stolen the ring and a bracelet with shells from a trip to Miami and given it to someone named, she thought, Genevieve. Maybe it was Genevieve, maybe she was named something else. She wanted that bracelet back so much she said she felt an ache in her teeth. She remembered the fact that she had played piano masterfully as a teenager and then gave it up for some reason, that had to be the demand of someone else; she could feel the desire to play in her fingers, though they had long since thrown the piano out. There was, in her body, she said, yearning for things, events, people, who felt essential.

Sylvia remembered her work for forty years—she had been a professor of rhetoric at a university, whose name she could not recall but remembered when you told her; she did recall the way her department head, who she now called the idiot, had told her no food in the classroom, no more bringing her homemade babka into the room. She remembered that meeting, as it was traumatic. "This is a classroom," the idiot had said, as though she didn't know that. "No snacks, no meals, just learning." It was a cruel proclamation, and the idiot was jealous of her babka, that was clear. The students voted her teacher of the year eight times, and then she had to sit in a classroom devoid of babka or other pastries, which was good for no one.

The department head had retired, leaving a half-eaten box of Thin Mint cookies in her office. Sometimes Sylvia remembered this, sometimes she awoke, shouting her name in her sleep. Sometimes she shouted at her father in her sleep; her father who worked at his brother's discount store in Flatbush his whole life and whose brain was too frozen with fear to go to college himself; finally, she had the words to answer when he called her a birdbrain, seventy years ago. Finally, she knew how to shut him up.

She did not talk very much. She slept and sometimes she yelled out in her sleep. We watched her as she slept, a still but active sleep, more active in a way than her wakefulness. She looked so furious and effective in her dreams. She looked deeply alive in her dreams, and how we envied that. The children, teenagers, fleeing toward love or even good snacks when they could, warned not to lower their masks, not to kiss, to not do everything they were supposed to be doing, vanishing into the cold day for hours, doing of course all that, or maybe not. Her son and his wife, crammed into a storage room off the main living space shaking with sound from Top Model shows, with the sour job of having to tell everyone to stay put as the numbers of the ill climbed; they lay there, trembling, waiting for the mistake. Desire like a shovel, wanting to dig up the world. The apartment brimmed with all sorts of wanting. We were trying to slow down time in some ways, for it was sliding to no good place, and we wanted to speed it up in others; each moment squished us in like a cold wall.

And then one day her eyes flashed open and she made an announcement.

"I know my main problem in life," she said.

"What," we asked, eyes blinking open.

"It's her," she said.

"Who?" we asked, looking around.

"My problem in life," she said, "is Arlene."

SHE WOKE UP the next morning, refreshed and focused: she told us about everything wrong with Arlene.

"She doesn't let me get a word in edgewise," she said. "Everything is Arlene, Arlene. How great her sons are, how successful, how beautiful their children are, but how great are they if they don't want her to visit? Answer that. They said for months, 'No, don't come,' and then suddenly they allow her there for two weeks. Two weeks of listening to Arlene and her greatness. The woman talks all the air out of the room. Maybe they like it. Because that is all she wants to do. That is how she has talked to me. The great topic in her life: her. It's enough. I have endured this for, how many, fifty years."

The truth was (we all admitted this): there was something thrilling about her hatred for Arlene Moscowitz. Sylvia became all of herself, her whole self, accessed a deep and buried intelligence when she spoke of her resentment toward Arlene. She had a precise knowledge of all the ways that Arlene had offended waiters, all the hints about Sylvia's diet and the flyers with weight-loss plans slipped aggressively under her door, all the slights over fifty years. We were all crammed in here and tired and everyone wanted the bathroom at the same time, in a sort of uncanny wave of urgency, and no one would do their chores, meaning the apartment had a constant low stink in it, which was really the constant simmer of fear. But when Sylvia began to talk about Arlene, we all stopped and listened.

In those moments, it did not matter what she remembered or not; it did not matter what we remembered. Suddenly we were all awake to feeling, her feeling; there was a clear and organizing principle to it; the world was wrong because of Arlene. It was as though a bell were ringing, though there was no bell; there was a clear sound, though there was (except for the blaring TV) no sound; she had utter clarity when she spoke about Arlene; it was as though she were suddenly, again, herself, which was a mirage, flickering, but bright, and we could not miss the moments she was there.

WE LISTENED TO Sylvia talk about the lamentable qualities of Arlene. But we sensed her glancing at the door, waiting for a knock. It was a waiting that had evolved from the past; before, between bans, Arlene dropped by on schedule, afternoons mostly, sometimes evenings, a couple days a week. But a few weeks ago, her children had said they wanted to bring Arlene to Ohio. Mostly, during the day, Sylvia said almost nothing, but after dinner, one day, she looked around and asked where Arlene was.

"Did you hear her knock?"

Usually, yes, but for the last few weeks, no.

"I heard a knock."

She got up and went to the door and looked for Arlene; surprisingly, she wasn't there.

Sylvia kept looking at the door, waiting for the knock, sometimes opening the door, peering outside, and closing it. She waited. She held a very still position, that contained the waiting of almost a century, the waiting for her sister to get up out of the street, the waiting for her husband to come home, the waiting for her department head, the idiot, to retire. She was good at waiting, she sat in that position as though carved into rock. And then one day while Arlene was away, Sylvia turned sour with waiting; one morning she made a grim announcement.

"I'm afraid," she said, "that Arlene is dead."

Could she be dead? It was not impossible, considering. Sylvia did not quite understand the torrent of death across the city. But we had not heard anything about Arlene. We scanned the street as we took her on her short one-block walks with her walker, seeing if Arlene was around, looking for her spiky wig. "We would hear if she's dead," we said.

"Why isn't she knocking?"

"Remember she said she was going out of town."

Sylvia became convinced that Arlene was dead. It was something she thought of, suddenly, throughout the day. "Arlene died," she said. "She died and she is in her apartment alone. Rotting." Sylvia looked at us, eyebrows lifted with an expression of sorrow and the sense that she had finally pulled rank.

"She's not," we said.

"How do you know she's not?"

"Arlene is out of town," we explained. She was visiting her children in Ohio.

"That's not true. Her children hate her," she said.

"They paid for her ticket out."

She looked at us, blinking. "Why didn't you fly me out?"

"Sylvia, we came to you. We came to take care of you."

She sighed, closing her eyes.

"Yes. Stay forever," she said.

SHE WOKE UP and stared at us, with an expression that unnerved us, as though we were gauze. It felt like a criticism, though we knew it was not. We had different responses to the stare. The teens became aware of their hair. They said they wanted it to look good during Zoom classes. They had lush, brown hair, and stood in front of her and combed their hair vigorously, gazing in the mirror. They had so much hair. They poufed it up with gel that filled the room with a sharp sweet smell. Sylvia watched this with great interest, as though watching a movie.

"Do you want something to eat?"

"Yes. What do you have?"

They brought her sliced apples, a yogurt, a sausage. They were glossy, vibrating with eagerness, the desire to hurl themselves into the world. They were beautiful and also dangerous.

She watched them and gently touched her hair.

"I need to shave something," she said.

"Where? You look fine."

She stroked her hair, tenderly.

"Someplace," she said. "I feel it."

ONE DAY, SYLVIA announced three things. Arlene was dead, her body was still inside her apartment, and Sylvia wanted to barge into the apartment and get her out. She's there, she said. Sylvia wanted to knock on Arlene's door now. She also had a dilemma. She wondered if she should lend Arlene the mother-of-pearl necklace she had always ogled, though lending would not be the right word to a dead person. This became the battle within herself—should she lend Arlene the necklace?

"Do you think she will appreciate it?"

"I don't know."

"But what if I want to wear the necklace with an outfit now? When I go out to dinner? It would be gone. Forever. Gone."

Someone had an eye on her most of the time, but one morning, Sylvia got up from her breakfast, put on a dress and shoes by herself, and headed to Arlene's apartment to see if she was dead.

Sylvia pressed the button on the elevator, took it to the seventh floor, got out and banged on 7.

"Arlene!" she said. "I'm here! Say something!" She was afraid of finding Arlene alone in her apartment; she had to be the one to find her. She would walk in just before she passed into death and yell at her so Arlene would jolt awake and accompany her to the diner, where they would sit in their favorite booth and eat something delicious, maybe omelets or pastrami sandwiches or maybe a cinnamon babka. "Arlene!" She banged and banged and banged on the door several times, she said, and finally a tall Asian woman in jogging shorts (why was everyone now wearing only jogging shorts?), with hair dyed oddly, a pinkish color, and spiky the way Arlene's was, opened it and, over a pale-blue mask, looked down at her, with an annoyed expression.

"What's going on?" she asked.

"Where's Arlene?" demanded Sylvia. "Is she there?"

"Who are you talking about? We live here. No one is here by that name."

"But this is where she lives."

She peered into the apartment, the same layout, the same large, grimy windows overlooking the plaza, but—not the same couch. Not the faded green sofa she had sat on for years. It felt as though that sofa were in her own home, she knew it so well, had in fact (twice) spilled coffee on it when Arlene wasn't looking and wiped it up; she had memorized all the sacred stains and creases in it, the maroon blotch from a glass of wine on the left cushion, the small tear near the bottom from Arlene's cat clawing at it ten years ago, all the times she had come and told Arlene about her own difficulties with her children, the death of her husband, the insubordination of her dishwasher. The couch was like a map of her own feelings.

Instead, there was a sleek orange leather couch, one she didn't recognize. Her heart chilled. It sat there, hulking. She wondered—had Arlene been kidnapped, what had happened—

"I'm sorry, you have the wrong apartment," said the woman. She looked at her with a probing expression. "Are you okay?"

Of course I was okay, Sylvia told us. Who was this woman who had the same haircut as Arlene and where was Arlene and her sofa? That sofa! I knew every inch of that sofa!

"I'm afraid," said Sylvia, because she said, nothing made sense, and the absence of the couch made her feel as though she were standing on nothing, air—she glared at the woman and said, "You stole her couch."

The woman then stepped out of her apartment, locked it, looked curiously at Sylvia and marched her downstairs to the man who stood by the door, and said, "This woman knocked on my door. Do you know what apartment she is in?" The doorman nodded, and said, "12F." Then he asked Sylvia, "Can you get there?"

"Of course I can get there," said Sylvia. "My god."

She sat on the couch eating some almonds we brought her. "Where was Arlene? Why was she not in her apartment?"

"Arlene lives in 11J," we said.

"She does not."

"Yes, she lives in 11 J."

"Well," she said. She smiled, carefully.

"Don't let her in if she knocks," she said. "She is still banned."

WE WALKED BY her as she watched Top Model, and her old selves were trapped in our memories, like swift butterflies. The old selves knocking around in our heads. Sometimes we mentioned them to each other. The time she had her rhetoric class over for end-of-semester pizza, and one student left with one of her many brass cat figurines in her purse; when she found out, Sylvia let her keep it but made her write an additional essay about why she felt the need to steal this cat. The time she bought you a halter dress from

Century 21 that she then asked if she could borrow. The time she planned a birthday party with a scavenger hunt that stretched across the entire apartment complex. The time she threw a shoe at you, for a reason still unclear. The time she spent three hours trying to convince you why a certain Academy Award–winning movie was crappy and never deserved any award. The time she called your school six times to complain about the fact that Jesus was mentioned in the prayer for her son's high school graduation. The times she called you darling.

"Do you want something to eat?" we asked.

"Yes."

We sat with her, mostly in silence. There were so many of us here, the silence was a way of making space.

"Sit with me," she said.

We did; we watched her chew.

We waited for her to start talking about Arlene.

ARLENE WAS IN Ohio for a couple of weeks and then one of us spotted her in the supermarket. She was palming some avocados, looking at the price, putting them back. She looked trim in her leopard-print jacket. She smiled, a big, bright smile, not a smile, no, but there they were, her glowing bright teeth. She insisted on wearing a mask incorrectly, like a necklace, as though wanting on some level to be part of a larger enterprise of cooperation, but also to undermine it.

"Oh my god, how are you? How's Sylvia? I have to see her."

"She's—you know. She's okay."

It felt like a betrayal to not present her as an equal. Arlene regarded an avocado, sighed, and dropped it in her cart.

"Well, tell Sylvia we have to go out to lunch. My treat. Soon."

She had returned early from Ohio, apparently. Her daughter wanted her to stay longer, until March, but Arlene had, would you believe, an audition for a commercial. For a medicine that cured reflux, she was supposed to sit at a café sipping a cup of coffee and look refreshed. We heard her say this to anyone who would listen, it seemed untrue but maybe it was true, or Arlene's sheer truck-like belief in it made it true. We huddled from the cold and searched the TV for Arlene's face. It was January 2021. We were waiting to get Sylvia a shot. We noticed that Arlene, the cheerful biohazard, went to the market in the afternoon; we tried to time Sylvia's fifteen-minute walks around this.

But then there was a beautiful day, and we were taking Sylvia outside for a moment, and we walked, the sun flashing on the cement plaza by the building, and the world was filled briefly with a cold sunny light. We walked through the winter sun in our coats, and Sylvia was awake to the world today, she gripped her walker and trod solidly around the block. It was a day that didn't seem too bad, a day when we could all survive each other. Then we saw, down the sidewalk, the familiar gray puffed coat, approaching like a small, determined cloud.

"Sylvia!" exclaimed Arlene. "Finally! I'm back!"

Sylvia stared at her, her face becoming still, as though there was something crucial she had to remember.

"Where were you?" Sylvia asked.

"So many places. Sylvia. So much to catch up. My family, they are beautiful, then I had to come back for the audition, I have to tell you, I knocked them out, I did, Sylvia! I'm waiting to hear back. They said they'd call me in a few days. It's been six. I think that's still a few, don't you? And I met the most wonderful man, would you believe, he's seventy, a child! I met him at a coffee shop. A retired teacher, plays tennis, nice body. I saw him twice. He laughs, he laughs at my jokes! So much to talk about—"

Her speech had a torrential quality, as though she could not stop until we were all drenched. She had the lurking belief that she would be stopped, but we were shy around her somehow, her force.

"Oh," said Sylvia.

"Sylvia, you need to brush your hair," said Arlene. "Why is it standing up like that?"

Sylvia had thin silver hair that usually we combed after a shower, as she held still, arching into the comb like a cat. This time we forgot, in our rush to get her into the sun. Sylvia reached up to touch her hair; it was a white flame.

"It's not," she said.

"Wind," we said.

Sylvia eyed Arlene's wig, which was slightly askew, revealing the woman's scalp, pale, with a few hairs.

"He laughs at you?" she asked.

"No, no. Sylvia," said Arlene, lowering her mask so Sylvia could hear her—"He laughs at my *jokes*—"

We stepped back.

Sylvia gripped her walker and gazed at Arlene with a hazy

expression, both trying to place her and feeling their history hardening like a concrete mold around her. Their long structure of friendship, of diner episodes and shifting rank. Sylvia stood in a position of listening, and Arlene too, as though she had been waiting for weeks for this position, to be part of a conversation. Suddenly, Sylvia's eyelids fluttered as though she had seen the entire sun. She turned her walker and began to head quickly back to the apartment.

"When will I see you?" called Arlene. "When? Sylvia? Let's go out!"

Sylvia was walking, with great speed, toward the brick building. "Soon!" we said, following Sylvia. She pushed the elevator button and stepped inside.

"We'll see her sometime," we said, carefully, hoping she would not remember.

Sylvia stared at the numbers flashing up: two, three, four, five, six.

"Maybe," Sylvia said.

WE SAW ARLENE move through the neighborhood—in the supermarket, at the CVS, sitting in the concrete plaza between the buildings, always talking to anyone, always in midthought. There was something we admired about Arlene, sealed as we were in our carefulness, there was a ruthlessness to her thrust into everything around us—the errant conversation, the line in the supermarket, the elevator; it was as though Arlene, more than any of us, was aware of her potential to vanish.

We woke up, opened our eyes, checked the fact of our own breathing. We sat waiting for Sylvia to wake up, listened for the soft roar she made.

We waited for the approach of Arlene, a bright comet, circling, waiting to crash into all of us.

ONE DAY, IN the market. Arlene by the tangerines. Picking them up, gazing at them, her dark eyes, and her eyelids, sad.

"Hello," we said.

Today she was properly clad; her eyes shone over her mask.

"Please. I have to drop by and see Sylvia. We have to go out to lunch. I'll come by this afternoon. I have so much to tell her. I'm so lonely. Have you ever been this lonely? I'm just sitting there most of the time. It's torture!"

"It is so hard," we said.

"Do you know what it's like not to talk to another person? I don't think so. I don't think you know at all. I go through a day and I don't talk to anyone, except at the supermarket. Alfredo at the deli talks to me. That's it. I need to take her to the diner. That's all I ask."

Our hearts exhausted. Arlene's loneliness like a boulder, weighing down the air.

She was perched, voice hoarse, beside the frozen foods, the glass doors opening and closing and releasing clouds of frost behind her. She never quite looked old, in some spectacular trick of light, but now she did.

"I want to take her to the diner," she said.

She gazed at us, waiting for approval. How we wished they could meet and sit in a red banquette in the diner and argue and ban each other as they had before.

"You know that she is different, Arlene."

Arlene peered at us with a troubled expression, as though we were standing in sheets of rain. And had forgotten our umbrella.

"You know that her memory is, well—"

She crossed her arms in front of her and shivered.

"Don't underestimate her," she said. "Don't ever underestimate Sylvia! I want to see her. When?"

"Soon."

"No. When. Where? I'm asking. Give me a time."

"Next week."

"I'm taking her to the diner now."

We admired Arlene's determination, and we were afraid of it.

"No. The apartment. With these on."

"The diner. I miss the BLTs."

"The apartment."

She was primed for battle, which meant she was terrifying.

"The apartment. And you have to wear one of these."

She paused, opened the supermarket freezer, grabbed a package of blueberries, slammed it. She closed her eyes, and then opened them, and said, "Okay. Yes. I'd love to."

"Okay."

We looked at her, with some skepticism; she saw this instantly.

"What do you think I am? She's my best friend. I treasure

her. Over how many years. We have to talk about—" At the market, people rushing, eyes steely, she held out her arms in a grand gesture and said, "All of it!"

SYLVIA GAZED OUT the window, waiting. She looked up when we told her that Arlene was going to drop by, that they could talk if Sylvia sat on this couch and Arlene on that one six feet away and if, if, if they wore their masks the whole time. The sirens ongoing out on the street, that wailing. The flimsy pieces of cloth, the armament for Arlene's visit. The visit was an event; it was something to look forward to. Sylvia nodded and said, for the first time in days, that she wanted to shower. She dropped her clothes and walked into the shower, and we rinsed her hair.

She sat on her bed as we held up shirt after shirt. Finally, she nodded at a long silver skirt and a sequin top she had worn for New Year's. We missed her hatred of Arlene, we missed it terribly, we missed who she was when she felt that much, we missed her focus and determination, how it lit up the dim apartment, the dreary world. We hoped Arlene would help her wake up to any feeling, Arlene always victorious in this realm. We loved Arlene, we did, for her ability to distract Sylvia in this way. We sat with Sylvia, in the dim apartment, and waited.

WE HAD NOT really set a time, but at 5:00 p.m. there was that sharp knocking. Sylvia had woken from a nap and was sitting, blinking, in the day, or whatever it was, which glopped, cold and gray across the floor. Arlene burst in, dressed up for the occasion in her short leopard jacket.

"Sylvia!" she said, as though her friend were a dropped nickel. "There you are!"

They looked at each other, Arlene standing, half on her toes, looking as though she wanted to topple into Sylvia, perched on the couch.

"You're all fancy," said Arlene. "Is there an event?"

Sylvia peered at her, blinking.

"You," she said. "I think you."

Arlene stepped in, closer, nodding. "How are you?" Arlene said. "So much has happened. Tell me everything."

Sylvia was quiet. "Not much," she said.

"Oh, I know there's something," Arlene said. There was a pool of quiet between them. "Well," she said, "I've been great."

What was terribly clear was the truth that she was not Sylvia, that Arlene was still able to move through the world on her own. It was, we all knew, a temporary triumph, yet it still was that, and it was a competition Sylvia had lost. We all sensed this, and the plunging sorrow. There was no way to combat this; now that Arlene was here, we were hostage to it.

The dark-gray light of dusk flickered across Sylvia's skirt.

"Do you know I may get the commercial?" said Arlene. "They called me back. I have to practice." She stood, hands on her hips, in the middle of the room. "Harold!" she called. "My stomach hurts!" She clutched her stomach. "Can you hand me my Duroflex? Please! Harold!"

Arlene's performance of pain was very convincing.

"What is happening?" asked Sylvia, looking at us.

"I'm acting, dear! I'm rehearsing, actually. My stomach doesn't hurt, really it doesn't—"

"Oh."

We applauded, loudly. "Arlene, that was convincing," we said, all of us an audience to Arlene, her victory of impersonating someone else. She turned around, bowed, and placed herself, beaming, on the couch.

"So tell me what's been going on," said Arlene to Sylvia. "Have you been doing anything recently? Take any classes or what? Remember that opera class we took at the senior center? That day we listened to *La Traviata*. Remember. That teacher. So cute. So good."

Arlene was swathed in her innocence like a silk cape. It was almost enviable in its absolute blindness, her determination to interact with the former Sylvia, only seeing who her friend had been.

Sylvia gazed at her. She seemed to be doing some sort of evaluation. "Wait. I have to give you something," she said.

"Oh, what?"

She rummaged through papers on a side table and lifted the necklace she wanted to present to Arlene.

"This is for you," she said, holding it out to Arlene. The necklace turned slowly in the gray light. We were hushed in the presence of Sylvia's generosity. Arlene's eyebrows lifted and her eyes crinkled in a smile, and she stepped forward to take it.

"I can wear this on my next audition," said Arlene. "It will be great—"

Sylvia started to hand it to her, but as she moved closer to Arlene she looked into her eyes, and then Sylvia jerked her arm back.

"No," she said.

Gripping the necklace, she stepped back from Arlene, who eagerly eyed the necklace, glinting in the dusk.

"Sylvia! What a thoughtful gift. I accept it!"

"But." Sylvia pressed the necklace to her chest.

"Honey," said Arlene, her hands outstretched. "You can give me a necklace. How kind! I accept."

Sylvia's eyebrows lifted.

"No," she said.

"Why not?"

Sylvia shook her head. She covered her eyes with her hands.

"What's wrong?" asked Arlene. "Can you tell me?"

"I can't."

"You can! What's the problem?"

"Because I remember. You were dead," Sylvia said, her voice trembling. "I know. Arlene. You were dead."

Arlene gasped and she clutched her stomach as though wounded. "Sylvia! I am not dead. I was out of town. And I just went to an audition."

"I knocked on your door," Sylvia said, pointedly.

"You did? When?"

"I knocked and knocked and kept knocking," said Sylvia. She slipped the necklace over her head and gently touched the shells.

"For god's sake," said Arlene, "I was on vacation. I'm

alive." She was. In fact, she did not just look alive, but alive and misunderstood. "Sylvia," said Arlene, lunging forward and sitting beside Sylvia on the couch, "I am alive. I am here! I am living, breathing, me! I am in your apartment, and I am so glad to be here, and I have been waiting for weeks, it feels like years—" She looked around, her eyes a little damp, and then, in a swift, terrible motion, lowered her mask and smiled brightly, lovingly, at Sylvia. "See, dear, it's me—"

Arlene's face, her lipstick, her wig tilted on her head like a beret.

"Arlene!" we snapped, when we saw this. "Remember the rules. Put your mask on. Now!"

"You were dead," Sylvia said, firmly, now also (no!) sliding off her mask, staring at Arlene. "I saw you. I think. I thought you were dead."

The two of them. Breathing. We gestured at Arlene and Sylvia to put the masks back on. Arlene rose, too slowly.

"Sylvia, look at me! I am standing before you. How would I do that if I was dead? I am right here!"

Sylvia held her necklace, her fingers gripping its presence, its solidness, and regarded Arlene with an expression perfectly balancing confusion and authority.

"If you were alive," she said, with great firmness, "you would have answered the door."

Arlene shook her head, her mask around her chin; she observed Sylvia, Arlene's expression both annoyed and shaken.

"Touch me," said Arlene, holding out her arm. "Go ahead!"

"Arlene!" we said. "Later! She's tired!"

Sylvia glanced at Arlene's arm. She did not move to touch it.

"I'm not tired!" said Sylvia, glaring at us.

We thought of Arlene, moving maskless through the supermarket, we thought of the sirens, and we moved closer to her, gesturing to her to put on her mask.

"Why are you all looking at me that way?" asked Arlene, backing up. "What's wrong with you? I'm here. I'm standing here. All I want is to take Sylvia to the diner. Is that so much to ask? Come on, people!"

Arlene stepped out and slammed the door. The apartment trembled. Sylvia sparkled, nervously.

"I'm right," said Sylvia. "Arlene. I know. Why does she say that? I know she was dead." She slowly lifted the necklace over her head and set it beside her. "I don't understand. I am the one sitting here. I am living." She sat, her eyes suddenly bright, wet. "I am alive," she said. "Me."

She stood up, went to the door, and opened it and looked up and down the hall, but Arlene was gone.

The hallway was silent. Arlene would be back; she was always back, like a foamy, relentless tide. But one day Arlene would come up to the door and knock and no one would answer.

Sylvia touched her eyes.

"Sylvia," we said.

She put her hand in the middle of her chest.

"I'm alive," she said. "But."

"Sylvia, what?"

Tears fell down her face, one after another.

"I'm alive, but my heart"—she paused, thinking—"my heart feels shaved."

THE NIGHT FELL quickly, and the air outside was starry and gray in the approaching dusk. That family dinner was like all the dinners, the boiled carrots, the sausage on the plate. We all ate, but we moved as though our skin was tender. We were glad Arlene was gone, for the moment, but where was Sylvia's glorious and relentless anger? We needed it, we needed to hear her complain about Arlene, needed to hear the story again about the diner, about the fee for the challenging guest. We wanted to ask again about that muscular fury, for there was an unspeakable sound, something else we all knew, too, rising up outside the apartment, silent and terrible, approaching.

Sylvia cut her meat into pieces and ate it. Then she touched the necklace again, and rubbed the shells, thinking.

"You know, you need to tell me something," said Sylvia. "I need your opinion."

"Yes. We will tell you."

"What do you think?" she asked. "This necklace. Should I give this to Arlene?"

THE LISTENER

The patient called without a referral, but the therapist, Saul, had an extra hour, so he said to come in. "I need to talk to you," the patient said. His voice soft, a softness that Saul recognized. The feeling of a voice about to crash into grief, that trembling. He opened his book and looked, though he kept most of the afternoon free.

"I have two p.m. open," Saul said, trying to press down the eagerness in his voice. "Tell me your name again."

A pause. A question like a hand or a knife. The sharing of a name, a revelation. Some offered it eagerly, wanting to be known, to be suffused in that particular light; others kept their names shoved in their pockets, in darkness, until they handed over their insurance cards. Saul waited.

"My name is Herman." A moment. "McSmith." And then a rush, "Thank you, doctor, thank you for seeing me—"

This did not seem like an actual name, McSmith, or Saul had not heard it before. This was the first thing Saul noticed. But the gratitude was palpable, real, and it nourished him.

Later he remembered, too, how he felt in the chair, the feeling of stillness. At this moment he did not feel that sinking, he was simply sitting, like a regular person, in the chair. A suspension, a balance, the gift of floating, of being.

"You have what insurance?"

Another silence. "Aetna."

A reasonable exchange; he had insurance.

Saul had tried to find the patterns to the times when he felt he was sinking, his body falling to the bottom of a sea, and the times when he felt more alert, when he was suspended on the surface of the world. The moments when he thought walking one block might not empty him. The bad days he sat there, conserving all he had, counting the steps to get to the door of the waiting room to let in the next person. These days, there were fewer people waiting.

This week was better. Today, the moment he told Herman McSmith he could come for an appointment, he felt his weight in the chair, the blossoming thrill of that stillness. This moment. He was not going to waste it—those moments when he was merely a therapist who saw patients.

"Okay. Bring your card. Suite 1201. See you at two."

THE PALM TREES outside the window like a stand of green fireworks, frozen. An explosion caught over and over. The luxuriant, astonishing propulsion of Los Angeles, the flowers in the desert. This morning his 10:00 a.m. said he wanted to eat his arm. Saul watched a single cloud move across the vast blue sky. The 11:00 a.m. said he had one more sunrise and that was it. Saul flinched when he said this and looked more closely at him. His patient stretched an arm along the back of the couch where he sat, a gesture that appeared intimate even though it wasn't. He said this gleefully. Saul, hands clasped, watched him carefully; he turned his mind to this comment, one more sunrise. He asked him if he had specific plans for harming himself.

The 11:00 a.m. flushed as though he had been caught, he laughed.

"I don't know, haven't thought that far."

"Why do you want this to be your last sunrise?"

He let the question into the air and waited. He watched the 11:00 a.m., a large, silver-haired man whom he had seen for two years, who shook his hand firmly and said, "Hello, Saul," at their first meeting, as though they were going to complete the sale of a car, and who had a deep laugh but whose blue eyes were frightened. The 11:00 a.m. put his palm on his chest occasionally, as though soothing a burp, though it also seemed like he was checking for the presence of his heart.

"My wife is a bitch."

He said this softly, and then started the reasons—she would not let him see his children, because she wanted them all to herself, she felt she owned them, she was still mad because he spent the night with his coworker on that trip to Houston, had let her into his bed because she kept touching his wrist, her blouse fell open, she smiled when he looked at her breasts, she thought he was compelling in a way his wife did not, but the sex was nothing, she just lay there wanting him to touch her in a particular way but did not tell him what, he thought she would touch him in some way that would make him fall out of himself but she seemed bored, her gaze flickering away from him, toward the ceiling, toward something, and he was embarrassed to look at her face, instead kept noticing the hotel-room decor, the lampshade with seashells hanging from the brim, which reminded him of the sachets in his wife's dresser. There had been no joy in that moment; his wife didn't understand that. What did people want? What did anyone want?

Saul listened and this was when he felt most in himself: the listener. It was as though the whole of his being organized itself around this role, this usefulness, a bending tree.

He had cultivated his own discipline this way and it was one that he was proud of, one he had discovered himself, one that his father, fleeing Russia at the beginning of the century, did not understand. His father, who could not hear out of one ear because of the way a Cossack once hit him, awoke at dawn and manned his clothing store in Des Moines until ten at night. His father, the master of counting, counting the product in his store in Des Moines, counting the number of shoes on the shelves, the number of shirts, the proportion of light blue to white, the precision of a markup, standing in the cold light of the morning, counting. He wanted to make sure everything was accounted for.

When Saul said he did not want to become a surgeon, which his father wanted, someone who sawed open a person and fixed their back, their lungs, their heart, his father leaned toward him with his good ear as though he had heard incorrectly and said, "What? People's minds? How did you fix them? Why go to school for that? What did you need to know?"

Saul's hands trembled. He could not open anyone up. The other surgical residents joked about the patients, but he remembered the fear in their eyes as the anesthesiologist prepared them to go to sleep.

So he did this, became a psychiatrist, with training in psychodynamic therapy. He trained to listen.

It seemed, when he began his practice, a miracle that any patients walked into the office. They walked through his door and sat down and began to speak or avoided it, but they looked at him and assumed, in a startling way, that he knew what to do. Now he was used to them, these privileged but frightened men and women in Los Angeles who told him their secrets. A vice president of a multinational beverage corporation clasped his hands tightly, describing how he couldn't sleep because he dreamed his mother would strangle him. A renowned biology professor stared, depressed, at the floor because the department head reminded him of his cruel brother. A mother who was always half an hour early and who was distraught that her daughter resembled a skeleton. They did not know him, or they knew him just as the person who would take in and figure out their words, which was both a throne and an erasure.

He listened to the 11:00 a.m., asked him if he had any specific plans for harm, but he became convinced that the

11:00 a.m. was exaggerating, the threat was not serious, there were fragments of light in his ranting, in his description of a vacation with his children.

The 11:00 a.m. rose to go. "I'll see you Tuesday," he said, curtly, as though embarrassed.

The office was abruptly quiet. Saul wrote down some notes, dropped them into a file, checked his answering service. Nothing. He looked at his phone. A missed call from Leo, his son.

LEO CALLED LAST week. It was the first time Saul had heard from him in two months. Their son had become a real estate agent, and their calls were short and polite, with a false jolliness, as though Leo were evaluating him as a client. Saul listened carefully to his statements, "I'm fine," wanting to hear more from the word. What was that word? He heard it many times a day, but from his child it felt like a dark pool. He could not see through it.

Leo's childhood so far away, a hazy continent. He remembered certain moments with so much clarity it was as though he were there, breathing. He remembered when he pretended not to see his son during hide-and-seek, his rush of brown hair always visible behind a hedge in the yard. His delight when he was found. Saul remembered sitting on bleachers, cheering for various sports, surprised by the way Leo kicked the sand at second base, distracted, tossing popcorn at a squirrel, so different from his own excitement about the game. He remembered the smoothness and ease of his love for his child, the love funneled into a torrent of advice: how to choke up on a bat, how to stand up to your friends. He wanted, above all, to be helpful, to provide the routes to make Leo's life easier than his own.

When he was in his forties, and Leo was fifteen, Saul became ill with a fatigue no doctor could understand. He was part of the world and then, quickly, separated from it. He waited days and then weeks and then months, trusted his body, which had served him so well, to return to itself, but it was as though it had become a criminal. He felt hot and cold, he awoke exhausted, he sat in the office with his patients, counting the hours until he could go home and collapse, trying to sit perfectly still, relax his body so his mind could focus. The doctors ran tests but couldn't figure out what was happening, became confused and contemptuous, and Saul tried to diagnose himself, keeping elaborate charts of his activity and supplements. Sometimes his body would rise from its murkiness and he was almost himself, he felt all right, for a day, two, seven. He gradually understood that the person he had to listen to most closely was the stranger who had inhabited him.

SAUL REMEMBERED LITTLE from his son's adolescence. Those years, his whole being was focused on the task of getting to the office, sitting in his chair, listening to the sorrows of others. Everything had to be measured, his moments talking with Leo, his walk from the parking structure to his office door. He tried, a few times, to talk to Leo about his illness, ask him how he felt about it, a conversation he knew was ridiculous even as he initiated it. His son, seventeen, eyes distracted; he wanted to be anywhere but with this new, depleted father. Leo always responded with short answers, as though his father's questions tried to excavate something he did not want to share. Saul remembered holding the same attitude toward his own father, watching him slowly, compulsively, count the shirts in the store, but it seemed impossible that this disappointment would be turned toward him. Saul got up every day to go to work, gripped the steering wheel of his Buick, wondered if this would be the day he would give up and turn around and go back home. But every day he moved forward, he wanted his son to notice this. But Leo never did.

NOW, SOMETIMES, SAUL pretended he was a customer looking for a house and tracked his son online, on the Coldwell Banker website, where his son posted the properties he represented. He read the descriptions of the houses, the promises they offered: *Luxuriate with your friends beside your expansive pool, sit on your glass balcony with your morning coffee and gaze at dolphins in the Atlantic.* Saul was relieved by this, by his son's job, his slow journey into adulthood, and he had found someone who would mentor him, a man different from him: a guy named Alan Fontaine, whose photo was in magazines that their son sent him, who filled out his shirt like a football player, and held out his hands to potential buyers with a welcoming gesture but also as though he wanted to crush them. Leo was doing well working for Alan Fontaine, was learning how to sell homes. Alan looked like the type of guy who walked across the street and didn't think about it. For this, Saul resented him.

Leo called this week with what he said was a simple request. Get on a plane and come see them. "We showed her parents around town last week," he said. "We took them out to dinner at this Thai place we like. They loved it. Her parents travel everywhere." There was a tone of bragging in his son's voice, attaching himself to this other family.

"They keep asking and they say what's so hard about a plane? You can do it. You've been looking good. I bet you can. Just get on a plane and fly for five hours to meet them."

Leo wanted a simple thing—for him to meet his fiancée. He wanted him to board a plane and fly to Miami, where he lived. He wanted his father to come and see his adult life. Was that such an onerous request? Leo saw him as better now, he clutched his stronger father inside of him. He did not understand how the measuring, the care, could maintain him for weeks, but that a walk through the airport could deplete him. Leo did not know how Saul imagined himself there.

Saul thought they had been close, meaning he thought his son would follow the plans he wanted for him. He had imagined his child living down the street, becoming a therapist himself, discussing patients with him, asking him advice about one difficult patient or another. Saul had not predicted Leo's difficulties; he had been a miracle, a child who had been given more than he had, who was listened to, who came from an easier soil. He recognized in his child a sharp restlessness that he noticed in his own father at midnight counting shirts in his store.

When Leo began college, the restlessness turned to panic. His mind could not settle down to study, he was unable to sleep, and then Leo dropped out. He sat in his room like a potted plant, wilting. Saul watched him, fearful that he would tumble into a place irretrievable. His son got a job as a custodian in a high school, a job that he could concentrate on, he moved in with friends where the apartment stank of weed. Saul lay awake beside his wife, his love for his child pooling uselessly in a bucket. He wanted to pour it all over the world, he wanted to pave a path for his son; he wondered what to say to calm him down, knowing there was nothing.

And then Leo's anxiety passed. It happened sometimes. Saul waited, eagerly, to be consulted, to offer any advice, but he was asked nothing. He felt shut out of his process in figuring it out. His son quietly found some therapy or some friends, he moved to another city. He slowly got better.

Now Leo did call; they had brisk discussions in which he issued reports about his life. He spoke in a way that was formal and also in a rush; he wanted to plunge himself into the world as though it would melt in his fingers. He was rising fast, walking people through condos and estates that overlooked the ocean, telling them how they needed this bedroom, these closets, this glorious view. Saul admired his energy, his pride was billowing, uncontainable. Leo sent him videos of himself for real estate sites walking through airy, empty living rooms, perched on rented couches, drinking a glass of wine, a performance of ease and mastery that people yearned for, that Saul knew was a lie, but that his son perhaps wanted to believe was real.

"I wish I could," he told his son.

"Try," his son said.

"Do you think I don't want to come?"

A pause. "Maybe," Leo said.

"Yes, I do," said Saul. "Why would you think I wouldn't?"

He could hear Leo thinking, that slow circular sound.

"I don't know. I've just—had it."

"With what?"

"I'm getting a call," he said. "I have to go—"

"What's wrong with you?" said Saul sharply, a knife rising out of his mouth into his voice, his own father's voice. "Don't you know—"

Saul knew that he could not do what Leo was asking. How could his son be this dense? All the steps to get there, a stairway rising, an infinite number of steps, his body fading with each stop, an insurmountable task.

"Do I know what, Dad?" asked Leo. Saul did not know how to answer this. Do you know what I feel. It shocked him, the disparate ways a struggle could shape you—it could open you up to the sorrows of others or it could harden you.

"I'm just—" Leo said, "I just want you to come." His son's voice was soft, suddenly. He hung up the phone.

SAUL SAT IN the empty office and shivered. He needed to lie down. He went to the couch and stretched out, closing his eyes. He needed to get some rest into his body before the next person arrived. The doctors had no clear suggestion for how to manage the fatigue. He imagined shoveling strength into his torso, his arms and legs; he lay very still, pretending he was dead, trying to let his body rest.

After a while, he sat up, blinking. His mouth was dry and tasted bad. He went to his desk and put a mint in his mouth and waited for the next patient.

HIS BUZZER RANG. Who was scheduled for 2:00 p.m.? He remembered the call. The new patient, Herman McSmith, had arrived. He was the first new patient in several months. Saul felt a ripple of excitement, stood up, smoothed his shirt, walked to the waiting room, opened the door.

A man was sitting in one of his chairs: the first impression was of slightness. Age unclear—early thirties, forty? A sunburned face. Thinning blond hair, not quite combed. A light beige jacket, similar to one that his son wore. But his son combed his hair, precisely, always. This man looked like he was hurled from the sky.

"Mr. McSmith?" he asked.

Saul could not quite identify the expression on his face. Surprise. He was surprised he was here, he was surprised he had finally come into therapy.

Mr. McSmith said, "Your secretary? Off?"

He did not understand the question.

"Who?"

Saul held the door open, and Herman walked into the office. There was a sigh, like a balloon released.

"You can sit wherever you'd like," he said.

Herman looked around the room, at the couch, the chair in front of Saul's desk, the chairs for couples across the room. He shoved his hands deeper into the pockets of his jacket, and then lunged toward the seat at an angle from Saul's desk. It was the seat where Saul could see the patient most directly.

"So tell me what brought you here," said Saul, settling into his chair.

Herman folded his arms and clutched himself for a moment, and let out a sound like a laugh, but not a laugh. "Why?" he said. "I found you."

There was a softness in his voice, and something pulsing underneath, muscular, like a dolphin below waves. There was a hint of an accent Saul could not place; perhaps Eastern European.

"You did," said Saul. "How did you find me?"

"I opened the phone book," said Herman. "And there you were."

He smiled with part of his face, not a real smile. This was nothing surprising or new. Saul was used to being examined by the patients; he let Herman's eyes rest on him, take him in. He enjoyed this moment, this sense of importance. A cloud breathed across the sky, and the room shifted with sunlight. Herman winced. Saul rose to adjust the blinds but Herman put out his hand.

"Don't move," he said.

"I'm just fixing the blinds—"

"Don't."

Saul stopped and settled back. Herman was very anxious. He wondered what he was doing to make him so anxious.

Outside he noticed the magenta froth of bougainvillea draped across the stucco wall of a restaurant, the throb and lace of color so bright he could taste it, the way California surprised him, over and over, in its gaudy, extravagant beauty, the way he sat in his office and wanted to wrap himself in the red petals, the silvery honeyed air. How did anyone know how to stagger through it? He had looked at this view for forty years, and it was both very close and achingly distant.

"So," said Saul.

Herman's jaw trembled. "I have a problem," he said. His voice sounded rehearsed, on the edge of tears.

Saul was very still, listening.

"What do you want to talk about?" he said.

Herman's lips pushed forward and back, a twitch. He reached into his pocket and brought out a gun.

SAUL LOOKED AT the gun and Herman's hand, pointing the gun at him. This was not the answer he expected.

"Please put down the gun," said Saul.

"No," said Herman.

Saul's heart was still and started galloping, his heart knowing what was going on. Saul was grateful to his heart, its brisk, knowing intelligence. What he felt was not energy, but something else, a thrumming that kept him sitting up. He had the curious sensation of not being able to think, and he was aware of not being able to think. He watched Herman's hand on the pistol.

"I picked your name out of book," said Herman. "I just put my finger on you and called you up and you said come in."

Saul felt a dampness under his armpits, and somehow he found the words: "Put it down."

"No," said Herman. He was still, in an unnatural way, like a statue.

Saul felt his thoughts organizing around one point—he wanted to get out. It was not an unfamiliar thought; he had thought about getting out during sessions he was so tired he could not stand listening to another word. Now he imagined getting up and walking out of the room, thought it so fiercely he wondered if he were doing it. But no one would be in the gray hallway, no one was ever there. It would be like walking into a wilderness. The other people with offices on this floor—doctors, accountants—locked in their own lives, working. He wanted to get up, move faster than a walk, move faster than any human, become a blaze, a wind, a tumble.

"Why are you here?" Saul said, now meaning something different.

Herman's face flickered. "I have no job," said Herman. "There was an accident."

There was no knowing if this was true. The man's face seemed small, his features bunched up in the middle of his face. He resembled a kind of dog, a pug maybe, his eyes a little surprised.

"I'll give you money," said Saul. "I don't have much, but I can get my wallet out of—"

"Wallet, no," Herman said. He laughed, a sort of laugh. "I'm not dumb."

"I don't think you're dumb," said Saul. His brain felt like a troubled, wrinkly thing, with no thoughts. Or his thoughts were simple. He wanted the man out, or he wanted the gun to drop so he could shoot *him*, he could lunge forward and grab it. Then how would he get him cleaned up out of the office? How would he get the stain out of the carpet? He could shoot his leg or he could shoot him in the head. Why was he thinking this? Saul wanted him dead. He noticed how quickly that desire flared up, a desire almost joyous and uncomplicated.

"Listen," said the man. "No wallet."

"You need money for your child," said Saul.

Herman's eyes narrowed and he clutched the gun more tightly.

"For your wife," he said. "Your father."

"My son," said Herman. "Stupid boy, in an accident—"

"I have a son," said Saul, quickly, and watched for a weakening, a moment of opening; he had to believe in this, the force of connection. Herman looked at him and smiled that peculiar smile.

Herman said, "Get up, we're going to the Wells Fargo."

Saul stared at him.

"I can't go to Walls Fargo," he said.

The man's face flickered.

"What, you can't?"

"I'm—" How did he explain it? "I'm injured, I'm not able to—"

"Wells Fargo. Now."

Herman thought Saul could just walk to the bank. It was an astounding misunderstanding, hilarious, almost.

"Not Wells Fargo. B of A."

"Why?"

"I have more money there."

No. It was closer. He could estimate the walk in his mind. The bank, there would be people inside, someone would take Herman down. Out the door, about thirty steps past the gym, across the street. A concrete wall along the sidewalk to sit down on. Or he could collapse on the street. That might be useful, in an ironic twist. Or Herman might be the type of criminal who abhorred weakness, who would just point the gun at him and shoot.

"How much?"

"A lot," said Saul. "Thousands. It's there. For your son."

Was this the right thing to say? He could pretend it was not a crime, here in his office, but a gift. He was helping Herman support his son. Herman, a father. Something besides a criminal, yes. An attempt to make him something other than what he was, standing here, now. Herman stood up.

"Let's go," Herman said.

SAUL WANTED TO get out of the room, it felt close, he felt Herman's breath, damp; he wanted to see the face of any person, anyone with an office in the hall, the pompous Dr.

Orson, another psychiatrist, who stopped referring patients to him when he heard he was ill, the gentle Dr. Pampas, a dermatologist, who always held the elevator door for him, the energetic Mr. Ortiz, an accountant, who always pushed past Saul, thinking he heard a phone ringing in his office, a ringing he could not miss. No one was here. Perhaps they had all planned it, they had all told Herman to set up an hour with him, that he could be dumped out like trash in the hallway.

If Herman shot him that was all they would talk about—not the fact they never saw him, not the fact they avoided him, not the patients they had scooped up because he did not have enough hours to schedule them. They would talk about how he had let Herman into the office without a referral, and they would set up a security-alert system to protect themselves.

Saul felt alone, that familiar feeling. He hated them, as he realized it was what he had felt for years.

He did not know what to do, so he kept walking. They rode down in the elevator, twelve floors, each time Saul hoping the elevator doors would open to someone coming in. But the numbers floated down, twelve, eleven, ten, nine, eight, seven, six, five, four, three, two, one. The doors opened. The lobby was empty, shining gray marble. The security guard who stood at the desk, a cheerful woman who appeared to be unarmed, of course wasn't there. They walked through the lobby to the street, the sunshine glazing the sidewalk. The cars rushed past, the cruel steel bodies. No one opened a door for him. No one was going to stop.

"Walk," said Herman.

IF SOMEONE SAW them together, they would think they were possibly friends, or related, their shoulders almost touching. Saul walked slowly, Herman right behind. The fear had the peculiar effect of subsuming the exhaustion, for the moment; his heart was rattling on. He did not know what his body would do under this immense fear. Saul was pretending to walk like a regular person, he was doing the usual calculations, one step at a time.

"Talk," said Herman. "Like we are friends."

"Talk about what?"

The streets empty, the streets of Los Angeles often empty of anyone walking, the sun too bright, warm on his scalp.

He knew why he had not asked for a referral. He wanted to prove something to himself, to be normal, to have a regular day. That urge, swimming around like a whale under the ocean, rising up with great power and breaking through. Other people did this, why couldn't he? He was aware of the seam in the world where it broke apart, he sat with people whose seams had broken every day, and it was the most basic yearning, for the world to move along in a predictable, ordinary way. He had wanted Herman to just come in and get help. And now this.

"How much money do you have," said Herman, eyes scanning the sidewalk, the street.

"I don't remember. Not that much."

"My son. He needs a lot. Thousands. The accident."

"What? What does he need money for?"

"Everything. Car. Teeth. Steaks."

Was this it? Was this—car, teeth, steaks—the key to everything? Father, son. What? Herman needed something, but Saul just did not want it to be from him.

THE BRIGHT LOS ANGELES light now made his eyelids hurt. The office buildings gleamed, mirrored. In twenty steps they would pass the gym where people ran on treadmills, faces blue lit, staring at the window. He tried not to look when he would walk by on a regular day, but now he was eager to see them, their energy, he wanted to be near it, for now the people were potential helpers, they could see him and come outside.

But how could he indicate his situation? He was so used to pretending all was fine, to impersonate a person feeling fine. There was just one person on the treadmill today, a young woman thunking on the moving ramp, her eyes fixed on the television. She did not look up.

He felt a rush of heat through his body and sat down on a bus bench. He closed his eyes.

"What are you doing?" asked Herman, looking around.

Saul breathing. Why had Herman signed up for an appointment? A psychiatrist, an easy target. Did Herman even think this through? Did he know how a psychiatrist worked? He should have kept something in the office. A gun? A bat? He hated Herman for releasing this fear. His body surging toward it instantly, a cry of loving itself. He was surprised, frankly, at the way this love revealed itself in him.

"Get up."

Saul watched the gun.

"Just a sec."

Herman stared at him, his clear blue eyes.

"Your son," said Saul. "What happened in the accident?"

He was embarrassed by his reliance on this—a question. He could not stop himself.

"Car crash," said Herman, quickly. "Not his fault." He stood very straight, a stance that Saul recognized, the stiff, inflated posture of the helpless. "He can't eat anything, he likes to eat, who doesn't like to eat."

"That is terrible," Saul said, listening.

"Yes," said Herman, his voice quiet. "Get up."

HE WAS NOT going to ask Herman if he could hold his arm while he walked, he would not, he would not, though Herman might welcome that.

"Terrible accident," said Herman again, sharply. "We were in a race. People were shooting at us. We were almost out of the way. Then crash. He's not dead. Everyone else is dead. Cars all over the highway. My cousin, my aunt. What do you do about this, doctor? You can save them?"

No, he did not want to save them. He imagined Herman strewn across the highway, too, and took a breath, as he felt he should answer carefully. Saul was formulating a thought when his pocket vibrated; he was getting a call. He took the cell phone out and pressed the answer button before he could stop himself.

"Another thing," Leo said.

He almost laughed at the cheerful insistence of Leo's voice. Now? Herman looked like he might lunge for the phone, but Saul held it hard. Help, he thought. If his son loved him, he would hear his fear. A rush of cars flew past; Herman was so close to him, one hand gripping the gun in his pocket. Help, he thought.

"I'll buy you plane tickets," his son said. "Allow me. A gift."

Saul kept his eyes on Herman.

"Come to Miami," his son said. "Or somewhere else. A vacation for all of us. Hawaii."

A vacation. Ha. It was a dream to propel himself across the street, into the bank.

"Dad. I think you'd like Maui. I went there with Naomi and you wouldn't believe it. We could swim. The water's warm. We should go."

He kept his eyes on Herman, but felt himself tugged by his son's eagerness, his inability to comprehend his limits, it was both naive and and absurd and beautiful, and he wanted it to lift him into the phone, away from all of this. His optimism, a cradle.

Herman grabbed the phone. "Shut up!" he said. Saul heard a sound of surprise from his son inside the phone. Oh no. He was suddenly less worried about Herman than his son's anger at being interrupted. What would his son think of him? He would feel insulted. Everyone in the world felt insulted.

"He's busy!" said Herman. He stared at the phone and then threw it into a bush. "Everyone stop talking!"

He exclaimed this brightly, as though at a dinner that had

gotten too loud. Saul looked at the phone in the dirt. It flickered dark. Leo would not hear his call for help. But then Saul also would not know what his son would do, or not, to help him.

"Get up," said Herman. "We're going to the bank."

He felt a flare of panic in the base of his spine. The panic felt distant but precise. He wanted his phone, sitting in the dirt.

"Walk," said Herman. "We're almost there."

He felt Herman's hand grip his arm and stand him up. Saul felt himself propelled by Herman's hand and his walk, without having to do as much himself, Herman was moving him, he felt his fingers clutching like a huge repulsive bird, his fingers digging in, the way Saul held Leo's arm when he was a child and trying to get him to listen—but Saul had been gentler, or he hoped he had been. He guided his son firmly before he became ill. He remembered Leo struggling under his grip and telling him, no, it was time for dinner, don't run away. The thrashing force of a child, the feeling of his son wiggling away, over and over, at four, at eight, at twelve, at eighteen, how had he gotten Leo to listen, had his son heard his own violence, what had he said that was wrong?

"Don't," he murmured to Herman, who smelled of onions and old sweat, a smell of disorder. Don't touch me, don't move me too fast. Don't look like you know me. Don't kill me. There was the whoosh of doors and the sudden feeling of cold air, and they were inside the bank.

THE BANK RESEMBLED a theatrical set of a bank, in its innocence. There was the cool sudden slap of air-conditioning, the pink marbled gleam of the floors, a weighted, hushed silence of people waiting to receive their money. Saul slowed down; he felt Herman release his arm, and Saul surveyed the room, waiting for someone to see what was going on. There was nothing in his stance to show them, in a quiet but recognizable way, that he was in danger. All the years of pretending he was fine. He joined the line, looking at the people, knowing what none of them did—that Herman held a gun.

No one turned around. There were a few people in line, gazing at the air, a woman filled out a deposit slip. The tellers shouted, "May I Help You," from behind their bulletproof glass. He stared at the people in line, wondering who could save him. The young blonde girl with the UCLA T-shirt, shifting her heavy backpack between her shoulders and swiping hazily on her phone? The Black woman in a teal nursing uniform, involved in an intent discussion via text? The young salesman with a crisp white shirt, with smooth black hair, tapping his foot and murmuring as he watched the line slowly inch forward?

"Dad," said Herman, in a crisp, modulated voice, "remember how much you said I needed for the house."

No.

He was kidding.

The word dad was obscene in Herman's mouth.

"For repairs," said Herman. He glanced around, awaiting an audience. "The roof."

"There's no roof," said Saul.

Herman's eyelid twitched.

Saul looked carefully, away from Herman, his twisted

plan. Leo was shouting into the cell phone left in the dirt. Saul wanted to pick him up, he wanted to carry him as an infant to put him to bed, his son screaming, Saul standing over his crib, he wanted to be that man. Leo gazing at him believing he knew something.

Saul observed the others in line. Couldn't they tell that Herman was, obviously, not his son? He wanted to run out and find his phone and tell his son, yes, he would go on a vacation, somehow, they would all sit strapped to their seats as a silver plane gently lifted into the blueness, the clouds buoyant, creamy beneath them. He would be sitting beside them as they moved through the air, and it would be so easy.

He thought of how he walked through the world many years ago, that person contained within him, silent and yelling, a ghost, he thought of the way his body curved in, to swoop up Leo when he was running, a young father, chasing him, his breath, reaching down and lifting him up, on his shoulders. The rushing forward, the sound of his shoes on the dirt, the feeling of force, of tumbling, the thoughtlessness of his movement, the supreme innocence of a body that did what you said, Leo pausing, his small arms dangling by his sides, so small and hopeful, gazing around, and Saul grabbed him and lifted him up.

"Father," said Herman. (Father?) "The water has to stop pouring through. The roof. I can't stop it. When are we stopping it? How much do we need?"

Saul could not acknowledge Herman, could not argue with him; he would be identifiable then as a parent.

"Father, we have to discuss this!"

His voice, the fake pain.

"Next," the bank teller said.

The line moved.

He imagined them standing at the teller, crisp bills counted into Herman's hand.

A heat gathered in his chest and Saul saw Herman glancing away, his arms dangling loose by his sides.

His arms dangling.

Saul stepped forward and wrapped his arms around Herman's body, pinning his arms to his sides. Herman's arms thin, soft. He held the man still, the blonde woman looked at them and smiled slightly; oh god, she thought he was hugging him.

"Help!" Saul called.

His voice pierced the polite silence of the bank. He was embarrassed by the way he had disturbed the silence. But he could not bear the others thinking he was hugging the man who wanted to harm him. The smile slid off the blonde woman's face. The nurse looked up from her phone. The man in the crisp shirt cleared his throat, impatiently.

Herman's heart threw itself against his back, over and over.

"He has a gun!" Saul shouted. "Help! This man has a gun."

No one did anything. No one ever did anything. However, they were all now watching.

"Father," said Herman. His voice trembling. "Father. Don't do this."

"Stop it!" said Saul. "People. He's not my son. He has a gun."

The others were frozen, like idiots. They did not believe

that something like this could happen to them. Saul had not believed it now, or before. Or, more charitably, they did not know what to do.

"Father, I didn't say that," Herman said. He had to stop saying that word, father, who was that, he had not been who he had wanted to be. And he could sense that the others believed Herman, not him. What was it about himself that was not believable? Did they not see this most believable part of himself—that he wanted to be useful, that he wanted his son to know him, that he wanted to be able to just walk across the street and go home? His arms were numb with his grip and then Herman shook off Saul's hands in a violent twist and Saul stumbled backward and then Herman was running, out the doors of the bank.

A teller slammed the glass window down. Saul grabbed hold of the ledge by the teller, his hands shaking; a tidal wave of exhaustion was about to consume him.

The others in the bank stared at him. What did they see? A slim man just seventy, in a white shirt and a navy blazer, a father who had insulted his son, a father who wanted to hold his son, a father never understood by his own. What did it take for someone to see another, not just the person before you, but all the selves they had once been? They did not see him walking down the hallway briskly as a young doctor, unlocking the office, sitting in his chair and waiting for the door to open. They did not see how he was counting the steps across the street. He did not know how he would get back. He did not know how he could get to the dirt and his phone. He wanted to pick up the phone and shout into it, to say yes, this was what he wanted, to float together toward an island paradise, to sit beside Leo in the troubled air.

Someone had, in a late panic, tripped an alarm. Finally, someone understood that there was a crime. A shrill sound flooded the bank. The customers in the bank were shuffling out of the bank's gray light into the sunny street; a few stared at him. He held on to the ledge, and he waited for someone to ask him if he was okay. He tried to see out the windows, into the street, toward the eucalyptus patch where his cell phone lay, a shard of metal, people walking by it; he imagined them walking by so quickly, passing the broken phone that glinted in the sunlight, no one noticing how radiant it was in the sun.

THE COURT OF THE INVISIBLE

The courtroom is full; it is always full. The line outside stretches beyond the block, onto the next street, they wait there even when the air is cold and the sky is the color of ice. The citizens gather at dawn or before, they think they are smarter than the others and will get a better place in line, though many have the same idea, and have stood in line for hours; the lines scare us and we work fast because we cannot have them waiting. The line is polite, though also numbingly loud, everyone rehearsing, muttering what they will say. People practice their complaints in different ways. There is a man reciting his grievances in soaring, passionate tones, lifting his arms as though giving a toast at a wedding, there are the mutterers, who specialize in droning repetition that sound, together, like a mass of bees, there are the clipped, enunciating ones, who are afraid of not being heard, there are always a few shriekers. We, the judges, have learned to blot out the shriekers, though I admire them the most, their voices blaring over the street, ragged, a little crazed. I saw them as I rushed into the court each day, past the latest hordes, the number was daunting, the line of people vanishing in a variety of ways: some with hands fading to a mist, some with shimmering feet, some whose mouths or eyebrows were blurred, indistinct. The cries punctuated the line of people vanishing, waiting in the gray light of the dawn.

I had the easy job—I said, "You are guilty." The key was how to say it, and I will admit I loved saying it, looked forward to it, woke up in the morning ready to shout it. This was why I was a popular judge in this realm, my stirring delivery, but I was, in fact, not a judge and there was no one to sentence. The actual guilty parties were not there. They had gotten away with it all. They were everyone around us: employers and neighbors, they were restaurant owners and former lovers and coworkers and neighbors and random strangers in the supermarket and friends and parents and children and cousins and they were not accused of any crime except the ordinary and everyday cruelties, their own ability to trample over you. They were savage in the smallest, most ordinary ways. They stole the parking spot you'd waited patiently for and cut in line for the last bottle of the medicine you had to have, they spread lies about you at work because they also craved that promotion, they hoarded all the toilet paper and bars of soap, they told the apartment broker that you had suspicious bugbites and got the tour first, they insulted your children before an important test and made them afraid; they wanted everything when they wanted it and they were glad if you had none. They were, in short, most people in this country, and they wanted things, as we all did, of course—we all wanted love and safety and comfort, who didn't want that—but this was different, this was something unleashed, this was another level of rampant obliviousness, of mawing need. The crimes were not technically crimes, to be clear, they were not illegal, but they felt like crimes in their volume and consistency, they did, and now they had a physical result: repeated incidents, day after day, made your body go dim. Your skin began to shimmer, fade; sunlight fell through your hands. The people in this country were alive, their hearts beat, their blood flowed, but sadly, for the constant wear meant that parts of their body were becoming transparent, like cloudy water; the people in line were vanishing.

There were courts like ours all over the country, to counteract the invisibility that was now epidemic, to sentence the guilty parties who weren't there. Those who weren't there were simply living their lives, blithely unaware of the harm they caused, or (more likely) aware and unconcerned. Our courts had been set up in the last ten years; when there was a call for judges, I immediately signed up. They didn't ask for legal credentials but simply required the rich, ringing quality of one's voice. I had no legal background, but I was a master of outrage. I had been waiting for this. At my interview, I was told to sit expressionless as a man whose ankles shimmered, barely visible, explained, trembling, how his brother, who had been kicked out of his house and was living with them, demanded to use his car. It was the plaintiff's precious possession, it had been purchased by his recently deceased wife of thirty-six years, who loved driving it and took painstaking care of the upholstery on the seats; the brother ignored him and took off with the car, bought a thirty-two-ounce soda and managed to dump half of it on the passenger seat. The brother, the plaintiff claimed, refused to clean anything off, refused to hear about his wife's care of the vehicle or, for that matter, any memories about his wife, and when he left, appallingly, for a dinner at a fine lobster restaurant, without even inviting the plaintiff, the plaintiff ran after him, shouting, and when he looked down, his feet resembled static on a TV. I nodded, my face blank, while the plaintiff wept. His loneliness moved through the room like a stale wind. Then I did what I was hired to do: I shouted on his behalf, with increasing, raw intensity, "Guilty! Guilty!" to the brother, wherever he was.

I was hired.

We were hired for our ability to appear objective. The courts sought people who had not yet faded, who would sit, solid, corporeal, in front of the court. Vanishing was a sign of weakness; the sturdy mocked them and bragged about their ability to be fully seen. I passed a gym on my walk to the court, SolidBody, which had giant open windows that showed patrons vigorously lifting weights, admiring their almost naked, gleaming selves in the mirror. The vanished rushed, heads bowed, by the gym, while the sturdy gleefully insulted them.

Judges were expected to be especially intact. We worked out; we wore robes but the more popular among us revealed their arms, their legs, even cleavage; our solidity gave us a reassuring authority. I loved saying it—"Guilty!"—and each time I said it, my heart uncoiled. Others felt the same, I knew it, as they leaned forward and listened to that word: "Guilty!"

The courts were the idea of our president at that time, a man voted in because he seemed so reasonable, and reasonableness was a scarce quality, longed for with nostalgia. This was the first time the cruel tumult of daily life had finally, physically, eroded us.

The vanishing started before he took office, the first incidents in Toledo, Newport Beach, Chicago, Manhattan, Atlanta: a sixty-two-year-old man who mowed lawns for a living watched his hands evaporate after his neighbor broke the lawn mower and refused to pay for its repair; a teenager's face grew blurry when a classmate told her, right before a choral performance, that her large nose meant no one would want to look at her on a stage.

The vanishing was not physically painful—you could still use your hands, walk around, perform all your regular activities. But everyone looked down on the invisible. They were mocked and hid their status on job applications, and certain clubs banned the invisible from their gates. Those lining up at the courthouse crossed their empty sleeves across their chests, wrapped scarves around their fading faces, looked at the sidewalk, ashamed.

THE PRESIDENT TRIED at first to come up with a medical answer, to find a pill that would keep people from vanishing, but nothing worked. The pills, in fact, created unfortunate responses—people's immune systems fought back, making some bizarrely clear edged and present; your eyelids hurt when you looked at them. So the president, in a desperate move, an attempt to solve the invisibility epidemic within the dwindling federal budget, built these courts, with grand, oaky interiors, hired us to proclaim the guilt of the others, dressed us in elegant black robes. This was where people could bear witness to those who had harmed them. Some scoffed and said that the courts were a way of giving up. Why didn't the government fund—well, anything? What was the point of screaming into a room? We could not find a solution to the epidemic of invisibility. It was what the scarcity in our nation had caused.

Yet people lined up for their time in the courts, one by one. And when I said, "Guilty!" or shouted it, really, to the person who was not there, the person who was vanishing flickered a moment. It was startling, seeing the plaintiff reassemble, see hands or face reemerge, the sudden clear illumination of a body. Their expression when they returned—the slow throb as a body when I said, "Guilty!" and they flickered, not quite there, and I had to scream, "Guilty!" over and over, until my throat was raw. It was judicial, of course, but also almost holy. For then I would see that throb, that flicker, the plaintiff coming back, clear, precise—there. That shimmer of visibility—how beautiful it was. The shimmer to solidity, presence, and then, a hope lurking—to what? I felt that moment resonate inside me, a click. Not just because I was glad for the transformation, my role in it, but because I, too, wanted it. I had a secret, something no one could see under my gloves—the pale, trembling translucence of my hands.

I BEGAN TO disappear three months ago. I had become a judge a few months before. My whole life, I had wanted to be the person that others could not look around, that they could not help but see. I rushed into the courtroom with my hands in my robes, swathed in gloves, my forehead damp, smiling brightly as I walked through security. I made sure my gloves were fixed tightly to my wrists, for if they were sealed correctly, the gloves would appear to be filled with air.

I woke up at night, touching my arms, my hands, afraid I would detect other places that had melted away. I did not tell others that I checked myself nightly, that I ran my hands over my body, looking for the places that I could not feel. Everything was there, intact, I loved every inch of fat, every billow and dip, every roll of weathered skin. I craved my body for all the regular reasons and others, too. I was an organized person. My children, each with their vulnerabilities—one too small, one too gentle, one who tended, annoyingly, to repeat everything the other person said. But they were each so beautiful, so precise, each with long dark eyelashes from their father, each with a different laugh that filled the room with hazy light. But all afraid.

Fear was like a skeleton inside them, and each morning, before I left to find the parking spot, I had to stand up and tell them everything would be okay. All the parents wore the determined, frantic expressions of rabbits who did not know where to run. I was the loud mother who stood up at parent meetings, who started petitions; they tired of the sound of my voice. The children were tested relentlessly in their schools, tests that ranked them for privileges so mean as to turn your heart. The savagery among the children predictably grew worse around test dates, and I coached them to ignore the ways their classmates tried to trip them up.

I did not think I would be one to disappear, and I dreaded it, but when I did see my hands flickering one day it felt natural, as though my vanishing confirmed something about me that I had always known. There were a few times in my life when I had felt myself becoming invisible, though I did not, but perhaps that set the stage for my vanishing now.

The first time was when I was seven years old. My parents forgot me at a supermarket; this had never happened before. My father and mother were arguing about something, in the way they did often, their arguing a constant low wind. I walked along, in my state of listening and not listening, and I stared at the ice cream case, which held four glimmering packages of different ice creams, which somehow spoke to a loneliness I didn't know I had. I stood there, imagining the various tastes of strawberry or pistachio or chocolate and I was suddenly filled with a wild hunger that came from the depth of my body, wanting to find one that would fill me so I would yearn for nothing again. And then I heard my name over the loudspeaker. Singer. Joy Singer. Someone was missing, someone was gone, someone with my name, and I understood soggily that it was me.

My parents were gone. I later learned they had left in a big rush for a job interview, for a job with five hundred applicants and three spots. Maybe they had just been distracted by their argument. I listened to my name, knowing I had been forgotten and I looked at the people passing me who were not missing. I felt myself trembling. I saw a girl my age walking with her parents. Her father wore large black shoes that made a hard sound, like clapping. She had shiny hair that was orange, and eyebrows like birds, and she saw me gazing at the ice cream, and she walked up and cheerfully put all four ice creams in her cart. I was sure that she knew I wanted them, and she took them all. I was frozen there, in the aisle, for a long time, watching everyone around me, listening to my almost name float over the room.

I waited. After a while, my name stopped. I was still unclaimed and there was a staticky silence. I left the store, looking for my parents. I walked down the street, alone, and I remembered people looked at me strangely, but did not speak to me. I felt my body drifting, here, but absent. I thought of the little girl who grabbed the ice cream and I felt hatred ringing in me like a large, heavy bell. The anger at her was useful; it kept me from feeling fear. I was missing for longer than I understood—eight hours, as the day fell into night. I was pressed deep into the world and severed from it, and watched the sky, the hard blueness of it, become a deeper blue, and I watched the pale lights come on, like sudden, bright breath, in the streets. The air grew chill, and I waited.

WHEN MY PARENTS finally found me, they were frantic in an annoying way. I saw that panic in their faces, especially my mother's. They blamed me—why didn't you look for us? Why didn't you stay and wait?

That moment echoed, quietly, through my childhood, and beyond; I could be one who was left. I had friends move across continents, uprooted by their parents, a beloved cat fled for better realms, and finally, my father decided that he wanted to live with another lover, somewhere else. He left my mother and me. This happened when I was seventeen.

How strangely simple it was to be forgotten. My father was both resolute in his new life, and embarrassed, sending money but with bewildering, affable messages: *Here's a little something! Have fun*. I did not know how I existed in his mind, but it seemed I had, in some way, eroded. I awoke each morning with something I wanted to tell him, but couldn't, to show him that I still existed. But after a while, that urgency faded, as there was nothing I could say.

My mother needed to claim a new life, a new home, a job. She did not know what to do. "Joy," she said. "Help me. Joy."

I put my rage toward conquering the system. I would be this thing, useful, to her. I bribed apartment managers to find her a place to live, I created résumés that were fake but convincing, I became the sort of person who got things through any means necessary, I maneuvered her into an apartment with windows overlooking a small lake, she began to work as a salesperson at a hat store and became successful designing hats. For a brief period, she sold a particular purple fedora with a silver band along the brim and earned enough so that we flew together on a plane to Hawaii. People wanted what she could make. She was a small woman with pinkish skin who looked good in any hat, as though she had evolved into an advertisement for her product. "Joy," she said, holding out a hat. "Look at this one.

Joy." When my mother said my name it was as though I were creating the world; it lodged inside me like a bright coin.

There were other moments, as everyone I know has experienced, the moments in supermarkets, schools, offices, city parks, dinner tables, planes, highways, all the places where one was regularly eroded. Then there was the one that actually made me disappear.

I STARTED TO turn invisible because of what might seem like a small thing: a parking place. But this was a precious parking place because it gave me fifteen minutes each day with my mother. Now we lived on different sides of our city, and the only way to get from my work to the home where she now lived was to jump in the car and drive at high speed for twenty minutes. I had fifteen minutes until they closed the doors. She was old and her body was failing; we did not know how much time she had left. But she always brightened when I walked into the room. I tried to make those fifteen minutes slow down.

I was halfway through my life and she was at the end of hers, and now, when I sat with her, I felt immensely greedy, as though I wanted to eat her like that ice cream I was denied long ago. What did I want out of those fifteen minutes? We sat in a faded blue room and I wanted to absorb her, or the better parts of her. We told each other memories of the past, or how we remembered it.

"Remember when you had that house on that cliff overlooking the Pacific? That view. It was beautiful," she said.

"The house," I said. We never lived in such a house, but she seemed to remember it so clearly; I tried to figure out what she was talking about. "What was the view again?" I asked.

"You don't remember? The Pacific. Crowds of people on a beach. There was a line of palm trees at the edge of the yard, the flowers, what were they? Gladioli? My god."

Her specificity impressed me. But our apartment had a view of a concrete wall from one window. Perhaps we had seen the grand house on television, on a real estate show that featured fabulous houses. I couldn't tell her this wasn't ours.

"Remember when we went on a trip to the ocean and we were swimming and were surrounded by fish?" I asked.

"Yes," she said.

"I was suddenly panicking and couldn't swim and you carried me back to shore under your arm. You swam with great assurance and grace. I remember that," I said.

She nodded.

"And you built a castle for me with shells after to thank me," she said.

There was no such castle, but I wanted to know about the castle.

"Tell me about that castle again," I said.

"It was small but well-made," she said. "Mostly pink, quite sparkly."

"What did you like about it?" I asked.

She thought. "You spent a lot of time on it," she said. "Like a sculptor. You tried to put everything carefully in its place."

It was a curious dialogue, and troubling, of course, but

also, in our mutual construction of fake events, somehow satisfying. I wanted to discover who I was in her fantasies—an owner of valuable real estate, an artistic person, good with my hands. I watched the clock, feeling each minute leave my body. I felt as visible as the sun as I sat there, with her, burning.

I had to get home to help our children study for their tests, I had to get back to my sweaty life. When the nurse came, right at 6:00, and led my mother back in, and gazed at me as if to say, "You may leave." I stood there a moment. Could I leave? How did anyone leave a parent as they were fading? The doors shut for visitors at 6:00. Each time it felt monstrous but necessary. I did not know if I could, but each time I did.

ONE OF MY life's great triumphs (sad but true) was that I found a secret parking place, two blocks from my office, a sliver of asphalt behind a dumpster and a tree. I had slipped my car there one day and no one had noticed. It did seem to be a legal place. I had everything organized, to the minute; I drove at dawn to locate the spot, waited until no other cars were around to take it. I set a couple of trash cans in front of it. if I didn't find this place, I would have to walk thirty-eight minutes to reach my car after work and I would miss the visit, that island of time with my mother. That I could not do.

One day, I was driving to the spot (carefully, glancing in my rearview mirror) at the soft light of the day flushing softly over the road. I was thinking of all the things of the day—the way our oldest child had spent a ridiculously long time getting dressed this morning, trying to find the right shirt to give her luck during an end-of-year test; the way my mother had decided, with great generosity, that I had taught her to cook a soufflé. I was driving slowly, by cars that resorted to various strategies of dissuasion—barbed wire, jagged rocks, carefully affixed to bumpers—to protect their spots. Each day, I felt my body tremble as I approached the spot, a strange sensation as though I were wild with hunger, and when I set my car securely in it, I felt a deep satisfaction, as though I had killed and eaten a wild beast.

That day I paused as I was about to angle into it. The driver behind me had their headlights off. I put my car into reverse, and just as I was about to back up, the other car slipped into my treasured place, with the slick quality of an eel.

I could not believe it. Someone had taken the spot, the spot that I had found and successfully hidden for the last few months. I needed that spot. If I didn't have it, I would lose those fifteen minutes sitting with my mother. I backed up. Who stole this place? Who had not seen that that was my place, my scrap, mine?

I held the steering wheel and waited.

The other car door opened. A woman got out. Navy suit, orange hair cut in a bob. She looked perfectly entitled to the space, happy to have found it, and ready for work.

It seemed that I had passed her somewhere, perhaps in a dream. I was burning with rage I didn't know I had; it was a glorious rage. I could not park and began, in my car, to follow her. She glanced at me and kept walking.

"That's my spot!" I said. "I found it."

There was a soft prune-like look in her eyes, an expression that I recognized: she was evaluating me. I drove beside her, slowly.

"I own it!" I yelled, which was a lie. "You'll get towed. Get out of it!"

She looked up for a moment, wondering, but then, I guess, decided to take her chances and kept going.

I wanted, in my deepest heart, to run her over. I was surprised by my rage, the way it rose from the center of me. She walked faster, glancing at my car, her orange hair glowing, and I leaned out the window and yelled,

"You idiot! Move it now!"

I sounded out of my mind, indeed I did, but sadly, I did not regret it. I said what I felt. I had searched so long for that spot or, truly, that time with my mother that I needed, and I could not lose it. Her face was taut with fear; she ran.

SHE WOVE EXPERTLY through the thin streets and corridors of downtown; she was gone. I held the steering wheel, driving slowly, now searching for a place to put my car. I looked out at the great glittering sea of cars, shoved into spots. Those cars! I had never really looked at them. I saw a measure of time in all of them, each one holding its slot for a particular moment of love or ambition or friendship. I had a flicker, silver and sharp within me, a question stretching over all these cars—why were we in this situation? Why were there not enough spots, why were there cars surrounding themselves with barbed wire, why could we not do this most simple thing: transport ourselves to our desires, to the places we wanted to go? At least we could be allowed that. A honk pierced the air; I slid back to battling the day. I spent the next hour finding a spot, and finally did, blocks from everything, which meant I had to race out of work an hour early, and the senior judges might object. Then I saw my hands, and there they were, holding the steering wheel but just flickering, I could see through them to the wheel.

A sound fell out of me. I stopped the car and rubbed my hands. Not me. But yes, me. My hands were vanishing. A shriek stuck, like a shard of glass, in my throat. They were still solid, though a bit softer, perhaps the consistency of silk. I was frightened; sorrow thunked in me like a large drum. I was not becoming invisible, I had tried to beat this back for my whole life.

But I was.

I CALLED MY mother that night and tried to explain what had happened. "I tried to get to my spot in the morning," I said, "but someone stole it. Someone got there first."

"Stole it!" she exclaimed.

"Yes," I said, wringing my shimmering hands, trying to squeeze them to their normal status, which didn't work.

"Why don't you get it back?" she said.

"How?" I asked.

"Move the other car," she said.

"I can't do that," I said. My hands trembled, watery in the light.

"You told me to do that," she said. "You said, 'Send your hat to this person or that one.' You said, 'Just go ahead.' You said this to me a lot, as I remember."

I was a failure in the most basic, dismal way; I could not stop time, not that I ever thought I could. But still, this obvious knowledge was depleting.

"When will I see you?" she asked.

My hands were transparent but still they ached.

"Tomorrow," I said.

I HID MY HANDS that night from my family, wore gloves while I cooked, kept them on while I ate. I tried to change my hands to their old solidness in my mind; when I picked up this jar of ketchup, when I brushed my child's hair, this is when I hoped my hands would swell. But they did not. I kissed my husband while we made love but angled my arms so my hands never actually touched his body. I felt him shift, confused, around me, sensing something different, perhaps wondering if I wanted to try an unusual new technique, if maybe I just wanted to be taken, if me not using my hands during our wrestling was a sign of some other desire. We were deep into the middle of our lives, we wanted to find new desires inside our desires, what would make us feel alive, in our briefness, here? It was difficult not using my hands, and I felt a strange helplessness, in this situation enjoyable. I needed this helplessness, this unburdening. It felt like a trick, living side by side with this other helplessness that I felt every day as I tried to find the right spot. We pretended nothing else was happening in the world. We dug ourselves into this pretending. My heart pounded and he held me down, and my hands were under a pillow, and this was all an immense relief. He did not notice my hands, which was a surprise, he was wrapped like cellophane in his own desires, but I was grateful, that he loved me without seeing these flaws, or pretended not to see them. We lay together and breathed.

THE NEXT MORNING, I woke up earlier than usual. I set our children's lunches on the counter in the cool darkness, got into my car and drove into the night to get the spot. I approached it, slowly, my heart bumbling fast, and saw it, oh that beautiful emptiness, the space that held a clear vessel of feeling. My car swung in; I got the spot. Victory! She wasn't there. No one was. I closed my eyes.

A regular day shouting at the plaintiffs: "Guilty. Guilty." In the court, other judges looked at me; perhaps they heard a special intensity to my shouting.

I rushed out that night and left my beloved spot, and squeezed my mother's whole self, carefully, wearing my gloves, when I saw her.

"Not so tight," she said.

THAT MORNING, all felt well, or as good as it could be; my careful life had balanced correctly. All I could think of was the woman with the orange hair. I imagined I could keep her asleep in my mind, make her sleep for just an hour later, just enough for me to get the spot. "Sleep," I shrieked in my mind, or "Sleep," stated in my mind in a more polite manner, "Stay away from my spot, lady." But clearly, she didn't hear me, for after my next predawn excursion, she had gotten there first. I saw her car there and I felt despondent. My mind's demands meant nothing to the workings of the world. She wanted that space, too. This time I stopped, wrote a note on a slip of paper, and shoved it in her windshield: *Move.* Perhaps I could frighten her; maybe this would work. The next morning, the space was again empty; I slipped my car in. My heart relaxed; perhaps I had won.

I was plunged into a schedule of haze and uncertainty. I remember when my father had left, a sudden impulse to hide that remade itself into a grim desire to gather friends—I joined clubs for activities I had no interest in, I went to gatherings where I knew no one and resolved to talk to everyone in the room—I needed to insert myself into something. Now I would wake up in the morning, unsure if she would get there before me, haul myself out of bed before the first light. I zoomed through the darkness, gripping the wheel with my transparent hands, and my heart turned like a red siren as I approached the spot. Some days I won the spot, other days she made it, and we were engaged in a silent, vicious battle. This went on for a couple of weeks. My hands faded from a pale yellow to gray; the world shone through them to the steering wheel as though I were looking through a clear pond.

"Why are you trembling?" my mother asked me, as we sat in the lobby of the place she lived, the walls gleaming a bright lemon yellow. The paintings were all of sunsets: over mountains, cities, oceans, to the point it seemed a strange and aggressive choice.

"I'm fine," I said.

"You look afraid of something," she said.

"Why wouldn't anyone be?" I said.

She laughed.

"I'm scared," she said, "they'll run out of the chocolate cake some nights. It's not that good, but I like the icing."

"That's reasonable," I said.

My mother grabbed my arm, suddenly emphatic.

"Don't be afraid," she said. She smiled, gleeful about this new role of philosopher.

"Why not?"

She paused, thinking.

"What are you afraid of?" she asked.

There were hoarse shouts from distant rooms. Outside the window, the dusk twinkled, dark and hazy.

"Myself," I said.

THE LINE OF plaintiffs was long. I watched them walk in, and my pronouncements of "Guilty!" echoed across the room. The other judges, who pretended to ponder the charges for longer, drew out the moment as we were supposed to do. My invisibility made me feel more aggressive toward those committing the crimes, and more maternal toward the plaintiffs, their various shimmering selves. The other judges were more mocking toward them, behind their backs, muttering during our breaks as though eager to establish themselves as different from them; they seemed worn out. Our job was also a workout. My invisibility was a betrayal to the plaintiffs. I clasped my gloved hands beside the other judges, who inhabited themselves as though they were large marble temples, solid, impenetrable, eternal.

MY MOTHER WAS more authoritative; she also called me by another name. It was the name of a girl she had seen on television, and not even someone that attractive; this second fact was especially sad, somehow. I didn't want to correct her so as not to embarrass her. But who did she think I was? Then she remembered again, and said, "Yes, of course, you."

I felt more injured by that misperception than I wanted to be. How is our very self housed in others, and in ways we can't understand. We were shy with each other that day, somehow, and she found lots of things to fault in me. That day she saw me mostly as annoying, as though she were suddenly itchy and I was a rash.

"I'm tired," she said, "and I can't sleep."

Her face was tight with hope, as though I held the answer to this, though I did not.

"Close your eyes," I said.

She squinched them shut, and then they flew open.

"Doesn't work," she said.

"I mean, not now," I said.

"Just tell me when," she said. "Tell me what to do."

After this exchange, I was tired enough to sleep for both of us. When I drove home, I fell into bed and slept for twelve hours, and the next morning I had missed my chance for the spot. When I drove by, the familiar car was there. Of course. A fatalistic calm settled over me, knowing that she would take it, and then I had a flash of rage as bright as a steel plate in the sun.

It was early morning; the cars blossomed with the soft bright newness of the day. The street was empty; I stopped my car, got out, and darted to hers.

It was just a car, but I needed to destroy it. I had written *Move* on a note and that didn't work. I thought of my mother telling me to move the car; that was impossible. I felt myself wandering through the aisles of the supermarket, not knowing where to go, or who I was, as a child, and a frustration rose like a geyser inside me, and I picked up a rock. I raised my hand and threw it at the car; a window shattered; I ran.

IT TOOK ME some time to find a spot, partly because I was having trouble driving; my hands were fainter, surprisingly, with this act; I could barely see them as I gripped the wheel. I had become the sort of person who threw a rock at a car, and worse, broke a window, and worse, I wanted to do more.

I got to work. That day, looking at the plaintiffs, the other judges, I was more awake than usual; quick to sentence the absent perpetrators, I was so vehement the other judges shifted in their robes and glanced at me. "Guilty!" I shouted. I was afraid they would ask me to tear off my gloves and see my erasure, and I positioned my gloved hands so no one could tell there was anything wrong with me. I wondered if there was a special vanishing that came with doing a violent act, or perhaps a special visibility, but I did not feel any difference, besides the fact my hands were pale, like morning fog. But, oddly, the judges copied me; my desperation was convincing. I tried to test them during our break. I did not know much about them; we got to work, quickly changed into our robes, and found our places on the raised bench overlooking the courtroom. I wondered if they were fooling me. Perhaps we didn't speak to each other because our roles, though admired, and coveted, basically required the same skill as a game show host.

"Good work today!" I said to Horace, a man in his seventies, a wide gray beard. His eyebrows lifted.

"Why?" he asked.

"The way you leaned on the *Y*. Persuasive," I said.

He looked pleased at the compliment. "Thank you," he said.

We had had a variety of jobs before: elementary school teacher, speech therapist, bus driver, food service worker, attorney. We were not supposed to know who we were before, but it leaked out; Horace lived on his own, and was two months behind on his rent; Gwen was a mother of two and her partner could not get out of bed; Lara had been fired from several jobs because they said she asked for too much, too often; little bits of their lives sparked out as we shrugged off our robes and put on our everyday coats. We did not know what to say to each other, but we felt we were important. I needed to flatter them, to distract them from who I was.

"And the way you added the *so*. 'So guilty!' They liked that," I told Lara.

She smiled. "I like to improvise," she said.

They let us out a back exit so the plaintiffs, in their gratitude, would not swarm us. Occasionally, some would approach us, the plaintiffs now supposedly returned to themselves. I remembered a few—a man with short silver hair and an expensive suit that sagged on his thin shoulders, a woman who teetered on high red heels, a tall teenager with broken eyeglasses—they were still not satisfied—still, understandably, unfulfilled.

"That's it? Guilty?"

"Excuse me. I waited three hours for what?"

"That bitch insulted me! I need more than this! Where's my payback?"

"I don't feel different. I waited and waited and fuck it, I feel the same—"

There were only a few plaintiffs who said this, most were relieved by their new visibility and continued their lives. Today, though, particularly, after my attack on the car, I believed I was an unhinged person and also, sadly, a fraud. Perhaps the judges knew of my hands, or they knew I had broken a window, and they seemed to be speaking particularly to me. Walking away from the courthouse, faster than I usually did, I looked at the faces of those passing me, some crisp and solid, marching ahead, lipstick bright, hair gleaming, their eyes roving across the streets, I knew those eyes, focused and intent as hunters. They walked alongside those with parts missing, I could tell from the way clothes flapped too wildly around a leg, or a scarf was tied oddly around a face, the person who had vanished almost completely, shockingly, just to an arm, low to the ground, a trembling hand holding out a paper coffee cup for money—and I wondered if the invisible could tell I was a compatriot, or that those with roving eyes would see my similarity to them; I was clearly part of both groups, and I wanted to belong to neither. What other party, what other affiliation was possible? I rushed through the crowds, and it was just starting to rain, and the streets were slick and bright like patent leather.

THAT NIGHT, I reached my mother in time for five minutes of a visit. I rushed in, talking too fast, wanting to fill the air with words, not wanting her to detect what I had done. "How did you sleep?" I asked. "I have ideas to help you sleep. I have chamomile tea. I was thinking a sleep mask to block out light—"

She looked at me as though I were five years late with all of this. "Fine," she said, crisply. "I slept great."

"Good," I said.

"I just closed my eyes and was out," she said, noisily unwrapping a candy and eating it.

"I don't need any help," she said. "I think I am fine."

She eyed me with, I thought, a sort of suspicion. Or was it pride? She felt good today. The nurse looked at the clock and nodded.

"Well," I said, dangling there, both pleased and useless.

"I tried to move the car," I said, though of course I didn't go into the details.

Her face tried to understand what I was saying.

"That's good," she said, lightly. "Now. I'm tired. I'm going to sleep," she said.

I didn't know what to do but reached out and grabbed her hands; she squeezed mine, and her eyes flickered, and I think she felt the gloppy absence. She squeezed harder, but she seemed not to notice any difference in my hands. The action was the thing, that I seemed to have hands that were holding hers, that was enough, and that she was gripping mine, and her heart beat in my thumb, that relentlessness, over and over. Or was it mine in hers? And then the nurse said, "Goodbye, it's time to get ready for bed," and my mother turned briskly and walked off, and I went back into the thick, tarnished dark.

THE NEXT DAY, I got up and drove, with a sort of calm, to the secret parking spot. Somehow, I knew it would be there, that the woman with the orange hair would not. My heart beat in that familiar, troubled way, and then I saw the space and it was empty. There was room for me. It was there—I pulled into it and shut off the car. I looked around to see if anyone was monitoring me, if anyone cared that I was there; if anyone had seen what I had done. I flinched when I heard any other car drive by, got out of my car and locked it with slow, deliberate movements that would reveal me as a reasonable person. I wondered what the woman had done when she came to her car and seen her window broken, the shattered glass in her seat, on the lot. I was glad for a moment to look like anyone. I walked quickly to the courthouse, slipped into the back door and put on my robes.

There were many plaintiffs filing in that morning, and I settled today beside Horace and Lara, clasping my gloved hands and ready again to shout, "Guilty!" into the buzzing room. It had been a bad week for many. They crowded in, I was struck by how little I could see of them—they were bundled up in big coats and scarves but I could see the damage, the blurry arms, the erasing of lips, ears, legs. They stood, talking fast, trying to get their complaints heard, and they sounded the same, all of them, and then I saw her.

The woman with the orange hair.

She was at the back of the room, arms crossed, as though she were cold. I felt a flash of heat, looking at her, a feeling identifiable as embarrassment or panic, I wasn't sure. She was wearing the same navy suit she had been when she'd first parked the car, her haircut was the same shape, a conservative upturned bob, and she walked with the same swift gait she'd used when she swerved into the spot that first day. She wanted to be healed. I watched her move with the crowd, the lines funneling into our separate stations, each plaintiff moving through a corridor where they finally came to us. I watched where the woman with the orange hair was headed, and I tried to figure out why she was here, what part of her was disappearing, and why. I knew the answer to the last point, I did, though I did not want to think this, and as she got closer, I saw that it was severe—her skirt revealed that her legs were barely visible, half of her was gone.

My heart tightened. The plaintiffs had started to come in with more extreme cases of their bodies invisible, sometimes now with large swaths of themselves vanished. They spoke faster, sometimes almost unintelligible, as they described the harm done to them, and when the guilty verdict usually worked quickly, making their bodies assert themselves, swelling to fill their coats and pants and skirt, some had ripped off their clothes, grateful to see their shiny, solid legs and arms and buttocks, and wept.

I could see her face more clearly. She was someone who cared for herself—her hair was set as though she had been to a salon, her face gleamed with creamy pale makeup, her lipstick a matte red. She looked as though she were going to sign a business contract, but her skirt floated over a gap between its hem at her shoes. She gripped a piece of paper and appeared prepared to make a speech.

"I have a complaint," she called. Her eyes roamed the judges, as though she was going to pick one, but the plaintiffs didn't get a choice, they were shuffled by guards down whichever line was going faster, like the DMV, and the woman was heading right to me.

I thought of jumping up, feigning a stomach cramp, and running out. I started to rise.

"Judge Singer," she said.

I went still. Her voice was softer than I had expected, I guess making assumptions from the suit and her determined, marching walk. She sounded as though she were used to keeping her voice low yet controlled, like a kindergarten teacher. I thought she had picked me for a purpose, and my blood jumped, but I saw that she was just reading my name off the plaque on my part of the bench.

"My name is Ann Houser," she said, "and I was the victim of an attack."

I clasped my hands, and I swore that I felt my invisibility creep up my arms, a sensation of both heat and cold together, a feeling of confusion, of static.

"Judge Singer," she said, and I felt my neck chill when she said my name, though it seemed she was just trying to get in good with me, "I was the victim of an attack a couple nights ago. Or it was not me, personally, but it was my car. I have photos—" Some of the plaintiffs came armed with evidence and she held up some photos of the damage to her car, which she had carefully documented: glass glinting on the worn beige upholstery of the front seat, glass on the floor of the car, a close-up of a very sharp shard of glass. A few people shook their heads. It looked like the work of a lunatic. My face fell into an expression of concern.

"You may wonder why I'm so upset about a car," she said. "Why when I returned to my car after I found a spot, finally, after much searching, and saw this. This attack. I turned around and started running, trying to find who did it, I couldn't find them, the streets were empty. I knew I wouldn't find them, and I kept running and then this happened." She gestured to the bottom half of herself.

The vanishing was particularly profound; I shifted in my seat. Usually the judges were focused on their own plaintiffs, but her voice was high, like a flute, I noticed Horace and Lara examining her.

"What happened is that I'm someone who is starving," she said, and I sat up and looked more closely at her, as she did not seem extremely thin. "But mostly for one thing. I wanted other things when I was a child, I wanted it all, but then it focused. I have had a craving for a particular cookie, one with chocolate and a hint of peanut butter and maple and some other delicious thing I can't describe. It's not an expensive cookie, it's one you can get anywhere. I feel it on my tongue, in my throat, this desire for this cookie. It just happened one day and then it was something I wanted my whole life. I had a tendency to fall in love with small things, so much I felt faint. Friends, lovers, cities, movies, and the like. Sometimes in a sexual way, sometimes not. But I needed this cookie, this taste, or there was a hunger in me that made my stomach feel raw. I couldn't think of anything else, I could not."

The room was as big as an armory, and the many voices swerved, rolled over each other, but I could hear hers, precisely, in the din.

"I was not a picky eater as a child, I liked many things, but I fell in love with that cookie. I don't remember the first time I ate it, I grabbed it off some tray, but I remembered it. I was standing in the shadows of a huge church with my parents, who had ordinary lives, but had dodged a violence they wouldn't reveal. It happened in the land of their childhoods. On our street, which was a quiet street except for sometimes, there were often celebrations of life for someone who had killed themself. There were often candles, bottles of rum, posters of the person who had died. We passed these on our way to school. The celebrations were a determined effort to make a terrible thing seem okay. Our parents believed deeply in prayer. Otherwise, they seemed heavy. Their faces, their postures, their clothes even seemed to be made of lead. I felt that heaviness press on me and I felt like my brain was getting crushed. I thought of that cookie. It was a bright-green color, like a forest, and there was something about that taste that reassured me about the world. I imagined how I'd feel when I took a bite of it, and how chewing it I would not be like them.

"I know this is long," she said. "And I never questioned that hunger. It was mine. It was secret. I went along with my life, and some decent things happened. I wanted it, I'll admit, when I was first naked in bed with the man I married, after I tried to crawl into his body like a coat, I wanted it when I swore an oath to always be with him, I wanted it then when I fell in love with my piano teacher, for I wanted to learn piano so much, I even wanted it when I had my children, after I woke up with a tiny beautiful being beside me. I felt that salty yearning for a bite of that cookie; I wanted it whenever I loved someone, I had to have it then, I am embarrassed telling you this, that I held this hunger, that nothing was quite enough."

She paused and looked at me, at all the judges.

"Something is wrong with me," she said. "I don't know what happened. I feel that gnawing in my stomach, that emptiness, and I have to take a bite of that cookie, taste that particular sweet taste, and move on. I didn't tell anyone. And the worst was, my kids found those cookies in the backs of the cupboards in the kitchen. They found the small, chewed cookies and they took bites too, and I saw that understanding in their eyes, that terrible glint, that awareness of their own hunger, giant holes inside them, and I was ashamed I had passed that onto them in some way. I had."

She took a breath.

"What does any of this have to do with that parking spot?" she asked. "Well, this is why.

"I needed it because there was a place I had to go. Because, after I found out that my children had the same hunger as I did, that they were taking furtive bites of the cookie in the back of the closet too, that they too were doomed to this, I was ashamed. I was, judge, for I wanted them to be happy, I wanted them to be—well, full. Is that such a big thing to ask?"

She looked at us with a searching expression; I glanced away.

"So, of course, I looked for options. Too many to describe. And then I heard about this—a clinic, on Bay Street, right around here, where you could sit around and eat what you had a craving for, that one odd thing, and others would eat what they craved, a certain ice cream or a chicken leg or whatever. Someone had a need to lick the insides of candy wrappers; that was what he liked to do. It wasn't that this group offered any options, it's not like this hunger went completely away, but that you could sit around with people who had the same bottomless gnawing."

Her voice grew louder.

"I had to have that parking spot because I had to visit this place. We just sat around and ate our things. Do you know how glad I was when I found that spot? Do you know what that gave me? Peace, for a little while. Can't I just ask for that?

And then I came back to this." She held up the photos of the broken window again. "I ran into the street looking for this criminal, I wanted to beat him up, whoever it was, I wanted to grab his shirt and say, 'Why can't I have this, why not,' but there was no one anywhere, the person was gone, just doing this, wrecking my car and gone, and as I ran, then this—" She gestured to her bottom half. "I thought I was going to be completely gone, do you know! All I wanted was some moment when I didn't feel this hunger, when I could have some peace!"

I clasped my vanished hands inside my gloves. There were the groans of the others, examining the broken window.

"So please, Judge Singer," she said. "Help me. Help!"

Her voice was hoarse and terrible. It was my parking spot, I thought, I had found it. That fact clung to me like adhesive tape; I could not unstick it. How could I allow her that place, too? Whose yearning was better than another's? How did we all thrust ourselves into this dry air?

I had a job to do. I sat up straighter and leaned forward. Would the word come out of me? I felt it in my throat, stale, a piece of bread.

I opened my mouth. "Guilty!" I said, quietly. She was still, waiting. It was not enough. "Guilty!" I said. "Guilty. Guilty!"

Me. It was about me. But I had wanted so little it seemed, too.

Ann Houser was looking at me, more critically.

"Guilty!" I shouted. She closed her eyes. Then I saw—her legs reappearing, her body forming itself again, calves, knees, legs. Her body whole. I felt relieved that I could affect this, simply through the sound of the word ringing through the room; that she was returned to herself. I had this power, how did I have it? For she did not see this other element; she did not see what she had done to me.

"Guilty!" I shouted. My heart was a hard, sour nut. I felt a tumbling inside me, everything collapsing like a scaffold. What was left? Dust rose in my throat. I clasped my hands, aware of the nothingness in my gloves, how could this be? I did not want to be nothing. I looked out at the plaintiffs filing into the courtroom, all their glimmering wounded bodies. Was my own need, my love worth anything? The courtroom was packed. I felt a silvery propulsion in me that could be panic or maybe something else.

I tore off my gloves.

A gasp.

My hands were transparent, the tender thinness of clouds. The others looked at them as though at a nightmare. "Guilty!" I shouted into the room, to her, though she didn't know it, to the others. I wanted all of them to hear it—here were my hands, let them see my sorrow, too, see what my own love did.

Quickly, like leaves fluttering, a silence in the room.

A silence and then a few shouts. Ann Houser dropped her photos. The shouts: surprise, dismay. I was not solid, I was injured, too. I would be kicked off the bench, I held my arms out, trembling, my mother waiting for me in her far-away room. The faces of the plaintiffs were raw with shock: I was not what they had imagined, I had no authority, I was no different from them.

What would happen to my hands? Would I be able to

turn them back with my words, too? They flickered, gloomily, in the silence. And then I turned slowly toward the other judges. They sat in a row, their robes draped around them like dark satin curtains, large and solid. I waited for them to tell me to leave, or worse, for I had broken the contract and had no right to sit up here, beside them. Lara and Horace and the others stared at my hands—they saw, quite clearly, my injury. Lara let out a small laugh.

Then she slowly unwrapped something I had not noticed: the sleeve of her robe. Unspooling the heavy shining fabric around her arm. But as she lifted the fabric, I saw something I could not believe—she had no arm, or she had an arm that was also vanishing, that glimmered, faintly, like my hands.

She crossed her visible arm over the one that was absent. She did not look at me, as though ashamed. The plaintiffs stopped talking. Then Horace, kicking off his shoe to reveal this: his foot, half there. Juan, rolling up the cuffs of his pants to show that he was missing both calves. There were no stories, there was a silence in the enormous room as we all looked at each other, and we sat there, waiting for the word that would allow all of us to return to ourselves, to repair us, to exist.

DATA

She had lost all her data. The streets were cold and blue and still and a few people rushed by, their eyes glazed over their masks as they gazed into the chill air. They filtered by like paper dolls, sweetly, into the darkness, back from work. No line had appeared on the test. Yet. Everyone oddly polite, in the icy night, under the circumstances. In any case, the computer had to be fixed. She could run out and drop off the computer at the repair store and come back. There were twenty feet from the living room to the bedroom door where her child now waited to be released. Anna looked at that space. The windows flung open in the living room, the entire apartment, cold, a jacket moving in the wind. It felt like a wilderness.

It was just 5:00 p.m., but the sky was already dark. The streetlights clutched a starry light. She had done an idiotic thing—spilled water all over her laptop, right before a meeting. Her daughter now shut in the bedroom, the room full of yearning, thick as red clouds. In the living room, a meeting, bizarrely happening on Anna's computer, in some other silent world. She saw the water falling onto the keyboard, a clear wave from a mug, but so quickly. That was it. The laptop sizzled and went dark. Everything was gone. She thought she turned the computer off, but it continued to eat itself, hot and wild, and it seemed about to scream as she hurried down the street, the lights from the bodegas green in the rumpled dark snow. The computer store was full of people holding tickets for repair, making room for each other in the tender, quiet way people sometimes did now, sometimes, the silent steps people took to stay away from each other; it was buzzing with young men attaching computers to red cables as though infusing blood.

She saw a man, worn, bald head speckled, staring ahead intently, a mother gripping a child's hand; Anna pinched the nose of her mask, fitting it. Her breath was hot and meaty in the cup of the mask.

—Can you get my data back? she asked.

—If we can turn it on, we can do it, a guy said, with the poufy confidence of a surgeon, or a pilot. —We can turn them all on. Do you have anything important on there?

—Important, yes.

—Did you save it anywhere?

—No. Of course not.

He gave her a ticket.

—Get it back, she said, now afraid.

He moved with the techno swagger of the young, as though he was swinging on a star.

—What is on there that you want to save? he asked.

—This guy last week had to have a specific photo he took of his son in 1993. Just one he took with him on the Wonder Wheel at Coney Island, but the father said there was a smile on his face so big he had to see. One lady said she had spent ten years writing a novel and forgot to save it anywhere else. Then there was the wedding video that vanished for the couple that was about to get a divorce. The guy wanted the video, he wanted to study it, he thought he'd figure out what went wrong. He was hungry for that video, whoa. What do you want the most?

One thing? How could there be one thing. A red flare of greed; she wanted everything.

—We'll call you tomorrow, he said.

ALL THE BUILDINGS in her neighborhood were sinking into the street. That was how it looked with the mounds of dirty snow. They were large brick buildings, all forming a corridor that the sun passed through, in the middle of the day, the rows of glass windows hungry for light, filling with light, silver squares in the late afternoon, and then fading; they were icy in the cold, and they seemed to be sinking. The ambulances zoomed, the red lights like candy, glowing. When one passed, she felt she was almost inside of it, the steel walls of the ambulance rattling as they rushed down the freezing street. Or she was sitting beside a person, faceless, who was gripping her hand. There was her mother's face, there was her husband, there was her father, long gone, but somehow returned to ride in the ambulances. Why are you killing everyone, one could ask her, but that was cheap, she thought, in this current situation, where you could blink and someone was gone. It was the only rational way to think now, she did not know how else to think. She was rushing down the street, her shoes the wrong shoes, she didn't know what to wear to go out anymore, who did, she did not know what to wear at all, the shoes thin in the snow, and she felt herself rippling across the street, like the lights from the sirens. But there was no rippling, she was not fluid, she was contained in this body, herself, she was walking, she was still a regular person, on an errand, walking down the street.

Outside, the air was clear. She would have to order a new computer. She stopped inside the supermarket, gliding around the others, directed, trying to grab what her daughter liked. Strawberries. Vanilla ice cream. Triscuits. Gatorade. Vitamin C. What would help. She wanted to find the right thing.

Walking home, she wanted to see into everyone's windows, she looked up and could see small bits of life: the sheets used as curtains and the laundry piled up against windows in the rental buildings, in the fancier limestone town houses, the chandeliers shimmering in living rooms, dripping with golden light, the large TVs flickering, squares holding football players, beauty contestants, women screaming in dark lots.

Anna walked, feeling her freedom in the cold air, and wanted to stay out here as long as she could stand it. Out here, the air was the air, great gulping breaths. She had been waiting for the red line. Every time her child returned after she was out, after she was just out, being a young person, Anna tried to sense if this time she had carried it in.

When she and her child saw the line on the test, one that she had been dreading, the apartment suddenly became a dark thing, a prison, for both, the walls closing in, the not knowing. In the apartment, she ran around, pushing up the windows even if it was freezing outside.

—I'm fine, her child said. On the other side of the door, now shut in the bedroom.

—How do you feel?

—I am fine. I just told you.

This was not clarifying.

—Do you feel warm? Tired? Sore throat? Anything?

—No. I'm fine.

This was good news, but puzzling. Anna could feel the youthful energy busting up the room, screeching laughter on the phone. Anna wanted to be reassured by the laughter, but was wary of it. The sound made her heart relax. The sound of nothing wrong. She felt her mind curling around the idea of nothing wrong and then allowing her daughter into the rest of the apartment and then her mind snapped back. She wondered if her daughter was fooling her. She tried to shut her own mind.

—I'm sorry but you have to stay in there. You should drink something. I can bring you some tea—

—Why? Stop freaking out. It's not that bad. I don't feel anything. All my friends are going out. They're having parties. No one is that sick. You should see what they post—

—It could be bad.

—Or not.

—You don't know.

—So I'm coming out.

—Honey, not yet.

Anna said this, firmly, to the closed door. She felt a tenderness toward the closed door. It stood there, not talking back, protecting her. She loved the door with an embarrassing love. The door did not think of her as the police. The door shielded her from her child's expression, which she was, suddenly, afraid of—the unhappiness she was causing with her rules and her daughter's cool excitement as she made plans. Her daughter was going to sneak out in the middle of the night, she knew, make herself a snack. She had become the sort of person who was afraid of her child coming out to make a snack. That sweet sound, her child slamming a cabinet, breathing into the air. Breath that could, in its current state, prevent Anna from seeing her own mother.

She wanted to believe the illness was not that bad, she tried to convince herself, but she could not stop thinking; she could not wrap her mind around anything else.

—I'll bring you all the food you want, what do you want? Guess what, I bought ice cream. Plus you need to hydrate. What do you want?

—I don't want anything! I am totally sick of this! I'll just stay here two days. I am fine.

—It's five.

—Wendy got out in two. She said she felt fine. It didn't matter—

—You could go to a hotel.

Silence.

—I don't want to go to a hotel.

A friend said, —Just send her to a hotel! She'll be okay. The young people are okay. Your asthma. What could happen if you get it? Do you really want to risk it? The asthma was under control. She wanted to keep saying that. Maybe she would be one of the lucky ones. Or she would not. But she didn't want to send her daughter to a hotel alone. How mean that seemed. And would she be afraid, lonely, what if she got suddenly worse? The wind blew through the living room.

—I did nothing, her daughter said.

Anna was quiet, because her daughter really did do nothing, but unfortunately it was something. She went to watch a movie at a friend's apartment. Six people there, one had a sore throat but wasn't quite as talkative as usual. He was fine. Everything was fine.

It was nothing, she agreed, of course it was nothing, it was life, it was fun, what could be wrong with fun, how could she be against life, fun, she thought of them sitting in that small room, sitting on the couch and the floor, the tumbling clamor of their voices. Shoulders touching with love. The buildings tall boxes of sparkle outside the windows.

Their breath in the dim aching light.

—I need something, her daughter said, voice now crisp. —A photo. My seventh birthday. I'm jumping off a swing, I think. You know that photo? We're all creating a friend collage, I want that one. You have it, somewhere, saved. Can you send it to me?

—A photo? Um, how about tomorrow?

—Tomorrow? I need it now.

—I'll look.

Anna had read that if she pushed a towel under the door crack, air wouldn't get through, so she did that. She placed a plate with a cup of juice on it by the door and stepped away. She watched the door open. A hand reached out and grabbed it.

WAITING. SHE WAITED for the computer store to call. There was a feeling of heat in her face, then gone. It could be four thousand things. It could be a heat from the inside, flashing in and out. Her body monstrous in its shifting now. What the hell was it. There were too many endings falling through the air. Thump. Sirens sobbed in the street. The ambulance was in front of her building, stuck behind a UPS truck. People in their cars honking, that flat melody, impatient to move. The ambulance driver stepping out onto the street, gesturing to the UPS truck. —Move! Get out of here! The blue-and-red lights glittering like a carnival. The hopeful movement of the rest of the world. People walking briskly by the ambulances, to their appointments, to the office, to work, to the supermarket. Inside, time sludged against the wall. She sat very straight, feeling her breath, certain she sensed some shift deep inside her, then didn't. This heat, or another heat turning like a hot serpent inside her. What was she supposed to feel? How many shifts were there to keep track of? Each month now a prairie, devoid of the rising up and down, a freedom in a way but she still waited for the month to reshape itself, still felt a strange longing for that rush, that feeling of ending and starting again. She wanted to reach under her skin and turn herself inside out, not to stop any and all declines, but to know who she would be within them.

Besides the photo, her daughter was not requesting any particular thing, and she kept turning down offers of various beverages. In her room, her daughter doing an exercise routine, turning up the music high, doing jumps, thudding. The thuds were comforting, somehow.

THE SNOW FELL pale and quiet through the dusky softness of the streetlights. It was silent outside, the silence of snowfall. The windows were still open and bits of snow fluttered into the room.

Her mother called.

Her mother, eighty, sitting in her home halfway across the country, trapped now for two years, her lungs trembling in her chest, a situation that made any illness dire. The first few months, waving to friends across the street, then later venturing closer, to lunch outside, shivering in a sweater, now, in the winter, sent back inside. She had sent her a manifesto.

—Did you read it? she asked.

Anna had downloaded it but hadn't read it yet. It was—oh god!—now in the ruined computer.

—Why not? her mother said.

—I haven't gotten to it, Anna said. She did not want to tell her about her daughter.

—I make important points in it, her mother said.

—You can tell me what, Anna said.

—I say it better in the manifesto. Please read it. There are two parts. I think one needs work. I want to send them somewhere.

She wondered when she would hear from the computer repair shop.

—What are the parts?

—You know what they are.

—No, tell me.

—The first part is about invasions. Do you know that there are invasions of a vine first spotted in Arizona, now all over our neighborhood. They have taken over the yard of Shirley Maxwell, down the street. They are choking the trees there, there were three trees that had to be cut down because the vines got in the roots. You know what? They don't know what the vines are going to do to the houses. They could uproot them, they say. You could wake up and your house is on its side, all your furniture falling to the bottom, and you may actually sink into the earth from the pressure of the house. Can you imagine! Waking up and your dresser on top of you, etc. There are photos of houses in Brazil where this happened. Have you heard about this?

—No.

—There was a story of a woman who barely survived because she had been sleeping by a window and darted out just as her house was flipped. Can you imagine? So scary.

Her mother breathing hard, as though she'd run up a mountain.

—The second half is a list of activities I want to do when this ends. It has to end sometime, while I can think. And walk around a little. How long will this last, you know? So I would like to go sit inside a nice restaurant and eat a trout almondine. I would like to take rolls from a bread basket. I would like a meringue cookie dipped in chocolate. I want a waiter to come over and ask, Can I get you anything?

—I want to go with you.

—Remember Florence Samuels? Down the street. We were in carpool with her kids, remember.

A chill gathering in her.

—Dead. She got it when she went to a dinner celebrating her daughter's promotion. Half the table got it.

—Oh no.

—She was older than me. Two years. Maybe that makes a difference. Who knows. I hadn't talked to her in ten years but my god. Gone in two days. Benny Horwitz got it. From temple. Sometimes he blew the shofar. He said someone coughed on him in the supermarket. It wasn't bad, but now he can't drive because he can't remember when to put his foot on the brake.

Her mother's voice was strangely flat, reciting this.

—Anyway. Read the manifesto. Tell me if there is somewhere I can send it. I want millions of people to read it. When are you coming here?

A sneeze, lonely, in the other room.

—A week, Anna said, softly.

—I want to see you now. I can't believe you're real.

It had been months and months. She had a ticket to fly to see her in a few days.

—I can't wait to hug you, said Anna.

—I can't hug you, said her mother, firmly. I can wave to you. From the porch. Someday, someday in my dreams, you can come back into the house.

THE COMPUTER REPAIR shop wanted to give an update on her ticket.

—We're still examining the computer. We think tomorrow we can turn it on. We have a special tech coming in. He's going to try. The water damage was extensive. He says it could work, he's not sure.

—There's a chance? she asked.

—We try our best, there's always a chance! he said, chuckling.

His eyes scanned over the people lined up, holding their tickets, their ruined devices. The fact their mouths were covered made everyone look strangely peaceful.

—Don't lose anything, she said. —I didn't save anything.

THE APARTMENT WAS silent. Outside the snow had stopped. The blue night glittered over the dirty heaps; the snow looked like people huddling under sheets. Her daughter took long showers out of boredom, the bathroom billowing with clouds of steam. In the computer were captured hundreds of moments of her life. Her family, posed, on vacations, in moments that she could only remember in flashes. Children in Halloween costumes, clutching fairy wands and toy guns, standing in line at amusement parks, standing by her mother through decades. She stood with her husband in poses as young people, in those irretrievable costumes of youth. Triumphant as though they'd conquered something. Standing nobly on vistas at national parks. In large crowds, bubbling, at a bar. The photos all lies, showing only the joy or hope of joy at any particular moment, but she still craved them, needed to be reminded of them, wanted something to gather, to hold, for she did not know how those moments would live in her without them.

The children now taller, bored, a week went by and the week was torn with holes of silence. Where were they. They were with themselves. They were stars glittering in the dark sky, glorious, unreachable. They were where they should be. They swung home, sweaty, now and then, the walls clutching the sound of their voices, but they were like horses here, kicking things, too big.

Her daughter was talking to friends on her phone, shrieking with laughter. A relief to hear that laugh, that beautiful sound. Trying to hear something in her voice. Maybe hoarse? But nothing. Maybe her daughter was fine, the joke was on her. Maybe the other parents, the ones who didn't care, were right.

—How are you doing? she called, in a tinny, cheerful voice.

—Bored.

She watched the door. She wanted to burst in and hug her.

—Can I check your temperature?

—No. I don't feel anything.

—What do you mean, nothing?

—I am bored.

Her husband, texting, How is she?

She seems fine.

How are you?

I don't know. Okay.

This will be over soon.

She balked at his sunniness. He needed to be protected, he was older than she was. He was away, timing this smartly, traveling, and it didn't make sense for him to be at risk too. It was a strange calculation, seeing who could be thrown into the front lines. In fact, there was no calculation, there was just the assumption, on all their parts. What if he was the one who would beat it back?

I can come home, he said.

She did not know what to do. Say yes, let's switch, you come in, I'll go somewhere else? But no, it was ridiculous, she could already be exposed. It was better to be here, lurking by that closed door. Or there really wasn't another option.

No, you stay. I already could have it.

She saw the dots that indicated he was writing.

Remember to, you know, wear the mask and keep the door closed.

I do all those things.

She had done everything she needed to do to protect herself, but was it enough? For some, not everyone. There was no one protecting her, against the virus, against the anger gathering in the other room. The air was cold in the hall.

SHE DREAMED THE cat fell into a swimming pool. He was an orange cat and he sank, quickly, but sat at the bottom, looking around the aqua water with interest. He sat there for a minute, two, blinking, waiting. There was no time to get him out. Someone dove into the pool and brought the cat up, and he was silent, looking around. She took the wet cat into her arms and felt his soggy, solid weight. Then the cat leaped out of her arms and plunged into the water again, this time swimming, his paws slapping the water, though the cat did not know how to swim, though maybe he did, the water frothing up around him.

SHE TESTED NEGATIVE again. Third day. Watching the narrow space, the open white sky of the empty space. The gratitude fluttering out of her like confetti. The listening to the door, the waiting. She went to the computer repair store. Her daughter needed to print out her paper. She wanted to walk there, to feel the cold air. She had a wedge of time, walking to the store, when she felt free. She let her mind settle around sex. She wanted to get into a parked car and feel a hand on her breast, a finger inside her. It could be anyone, it could be the boy she dated in high school, flung across time into her neighborhood, it could be the delivery guy biking through the snow, it could be her husband's mouth on her skin. Everyone was huddled against the wind, in a hurry. She wanted to rob everyone on the street, take them for herself, and she wanted not to be in herself. She wanted an orgasm or a drink. She walked on, her mind blinking, red, blue like an ambulance; it astonished her that no one could see her glowing.

ON THE COLD STREET, on the way to the computer store, she passed a bakery. It was a grand opening, a bakery she had not seen before in her neighborhood. Already, people were filling it, as though they all had been personally invited inside. The store held a golden light and there were trays of pastries glowing in a case. She stopped for a moment and looked into the store. There was the quiet hum of people buying pastries and bread. She envied the ones who sat inside the store, eating, how brave or reckless they were. It could be both. The rates were too high. There were pastries she had never tried. There were croissants, some dusted with almonds and sugar, there were tiny cakes in oval shapes with glossy yellow-and-pink frosting, there were meringues in a frozen whoosh, a wave stopped midair. There were fruit galettes with raspberries jeweled in the light of the tray. There were napoleons with their layers of pastry, fine, crinkly, archaeological. There were cakes with scalloped curls of whipped cream aloft chocolate frosting.

There was a man staring into space ripping a croissant. There was a woman taking a large bite out of a cream-filled éclair. The women behind the counter wore light-blue masks, the customers sitting at the tables ate their pastries luxuriously.

The bakery was too crowded to enter and there were too

many people sitting there, faces gleaming, eating but she stopped and looked inside. When the door opened, a sweet warm smell came out into the chill air. She imagined what she would buy if she walked inside. She watched the woman eating the éclair, how she took a bite and placed the pastry down and gazed ahead, in a way that was gloriously ordinary, in a way Anna had done two years ago. It was beautiful in its casualness, that bite.

THE COMPUTER STORE was bright, and bustling, and people waited with tickets to find out the future of their broken machines. The repair associate, a slim guy who appeared to be permanently smiling at the dejected masses, saw her.

—You're here again!

—Is there any news, she said.

—What's your number? He tapped into his computer, peered at the screen.

She told him and waited. She wanted to tuck him into her pocket, have him give her updates every hour. He clicked the keyboard a few times.

—No, nothing.

—Is it still in progress?

—Yes. We are still working on it.

He was orderly, reasonable, and she did not want to wait.

—Tell me which photos you want, he said. —I'll look for them.

—There's one of a girl on a swing, she said. —That one.

She could not think of any others. It was a reasonable

question, and she had no idea how to answer it. To choose one memory seemed to degrade the others—they had been lived, too.

—All, she said. —Find them all.

She turned and rushed into the street before she could harm anyone, for there was always the chance she could—just with her breath—kill someone now. The heaps of snow glittered as she headed back to the apartment, waiting, waiting, feeling the heat of her cheeks in her hands.

—THERE'S SOMETHING IN the manifesto you cannot miss, her mother said. Sitting in the Zoom box, she looked so tiny.

—Sit closer, Anna said.

Her mother tried to scoot closer, but she appeared small as a doll, as though Anna could pinch her. She was grinning widely.

—What you can't miss is the paragraph at the end, her mother said. —It's very good, I think. About the person who ran out of the house when it was sliding into the earth. Why don't you print it out? Can you give me some corrections?

—What sort of corrections? Anna asked.

—You know, punctuation. How to make it better. Sharper. More publishable.

Her mother was shouting into the screen.

—Now!

—What?

—I want to publish it now! Before I'm dead! So people can read it!

—I can't print it out yet.

—Why not?

—My computer is broken.

Silence.

—How did you break it? You can't break it now!

—Well, I poured water—

—We can't waste any time, her mother said. Get it fixed.

SHE WOKE UP sweating and she was sure this was it. Now it would start. She almost wanted to get sick at this point. She could open the door and her daughter would walk out. The doorway would open and sunshine would pour into the room. They could sit together and eat soup and watch TV. The beautiful ordinariness of sitting with each other. There was the desire for this, to surrender, to open the door but there was also the dumb, relentless desire to batten down the tender walls of her body. She did not want to trade herself.

She sat up in the darkness. A single cough from the other side of the door. A rustling, then the sound of snoring. A silence like a velvet cat in the hall. Anna could not sleep. She stood beside the door, listening for a while, in the darkness.

DAY FOUR. Standing over the test like a hawk. The looming. There were meetings happening in the computer, somewhere, she could not access them. There was nothing she knew. She was freed. The test did its silent, daunting calculations.

Her daughter flung open the door and stood there, surveying the expanse of the world with a look of distaste. Anna couldn't blame her.

—What did your test say?

—I haven't done it yet.

—Do it.

—I still need that photo, her daughter said.

—I'm checking again. What do you need from the outside?

—I need my life.

It was strange in a way, the impatience of the young—they ostensibly had so many more days. She was the older one, the one farther along in this sodden march, who should be impatient to get back to her days but the ordinary days were burrowed down so far now, under the daily tumble.

—Diane's mother didn't care, her daughter said. —She just let her around the house.

Anna stared at the door. She stood between the door to her child's room and the door to her mother's house. The wind blew through the house and her feet were freezing.

IN HER DREAMS, the vines started to come into her apartment, of course, her dreams couldn't be more obvious, she was almost aware of this even in her sleep, but what she remembered about them was how shiny they were, stretching out through the floor, reaching up. She waited for them to do what vines would do in a bad dream, reach up and strangle her, or wrap arms around her and crush her, but the vines were not active, they pushed up through the floor and hovered in the air, small trees. She looked at them, waiting. What she noticed was their gloss, as though covered by sugar, candied, and suddenly all she wanted to do was eat them.

SHE THOUGHT SHE woke to the sound of weeping, but it was the ambulances, their cries, over and over, through the streets.

IT WAS TWO days later when she held out her ticket at the computer repair store and the man looked at the ticket, paused, and went to the back of the store. He walked back slowly and placed the computer on the counter.

—We can't get it, the man said. His eyes were not smiling this time, but frozen blue and sad.

—What do you mean, she said.

—The data is gone, he said.

She felt her heart tumbling and tumbling.

—How is it gone, she said. Where is it?

—It's in here, he said, tapping the silver top of the computer. —But it's gone, there's no way to retrieve it. We can throw it out and recycle if you want, or you can have it back.

—I want it back, she said.

He handed her the dead computer. It was steel, hard as it had been before. It felt so smooth and intelligent, though, clearly, it was not.

—Sorry, he said. —Be more careful. Usually we can fix it.

She clutched it tenderly and with care, though she could

have hurled it across the room. It held nothing, it held emptiness. It held dreams that she did not remember. How could she be more careful? Her whole damn life now was being careful. She put the computer into her tote and walked into the chill air. How could the information be gone? Where was it? There was a trembling at the borders of herself, the end of her edges, of everyone, all of them treading quickly across the frozen sidewalk.

All of it lost.

The sky was a heavy piece of tarnished silver, and she could feel its weight on her neck. She texted her daughter: Do you want anything?

No answer.

She passed the bakery again, looking into the golden glow of the store. Her heart swung like a sparkly pendant inside her. She wanted to go in. The door swung open and there was the soft warm sugar of the air. She paused and felt it as one customer came out, then another. There were a few pastries left, glazed croissants gleaming under the small pearl lights in the ceiling, square chocolate cakes with rippling icing, a drift of pink sparkles scattered across a plain of flat white frosting. There were a few meringues, in a pile close to the window, the tiny sugary froths of cloud.

She watched for a moment. The customer inside, no mask, was standing in front of the case, rubbing her fingers along the glass. She was eyeing these items, too.

Don't, Anna thought. She held her breath. There was so much she wanted. The woman at the counter nodded and began to place croissants into a box.

Anna pushed open the door; there was a soft chime. She rushed in so quickly she felt the others watching her. There were seven meringues left. She wanted them. More—she wanted them all. She stood in line behind the woman choosing her pastries, and Anne's feet were hollow with longing. The woman in line began to say something, and Anna stepped forward and said,

—No. I want these.

She was almost shouting, and she had cut in line. Her forehead became hot, another sort of heat. The customer and the worker at the counter were now rapt. It did not matter what they thought, nothing mattered but the meringues, the meringues, nothing mattered anywhere but those meringues.

She stepped in front of the other woman.

—The meringues. I want to buy them.

The other woman's eyes widened, staring at her.

—Excuse me, said the worker at the counter, eyes gleaming over her blue mask. —She was in line before you—

—No, said Anna. I can't.

She stepped forward.

—I need to get the meringues. Now.

What was she saying? She wanted the sweet, crumbly taste of meringue vanishing in her mouth. She wanted to eat all of them, to crawl into the meringue and live in it. Once, she had felt this way about a pot of chocolate. To luxuriate in something deep and sugary, to be consumed by its absolute and unwavering sweetness.

—I need them.

They did not understand this.

She did not know how she sounded. The pressure to sound polite. But at this point she wanted to be unreasonable, she was fine if she upset them; she just wanted the other customer to step aside so she could get the damn meringues. The customer put her hand over her mouth and started laughing.

—Well, said the other customer, her white hair artfully organized into a bob. —I'm not *that* hungry.

She was. She was that hungry. The worker glanced at the customer before her, who nodded and paid for her croissants. Anna stood, in front of the display of croissants, cookies with red jeweled berry centers, square cakes with smooth lavender icing, the flecks of chocolate on flaky tarts. The seven meringues, dipped in chocolate.

—I would like all of them please, three shipped overnight mail. She would send them to her mother, and she would share a couple with her daughter. —The others in a bag, please.

The woman sorted the tiny pale clouds into the box and bag. Anna felt relief that she could get these to her mother, to get her something; her body crouched in that box, too, flying to her.

She would bring the meringues to her daughter—an offering. She would have to tell her about the photo. Oh, all the photos. She had slipped another test under her door; one more day. They would sit and eat them together, in the same room.

"Thank you," she said, to the woman whose eyes were flat and annoyed over her blue mask. Anna smiled under her mask, and hoped the woman would see the smile in her eyes. Then she left.

The snow was heaped by the sidewalk, fat gray mounds that looked like a thousand people had stepped over them. The dark gray sidewalk was icy; she scanned the sidewalk for the dry places to step. She felt lighter now, holding the meringues. She had them. The sky was heavy and there was the shimmer of movement in it; snow was about to fall again. The apartment windows were squares of golden light. She slipped her hand into the bag and took out one meringue. It was perfect, a frozen whip of cloud, a wave of longing caught. She could not wait; walking through the dusk, her hands cold, she took a bite of it.

A bite. The sweetness, this life.

There were crumbles of lightness on her tongue, melting sugar and vanilla, and she walked, eating the meringue slowly. The walls of cold opened for her, she passed the golden windows and felt, briefly, that she was part of the world.

Her daughter would love the meringues. She could not wait to share them with her; maybe now her test would be clear. She burst through the door and toward her room. She called her name.

—I have something for you, she said.

The door to the bedroom was open. Anna stepped in. It was empty.

She said her daughter's name. Again.

The windows, just open, the wind lifting the curtains, the room cold.

Anna called her daughter's name again. But no one was here.

She was gone.

She was out of quarantine. Her daughter left, it must have been moments ago. But how? Where was she? There was a test sitting on the table by the bed. Anna breathed; she stepped toward the table, holding the meringues.

GLOBES

The darkness is the largest thing I have ever seen. We are sinking in it, and we are rising, we are not sure which we are doing; there are the globes, radiant, spheres of light cradling some of us, floating above earth.

There are so many types of darkness, here, above the planet. I have, in my time here, made a study of the dark. There is the dark of darkness, the absolute black flatness that I see when I turn away from the circle of bright blue. There is the complete dark, where we are swallowed and can see nothing of the outlines of our bodies, of ourselves. A pure, simple unlitness in which I wonder if I am still alive. Then there is the dark where one is just able to see, there is the dark roughened by stars, those faint bits of radiance. The dark that pretends we are glamorous and young, though we do not pretend that we are. There is the pale start of the light as another globe drifts toward me silently, and I am looking for the way the sky fades to a gray around the globe, then a light pearl color, a luminous tender shade like dawn, not the sky, not blue, not morning the way we had known, not day, just the declaration of presence. There is the light created when several globes collect in one place, a necklace of bright spheres stretched across the sky, each cradling one person, or two, or a few, each globe passing, a swath of goldenness where we are just able to see.

The globes float past each other, silent. I resent the silence here, the absolute nature of it, with only the sounds I make and the ones my husband makes, and I think about sounds I miss. I miss the most obvious sounds, I am embarrassed to miss them. The crackling of autumn leaves under my feet, a sound like the ocean. The rhythmic tap of a train. The way live music thrums through your body. The hard, swift sounds of people shouting. I miss people shouting in the street. I miss their longing for love, their anger.

Sometimes we shout, up here, in the globe, just to hear it. I shout in my sleep, my husband tells me. It wakes him up. This is hard because there is nothing to wake up to. He says I sound like I am in great pain.

To my embarrassment, I don't remember any shouting or any dreams.

—What do I say?

—I can't understand the words, he says.

WE HAVE TUMBLED up into the sky, trapped within the globes, they shot us up, one by one or two by two, or three or a few more, we detached from earth, and we tumbled up and we were floating, in these clear globes, in the sky. It happened quickly. We were lucky, or they said we were. We were walking to work, we were alert but not particularly afraid, or not more than any other time. Our fear was such a part of us it was not part of us, or we had cataloged so many fears (the plumes, the ephemeral quality of our work, the slow joking revolt of our bodies in middle age) we had grown so used to it that it had faded to a low presence, a shadow brimming always within ourselves. We had been told to prepare for the incidents, the long, dark plumes of blue air that arose, at peculiar moments, from the seams of the earth. The plumes unfurled, the color of the ocean, a deep sapphire blue, and they fooled us, and at first sight people were awed by it, moved even at what new colorful event the earth could produce, but then, within hours, many of them clutching their throats, dead.

There was no clear pattern for the release of the smoke—it had happened in Phoenix, in Miami, on a farm in Kansas, off the coast of Rhode Island, it could rise from anywhere and there was a chance it would rush up in a mass, at once. Communities sealed up cracks in their roads with anything they could find—hot asphalt, steel, duct tape. The wealthier ones bragged about their efforts, reupholstered their smooth, glossy streets with gravel and tar and steel, and ones that had less to work with filled cracks in with dirt and planted trees. They eyed each other, wondering.

Nothing worked.

Scientists drove long cameras into the earth to peer at the smoke, to understand what lurked deep within and could kill us. Their cameras sent back swirls of blue, the color of sky or water, that elicited a feeling of gratitude and awe—the sense that the sky, something pure and clear like it, was deep within the earth. Whatever was in the core of this earth was distracting and devious. Why had it developed now? How enormous the earth was, how strange what it held. My husband was somehow calmed by the beauty of the swirls. His fear was such that he liked to pretend anything ominous was the other thing. Was this new development an unnatural toxin or how the world now evolved? I found the calm people sweet but suspicious. I tended to clothe myself in fear like a thick winter coat; wearing it made me feel sensible and more alert.

The government, with great authority, declared that there was no need to worry about the rumblings in the earth. They had a plan to save us. The answer, they said, was found in globes. The federal government had contracted with aerospace companies and furniture companies to construct devices to protect us. The globes were putting thousands of people to work, and we saw this—we watched videos of the globes being built, saw their large forms perched like thousands of huge clear bubbles on scaffolds, rolled through factories, with several workers heaving them forward onto steel carts to demonstrate their heft. The companies showed off the globes, photographing them with pillows, seats curved against the clear walls. They told us that they would be as comfortable as living rooms and in them we would be safe.

We watched the news, chewing on our dinner, absorbing all of this. Hope hovered above our heads, like a bludgeon. My husband had been crushed into hope, feeling its garish weight floating over us. I felt its taunting heaviness and I resented it. Our son was eighteen and he went to school, literally armed with hope, giant weaponry stuffed in his duffel bag. His dorm bed was claimed, his wall plastered with posters in a matter of minutes. He had plans, he had people to meet. —You can go home, he said.

We were in our fifties and there were warnings within and around us: flares going off in our bodies, or the jobs slipping through our fingers, in the rumblings within the earth. We were tired but we wanted to live, whatever that meant: we wanted to walk by the ocean in the purple light of dusk and eat ice cream and of course kiss and breathe in the smell of flowers, of rose and honeysuckle. We wanted to have dinner with friends and we wanted to laugh and have people laugh at our jokes, even if they were bad ones. We wanted to listen to our son describe his day. We wanted not a lot, and we wanted everything. We marked our schedules diligently, like we had a future. The future was like a small green lizard, thinking about a safe place to dart.

We went to work, we came home, we waited.

Our government could build globes but could not predict when the incidents would happen. One day, I was walking down the street with my husband, and the sky became dark. Someone began to scream. I looked up and there were hundreds of shadows; the globes began to drop from the sky. They fell from a great remote military ship, floating at such a height it was invisible, the blue sky blotting with the hundreds of gray circles drifting to earth. They touched down with great slow gentleness. Doors flung open. No one knew what to do. Officials in suits rushed through the streets, pushing us in. It was very disorganized. It happened before we had plans to leave.

An official standing in front of us, murmuring into his silver phone, for one moment I could see his eyes as he regarded us. He hesitated; the official's gaze was cool, questioning. He started to ask us something, and then someone shouted, —Go!

He nodded to another official. The globe alighted in front of us, and they pushed us in.

My husband's cry as they shoved him in, —Wait, he said. —Why us. What about others. Our son was hundreds of miles away, in his life. Wait.

We tumbled up, shrieking. The earth behind us, falling.

We lifted up into the sky, our stomachs plummeting, our phones beeping with official messages: There is an incident in your area. The blue smoke rushing up from the cracks in the sidewalk, the smoke like blue fur, moving slowly across the city. The officials, in silver suits, encased in material denied the rest of us, pushing whoever they could into the globes, without reason, or later we would learn the reasons. The map of the continents below us, the blue pearl planet. The smoke curling up, silent blue pillars of mist.

Those we loved tumbled like dice across the world.

The messages that flashed on our phones. Where are you. Are you okay.

Where is everyone?

Where are you?

THE GLOBES MOVED slowly, through the soundless dark air. We did not know if we were alive, and that confusion made us feel small. We were dizzy, as though on the world's worst roller coaster, and the sky around us was blue, then quickly black. We were alive, or at least we thought we were. We had each other to ask, anyway.

—Are you dead? my husband asked, in a bewildered, polite way.

It was embarrassing to ask this.

—I don't know, are you?

We grasped hands, with hope, and waited for a message. What. A thrum in the palm. That throb, that insistence. We were so busy, we never listened to it. There.

—You're alive, my husband said.

I was happy, a happiness pure and enormous. Our hearts fell open and fireworks rushed in. We glimmered softly against the dark sky. We looked at each other, each smudge, each mole, each wrinkle, a gift; we looked at each other like celebrities, or babies.

I wanted, also, to apologize.

The earth falling away from us.

THE NEXT QUESTION, or at the same time, really, a thought so hard we felt it: Where is our son?

At this moment, in another universe, he was supposed to be in class. I did not remember which one, and that was personally shameful. I didn't keep track, I just knew that he was supposed to be doing his homework, and he usually was. It occurred to me that this was a good excuse not to be in class. I think that before I am afraid; I wrap myself in this thought for one moment, comforted.

The earth, that blue hazy sphere, so far, so quiet.

WE ARE FROZEN in an ice cube of fear. We try calling, we try Emergency Control, there is an automated message, we hold up our phones with his photo to others passing in their globes, and scream, —Do you see him, they look at us, hold up their own phones with photos, but it is too far, and we cannot see anything; all we can identify is our shared anguish. We lean forward peering, we bang on the globes.

We look at each other and want the other to do something. Could one of us please do something? The checklist: our son, silent; a sister, two brothers, accounted for, floating; an aunt, scattered friends, some neighbors. News flashing on our phone. Twenty-seven dead in our district; a senior citizens home; no globes in the vicinity. Hundreds in other cities. He would have been in class. We call his school.

A recording: Our university is closed as we tend to those affected by the incident. Please call again later to check on the status of your registered student.

WE CANNOT STEER these globes; we are carried. Our inability to move them highlights all our failings as parents; shame comes over us like a wave; the shame that unfurled inside us from the moment we brought him home and did not know what to do when he, a tiny, perfect person, began to cry. A good parent would have known, somehow, that blue smoke was gathering. A good parent would have known when the globes would begin to fall. We tried for years to be effective parents, to be hawks floating over the world. We tried to maneuver around the bullies, the bad teachers, we kept our eyes open, alert, but somehow we had missed this, in our vigilance, we had not considered the possibility of blue smoke cracking out of the earth.

Now we are full of useless activity for it seems like days; but it could have been hours.

We sit in various positions within the globe—cross-legged, legs stretched out, our backs pushed against the long curve. We try to move it, both of us heaving our weight toward one side, we make efforts to push it, we want agency, direction; there is none.

—You just lean on the northeast, um, curve of the globe, my husband says, with confidence that is touching but pointless. —On TV they said we would have functions of movement.

—You believed them, I say.

We lean and shove and our globe goes nowhere. What do you have to do to move this thing! We feel hapless and regret not going to the gym. The guy who floats by and shoves some sacks of food through the chute, who trundles by once and is supposed to bring us more (we hope), laughs, I think, when he sees us, fumbling to push our globe. We envy him; he saunters by, slow, majestic, bored.

—How do you make this thing move, I try to ask the man in the vehicle floating past us. —Tell me. Please. Is there an instruction manual? We did not receive it. We need to find someone.

He looks at us.

—Ma'am. You know or you don't. You ordered the premium

selections. The government will withdraw this amount from your account.

An account? Was there an account? How much will we owe?

He glances at us and appears to make a note.

OUR GLOBE IS not large. We try to jog in place as we wait. We sit next to each other, we do not have enough room, we press against each other, sometimes when we need space we sit back-to-back so we will not see each other, feeling the shapes of our skeletons against each other, we know the precise nubs in each other's backs.

I dream of people dying, some I knew, some strangers that I felt I knew. My aunt in Sacramento. The young assistant at our work. The mechanic who changed the oil in our car. The older woman who walked her dog in a park, the dog now trotting through the park, alone. Is this why I cry out in my sleep? Is it not people I know, but people I don't? I don't feel the loss of them and I do, deeply, in my dreams. I hear their names and I scream.

MY BROTHER, who is younger than I am, hears from his children. They somehow found one another, organized their globes in a circle, and are playing games in the dark velvet sky. He sends me photos, the five of them, floating, luminous, as though in water. They are becoming fit with group exercise. They even have formed a choir of sorts. They sing into their phones, watch each other's mouths from afar, and experience a feeling of connection. I look at this with admiration and envy. —How did you do this? I ask. —We cannot even find our one child. He says, —He will turn up. How can he know this? I have forgotten how to think. My mind cannot encapsulate time. He believes that there will be opportunities for profit, once they return to earth. I admire his optimism and feel ravaged by it. He believes the blue smoke was a one-time incident. I wish I could inhabit his mind, but it is so foreign to me.

My brother also has the gift of great confidence about the future.

IT IS A small globe, we take turns standing up, running in a circle, I can lie down, I send my waste out through a little chute. I try to cover myself when I do this, modesty feels like a grasping toward civilization, I don't want to let it go. I wonder when I will, when I won't care about that anymore. I look for the others, I want to see if there is anyone I know, any face I have had a history with, any history. The craving for home is like craving something to eat. Nothing fills it except the thing itself. I see others floating by, there is a woman in office clothes, sleeping. There is the couple sitting feet pushed together, pressing against each other as though trying to launch themselves out of the globe. There is the woman who is topless and dances, proudly, for everyone, as she floats by. There is a man in a business suit, crouched in his globe, hands on the curved clear wall, screaming. I see the cashier from the market, she is naked, clutching the back of a large man, I think I see a teacher from the gym, head in her hands. There is the bewilderment of people who are almost the ones you know, but not the ones you know. Some look lonely and some look useless and some are both. My husband shuts his eyes when people float toward him; they are the wrong ones and make him too sad.

The globe carries us through the cold wild dark.

WE GET UPDATES from the ground: the blue smoke has stopped. Teams that look for cracks in the streets, who are trained to detect the odorless blue smoke and sound alarms for people to move, to push them into globes, have stopped running; we see footage of them standing at corners, looking regal and bored. There are no more dead or they have been hidden; the city streets are clean, swept, empty, the buildings glittering, waiting for us to return. They do not tell us how to locate who is missing.

THE PHONE RINGS.

—Hi, he says.

Is it him? Is it a joke? No, it is him. The sky is dark navy blue, the stars glittering like broken chandeliers.

—Hi? Are you okay? Where are you?

—I'm fine. Somewhere over Antarctica.

—Where have you been? It's been weeks—

—It's been four days, he said. —I had trouble with my phone.

—Are you okay? Can we pick you up?

A laugh.

—You can't pick me up.

—What can we do?

There is a troubling silence.

—Why didn't you call your parents? my husband asks, the most embarrassing question in the world.

—They grabbed us out of class. They were shoving us into these things. I got one, I grabbed it with a couple of my friends, we're good. You can say hello to Henry and Gordon, he says.

—Hello, says a voice.

—Hello, we say.

We hear laughter.

—Who are you? Do your parents know? I ask.

But they are adults, and of course they find this question funny, or maybe tragic. They laugh at us, uproarious, for a few minutes.

—We're having a race, our son says. —These things can go fast. Some of our class is over Finland! They found each other. We have to get there.

—You have to press the controls on the side, says, I think, Henry.

—What controls? I ask. What are you talking about?

—The controls are on the—

There is static, garble.

—What? Where?
—Mom. Just lay on the—
—What? *What?*
—Talk to you later, he says, and hangs up.

THE RELIEF IS sudden and general at his presence of life, and then curdling into an unfortunate bitterness. He knew how to move and we did not. Why had he not been gladder to reach us? And what did he know about the globes that we did not?

WE LOOK OUT at the others, and there are two ways they are moving through the air—some, like ours, seem heavy as planets, pulled slowly by the earth's gravity, while others arc through the sky with the lightness of fireflies, the people within the clear spheres leaning hard on one side, one foot pressed to a particular spot in the globe, gazing intently at the dark. It is as though we have been given two types of globes, with distinct capacities, but they appear exactly the same. The other globes fly toward one another, they travel in groups, and we shout at them as they zip by, but they are too light, too capable, they resemble planets creating their own clear orbits, detached from the enormous, gauzy earth.

WE NEED TO be here together, we need to be here in this globe, but we are too close to each other all the time, it is too much, we try to sit so our limbs don't touch at least some of the time. He likes sitting with one leg up on the side of the globe, leaning down to stare at the earth. Our breath is familiar and meaty. I hate the smell of my breath, and I love it.

I DREAM OF passion, of us tumbling desperately toward each other. Mostly, we just sit. When the globe is swathed in darkness, the moments we cannot see each other, when all the other globes have vanished, the moments I think where are we, am I me, we grab each other, we listen for each other's breath, the fact of our presence here together startling, erotic. The moments when our bodies are all that exist in this nothingness. I dream of dresses and being pinned against walls, but that is only exciting if there is a chance of escape.

MY HUSBAND AND I look at each other's faces, the only ones we see day after day. We are fascinated by small things. The way our hair cares about nothing and unspools. The way our backs press against the curved sphere, how we try to sit away from it so our backs will not conform to it.

I START TO think I am seeing him in the spheres that pass us. Our son, that haircut, that has to be him. Or that shirt, yes. And not just him, others I was used to seeing. My friend down the street, I see her bobbed red hair, I know it is her, my sister, wearing the shirt I bought her at a sale, I know who they are. But then I don't as they get closer, as they pass by, and the disappointment of not knowing them makes my head feel as though it will fall off.

MY BREATH SMELLS worse, the smell of a dying animal. I don't know where it comes from, I do brush my teeth, even here. I don't know what is dying in me, besides the regular aspects, but the smell seems to indicate there is another form of withering. It concerns me. I want some gum. My husband does not, sometimes, want to kiss me. He will, however, hold my hand. The darkness outside makes us hold hands in a new way. Tighter. We feel each other's bones.

EACH NIGHT—or we think it is night—the government flashes photos of the world we are missing. There is a strangely desperate quality and frequency to these photos, as though the government is afraid we will reject the world, but of course we want to see it. We see photos of empty beaches stretching out like wrinkled beige scarves, of mountains sloping like great shoulders, of skyscrapers soaring on empty avenues. Come home to earth, the messages say, with a sort of wistfulness. Come walk the sandy beaches. Come swim in our oceans. Come dance in our cities. Come back to earth. We are ready.

These photos make my husband nervous. —They do not need to sell us our return to our lives, he says. —Why would they need to sell it?

The ones who can maneuver the globes are having too much fun, are too free up here. Their globes dart like clear golden bubbles, rushing by in shining packs, with a celebratory feel, as though at a wedding. They look like they are elastic, they stretch with the people inside them, they elongate slightly. Some of the younger people are distracted by their power within the globes and are forming racing groups across the sky. Who needs earth, says the wild rise and fall of these globes, and I too want to race with them, thrusting myself into the dark velvet of space. But where would they go? The marketing committee of the Earth wants their attention. I want to imagine other worlds, but I am also in love with the world below us. I wonder if this is a failing within me. They look like comets; we watch the wild, bobbing streaks they make.

THE MAN DRIVING the globe with food brings it to us and edges it into our globe with his skeletal arm. I am sick of the food he brings—I want a particular taco with the fresh cilantro at that place around the corner or the pizza slice that was so heavy with cheese it made the paper plate translucent. Then he hovers near us in his supply vehicle, which resembles a large, clear truck with stacks of food options inside. At first he is chatty, telling us how the reports from earth are very positive, how the scientists can predict the tremors the earth makes before the smoke rises up, and then, in a slightly bragging tone, how he had a very nice, indeed calming stroll by the beach, the gulls dipping over the glorious, shimmering sea. I wonder if he means to make us feel terrible. Then he grows serious.

—I need to ask some questions, he says.

He looks at us, his eyes arching in a judgmental way.

—What are your jobs? he asks.

—What are your favorite activities?

We answer, carefully, with an eagerness that embarrasses me; I watch his face.

—Can you make the globe move?

—Move where? we ask.

—Just anywhere. Can you make it move?

He writes something down and looks at us with a pert, expectant expression.

A shiver in the darkness.

—Yes, we can. Of course.

—Show me.

He holds out a notepad, leans back, and waits. His expression is weary and amused in a way that is alarming. My husband and I glance at each other, in our shared and voluptuous ignorance, and we shove our feet against the globe in the way we saw the others doing, try it with a flat foot, then pointed, then tapped, waiting for a blip, a jump, a heaving or urgency underneath, a sense of motion—but nothing. The globe has a hard texture to it, I realize it has not stretched like the ones that soar and move, I keep trying to push it, but it is stalwart, unmoved.

—It should work, I call to him. —Just wait!

A few minutes more of this and nothing.

He shrugs and the steel arm reaches out and raps on the outside of the globe. It sounds like he is knocking on wood.

—Thanks, he says.

—I have a small question, I say. —When do we come down? How will they do it? Can we help in any way?

I have other questions—why was it so easy for the others in their globes? What did it mean that our son did not call? What would we be now that he was free in a globe, zipping around the universe? How long would we have on earth, how long would we turn to each other in the night? I have too many questions, and ones the interviewer cannot answer.

—When? my husband asks.

The long steel arm deposits another package inside our globe. We open it, eagerly; it is two somewhat sad muffins.

—Soon. Enjoy! he says. He winks at us and trundles off.

WE BOB AMONG the others, who, in their globes, are in various states of mental disrepair. Some sit in their globes, alone, eyes closed; some stare at whoever passes as though they want to eat us. There are those who have mastered the globes and are hurtling around the rest of us, in a way that seems perhaps aggressive. Then there is a globe rising up beside us, it seems to be heading toward us. Its brightness flashes, blinds.

It is our son, again.

—Hi! How are you?

—Could be better. How are you?

—My classes are starting, our son says. —They want us to start next week.

—Already?

—Yes. I need lab fees for supplies.

Of course, the pay function on the phone is intact and remarkably efficient. Of course that works. We send him the money.

—Thanks, he says. —I don't know when I'm going down. Soon, I hope.

The globe lingers in the air. His globe has elongated and the others are in a corner, arguing. He does not quite leave yet.

—How was the sky over Finland? I ask.

—Fine, I guess.

—What was it like?

—I don't know.

—What does that mean?

—Oh, we couldn't hear each other. We all bobbed there, no one knew what to do. They're idiots. The whole thing was stupid.

His face narrows itself in sadness for a moment, resembling his face as a child, and I feel a flare of understanding across the hard clear globes. I see all his ages in his face, in a trick of light, and how his face will shift with fear and disappointment. There is nothing we can do to stop this, and I feel this knowledge like a hard nut in my heart. I look at him across the globe and I want to hug him but I can't, so I say,

—I wish it had been better.

He glances at us, and I see something, an appreciation, that particular light.

—We'll see you there soon, my husband says.

He moves to the edge of his globe. We sit in our separate

globes, and it feels as though we are together, sort of, in a way. Our globes tremble in the shadows, the brightness of the sun.

—Soon, he said.

AROUND US, the sky begins to change. It is, at first, a general, faint difference—the sudden loss of the golden globes, their luminous, precise brightness, the rapid diminishing of light. The globes begin to descend. It happens without sound, almost gracefully, each plummeting swiftly like an elevator heading to earth. The sky is scattered with the flashes of light and gold, and we see it happen, randomly: they are floating, then caught midorbit, and a force faraway stops them, fully, and they are suspended, still, held, in the darkness and then the globe punctures the white gauze of clouds far beneath us, the globe tumbles through them and is gone.

MY HUSBAND AND I peer out of our globe, watching the others. We debate whether we should ask to return to earth, whether it is a sound decision or a reckless one. We imagine the first ones are fools, they have decided to return to earth before the smoke was gone. In this scenario, we are smarter and superior in our residence in the sky, and this comforts us. But the images coming from earth reveal only things to envy: people walking across the street, eating dinner. We see people walking their dogs and getting into their cars. We see the seamlessness of ordinary life. Then it becomes clear that there is no decision being made by those inside the globes—that they are being pulled to earth, they have been selected.

THE GLOBES KEEP falling, like enormous glimmering drops of rain. How many people filled the skies up here; the number is astonishing. We watch them fall and wait our turn. We have not received a message about our descent, and we wonder. Were we rude to the man who brought us food? Did we forget a payment or to fill out a form? We run our hands along the globe trying to find something we have missed, but it is smooth and rigid and does not reveal any secrets.

Our son has started school. He sends us a picture of himself walking on campus. We look at the light, all the glorious light in the photo—the sun glinting off glass, the sun flashing on water, the sun—and we want to gather the sun like flowers, cradle it in our arms.

He sends us a photo of the crowds now assembling in his city, on earth. How normal everything looks, as though nothing strange has happened. We see people stretched out on towels on a green park. The skies are clear and young people tread across the earth as though nothing toxic ever rose from its core. It is a city I know, but there is something about it that makes me look closer. We look and we realize that everyone in the photos, everyone who has been brought down to earth, is similar in a certain way.

They are all in their twenties and thirties.

They are all young.

WE LOOK AROUND us, at those of us who are left, bobbing in their spheres. We realize that all the people left are not young. In fact, we are old. They are many versions of old—there are the very old, frail and standing and pressing their hands to the sides of the globes to maintain balance, there are recent retirees, who look energetic and mad they are stuck here, not on a cruise in the Bahamas. They are, to be fair, older than us, but some look our age, or are just faking it effectively. We are left here, too; we are those who are on our way to being old. We pass each other, the globes that are left, and we understand, and we regard each other with derision and surprise and fear.

Come get us.

Someone is shouting it in a globe near ours, and we begin shouting with them. We turn our phone to the Command Center and shout.

—Come get us!

—Come get us!

—Come get us!

So many other globes have fallen, there are now long stretches of darkness between us, like vast deep lakes. We pass each other, wondering why we have been left up here, though also we believe we know.

We pass the others, some more frantic now, some resigned.

We are here, suspended in the sky, waiting. I dream of the earth and the smell of the ocean and of the morning. Watching the sky. Our son calls and wants to know when we are coming back. This time he does not ask for money, he just asks where we are. —Soon, I say, though I don't know.

The darkness is the largest thing I have ever seen. We are sinking in it and we are rising, we are not sure which we are doing; there are the globes, radiant, spheres of light cradling some of us, floating above earth.

We wait for the moment we too descend, the moment we will sense the globe begin to sink, the way we will leave the deep-black sky, the moment we will take steps across the crumbled surface of the ground. We wait for the way the earth will rush up, closer and closer, the way our neighborhood and our city will reveal themselves, tree by tree, sidewalk by sidewalk, the solidity of the ground as we take our first step. We wait to be invited back to earth. We hold hands always now, and look out at the darkness, waiting. And sometimes we imagine seeing a gold globe rise from earth, small, then becoming brighter, more visible, and we imagine: This one holds our son, and he is on his way. He is coming to find us.

Acknowledgments

First, and with so much gratitude, to the magnificent team at Counterpoint Press: Megan Fishmann, Rachel Fershleiser, Andrea Córdova, Dan López, Laura Berry; and a huge thank-you to Dan Smetanka, for believing in my work and your editorial brilliance and friendship. To my agent, Maria Massie, for wonderful insight and nourishing support.

To the editors who published some of these stories: Harold Augenbraum and Meghan O'Rourke at *The Yale Review*, Melissa Pritchard at *Image* and David Ulin at *Air/Light*, and Bill Henderson at the Pushcart Press; what an enormous joy to see my work in your pages.

To those who have given me the privilege and opportunities to teach over the last few years: the crew at Hollins University, especially Thorpe Moeckel, Jessie Van Eerden, Jeanne Larsen, and Cathy Hankla; at SUNY Stony Brook, especially Julia Sheehan, Susan Merrell, Amy Hempel, Meg Wolitzer, Carla Caglioti, Christian McLean, and Paul Harding. Big thank-you to Sophfronia Scott at Alma College and the MFA faculty: Leslie Contreras Schwartz, Dhonielle

Clayton, Shonda Buchanan, Ben Garcia, Donald Quist, S. Kirk Walsh, Anna Clark, Matthew Gavin Frank, Jim Daniels, and Bob Vivian; your support when I read parts of these stories buoyed me up. And thank you to the wonderful Amy Margolis at the University of Iowa Summer Writing Festivals and Blake Kimzey at Writing Workshops. Huge gratitude to the brilliant Carolyn Ferrell and Matt Klam, for their kindness and generosity.

With love and appreciation and joy to dear friends and family: Margaret Mittelbach, Jennie Litt, Amy Feldman, Katherine Wessling, Jenny Schaffer, Malena Morling, Dana Sachs, Allison Robbins and Jim Jennewein, Scott Alexander and Debbie Alexander, Pamela Leri, Bill McGarvey, Eric Wilson, Natalie Plachte White, Michelle Plachte-Zuieback, John Altman, Lauren Gewirtz, Perrin Siegel, and Sean Siegel.

To dear Tim Bush, who always gave the best advice and whom we miss so much.

With so much love to my father, David Bender, how I miss your laugh and your insights and everything; to my mother Mary Bender, for being a model of strength and creativity and for your poems; and to Suzanne and Aimee, my beautiful and precious sisterhood, to our team.

And to the beloved treasures who are Jonah Siegel and Maia Siegel, how you open the world for me, and always, to Robert Siegel, my beloved partner, my home.

© Jonah Siegel

KAREN E. BENDER is the author of the story collections *The New Order* and *Refund,* a finalist for the National Book Award for Fiction. She is also the author of the novels *Like Normal People* and *A Town of Empty Rooms.* Her fiction has appeared in *The New Yorker, Granta, Zoetrope, Ploughshares, Story, Harvard Review, The Yale Review, The Iowa Review,* and other magazines. Her stories have been anthologized in *The Best American Short Stories, The Best American Mystery Stories,* and *New Stories from the South: The Year's Best,* and have won three Pushcart Prizes. She has won grants from the Rona Jaffe Foundation and the National Endowment for the Arts. She has taught for numerous MFA programs and is currently a visiting writer for the Stony Brook University MFA in creative writing and on the core faculty for the Alma College MFA program. Find out more at karenebender.com.